Reason to Leave

P. Addison Wentz & Anne Wilson

Designed and produced by:
Maine Authors Publishing
12 High Street, Thomaston, Maine
www.maineauthorspublishing.com

Printed in the United States of America

Dedicated to John Douglas Pillans
(See…we did finish it!)

Somewhere north of 0° latitude
and west of 0° longitude in the
North Atlantic Ocean

SANDARAY ISLAND

ORRAN ISLAND
6.4 nautical miles
northeast of Sandaray

"American traditions and the American ethic require us to be truthful, but the most important reason is that truth is the best propaganda and lies are the worst. To be persuasive we must be believable; to be believable we must be credible; to be credible we must be truthful. It is as simple as that."

—Edward Roscoe Murrow, American broadcast journalist and war correspondent, 1908–1965

Prologue

December 2014, London, England

Some of his thoughts to exact revenge had been incredibly involved, but that afternoon, watching the paddle boats gliding serenely past, a unique scenario took shape in his mind. *This will work! I'll get the son of a bitch this time.*

As he walked home, he continued to think and plan, but knowing the mental solitude provided by walking would soon vanish, he stopped on the front step of his apartment building for a moment, relishing the ingenious simplicity of this new idea. He smiled, oblivious to the sound of traffic, the comings and goings of the other residents, and the dark shadow in a third-floor apartment window across the street.

All three shots hit him.

Chapter One

March 14, 2012, Sandaray Island, Maine

A slight nudge indicated the ferry's arrival. It had been a bumpy, four-hour crossing from Rockland, but the captain knew his stuff, berthing skillfully despite the swell. On deck, several cars and a truck loaded with propane cylinders prepared to drive off, while passengers gathered up unruly children and litter from the long, early morning voyage. As the exodus began, he knew going back would not be an option. He took a deep breath, threw his duffel bag over his shoulder, and made his way down the gangplank.

Once on the wharf, he paused to take in his surroundings. Along the shore stood several small buildings supported on pilings, their jetties littered with tools of the lobster trade. Behind them, a dirt road snaked uphill past a collection of ramshackle sheds. A handful of fishing boats lay moored in the harbor but, to his surprise he saw little activity anywhere. The few cars and passengers disappeared in an instant, and he found himself alone.

He had only thought in general terms of how he would proceed once he arrived, but now, actually on the island, the enormity of what he had done finally hit home. *Where am I going to stay? How am I going to survive?* Even the harbor area, which he imagined had the largest concentration of buildings on the island, looked tiny compared to anywhere on the mainland. Maybe this wouldn't be as easy as he had imagined. Perhaps this whole idea had been a big mistake. He looked back at the ferry and considered, *There's still time to get a return ticket.*

A noisy truck heading up the hill caught his attention. It had definitely not been on the ferry, and there had been no sign of it parked on the wharf. He studied it with a mixture of curiosity and unease. It stopped in the middle of the road, and the sole occupant, a short man, got out and began scanning the harbor area as if looking for something...or someone. After a moment the man reached into the truck, retrieved a pair of binoculars, and continued his search.

Shit! he thought. *Is he looking for me? Have I been followed? Has someone recognized me?* Instinctively turning from the spying eyes, he pulled up the hood on his jacket and began walking as casually as he could along the wharf. He knew he was being paranoid, but he couldn't shake the feeling of being watched. *Those bastards have eyes everywhere!*

Eventually the truck started up again. Sneaking a look back, he watched as it made its way up the hill.

Sighing, he wandered over to a mooring bollard and slumped down, holding his head in both hands. He had to get a grip. *Come on. You can do this. You've come this far. This is your new start.*

He must have been there for some time because, when he finally looked up, the ferry had reloaded passengers and cargo ready to depart. *Last chance buddy. Decision time.*

He stood, grabbed his bag, turned, and headed off up the same road the truck had taken.

A large, garish sign depicting an old sea captain proudly announced Port MacKenzie. The whole place had a downbeat feel, probably typical of working ports on islands like this. He imagined there must be a town center somewhere—a church, some shops, and a post office at the very least—but nothing was immediately apparent. So he kept walking.

Not far ahead, he spotted two people entering a building near the crest of the hill. As he got closer, a sign swinging above the door indicated he had found Emma's Café. It seemed as good a place as any to start finding out about the island. A decent cup of coffee would also be nice. *It'll give me an opportunity to get a feel for the place while I get my act together.*

A small bell, mounted on the door, sounded as he stepped inside. The dining room was functional but nicely kept. The two people he had seen leave the ferry were now seated at a table near a window.

On the end stool, farthest from the door, a whiskered old man, dressed in a grimy shirt and paint-spattered jeans, sat cradling a mug of coffee. He felt the old man's eyes boring into him. He nodded to the old guy in acknowledgment and took the counter stool farthest away.

"Emma'll be right along," he called out. "She just went to get some more ballast rocks."

He wedged his duffel bag between the stool and the counter and looked around, wondering what "ballast rocks" were. The old man's eyes continued to scrutinize him intensely. He would need to get used to being an object of curiosity if he was going to survive here.

"You just come in on the ferry?" the old man queried. "Out here for a while or just till next week's boat?"

Desperate to tell him to mind his own business, he reminded himself, as the outsider, that island culture would be very different from the city life he had left behind. He reasoned the old guy, probably a walking encyclopedia, could be a useful source of local information. *Best not to offend him at this point,* he thought. He knew personal questions could not be avoided, but he didn't want everyone prying into his business or his past. By way of a compromise, he moved along the counter, closer to the old man.

"Seth Martin," he conceded, offering his hand.

"Kenneth Young," the old man responded, "but everyone calls me Kenny. Welcome to Port MacKenzie, Mister Seth Martin." The wrinkled, sunburned hand felt surprisingly strong, reflecting a lifetime of hard work.

Emma, a slight woman probably in her mid-thirties, arrived dressed in work pants, a man's oversized denim shirt, and a well-used apron. She had a pleasant face and the deepest blue eyes Seth had ever seen.

"More coffee, Kenny?" she asked as she held a coffee pot over his mug.

"Umm, yep."

"Welcome to Port Mac, what can I get you?" she said, turning to Seth.

"Black coffee and a 'ballast rock'…whatever that is," he replied.

"They're plain, glazed, or chocolate. Does that give you a clue?"

"It does." He smiled for the first time in many months. "I'll have a chocolate one, please."

She moved with the efficiency of many years' experience and produced a large doughnut and two mugs of coffee. "Here ya go," she said, sliding the doughnut and one mug to Seth. Grabbing the sugar, she sweetened the other for herself. "Are you here for long?" she asked. Then, without waiting for a reply, looked at Kenny and remarked, "Bet he's one of those newspaper folks, probably staying up at big bad Bill's B&B."

Seth's instinctive reaction proved the same as it had been to Kenny's question, but again he reminded himself of his reason for being there. He needed to go with the flow.

"I just got in on the ferry. I was told there was work here, and work's what I'm looking for."

"Well, out here, most folks make their living in the lobster trade," Kenny piped up, "but tourists provide a living for some folks too. You know anything about lobstering? Ever been a sternman for anyone?"

"Yes, once. I went with Charlie MacBride out of Round Harbor earlier this year while Vance Smith was away."

"Did ya now? Is the old son of a bitch still pushing that thirty-six-foot Novi boat around? Bet he hasn't finished painting it yet. So what the hell happened to Vance?"

"Vance is okay. He and Joyce decided to get married. They left their kids with her father and drove to Montreal. They were gone about two weeks."

"Huh," Kenny grunted.

"The old *Lazy Day* may not be the prettiest boat around, but Charlie knows his stuff. I learned a lot and made pretty good money with him."

As Emma topped up everyone's coffee, Kenny reported JB Thompson and Ronnie Moody were both currently looking for sternmen since old Lenny McLeod quit JB, and Tom Stanley had broken his leg.

"Thanks very much," Seth said, making a mental note of the names. "Sounds like two good places to start looking. You two have any advice on where I might find a room?"

"Bill Harris runs a B&B in old Captain DeVoe's house up the road," Emma offered. "He rents out a few rooms for way more than they're worth, but he's a pretty decent cook. That's just about your only option unless you know someone who'll put you up."

Kenny added that since both Moody and JB were out to haul, there would be little chance of finding them until after five o'clock.

6

"I understand, thank you. Guess my first stop is the B&B. So how do I find it?"

* * *

Twenty minutes later, Seth was still some distance from Captain De Voe's place. Despite two weeks of physical activity with MacBride, the weight of his bag and months of stress were taking their toll. He rested briefly on a fallen tree and took in the surprising beauty of the island. After a few minutes, he felt much calmer. *It's a funny, quirky place, but I think it'll do.*

* * *

Several islands lay between the mainland and Sandaray. Some were uninhabited rocks; some, like Walton Island, were occupied by a single farming or fishing family; and others, like Orran Island, belonged almost exclusively to the rich and famous. These secluded getaway places were basically no-go areas for nonresidents, but were maintained by local people from islands like Sandaray. It was good work if you could find it or were born into it. For over thirty years, Bill Harris's family had helped maintain one such property, the lavish holiday home of Sir Reginald Wilson, on Orran Island. Bill too had benefited from the millionaire's patronage, working as head cook on Wilson's hundred-foot superyacht.

Ten years earlier, however, he had left his cushy well-paid job to marry a mainland girl he had met during shore leave. With a generous cash wedding gift from the Wilson family, Bill and his new bride moved to nearby Sandaray where they bought and renovated Captain Daniel DeVoe's run-down but handsome mansion, and turned it into a successful B&B business. The house boasted spectacular ocean views, fine period features, and even a widow's walk. Now in its ninth year of operation, DeVoe Lodge had lasted eight years longer than Bill's marriage.

* * *

It took Seth just over forty minutes to reach the lodge. He walked around to the seaward side of the building and onto the porch. The door, slightly ajar, allowed him to peer in. "Hello. Anyone home?"

Immediately, a slight man with a noticeable dowager's hump and graying hair tied back in a short ponytail, appeared in the entryway.

"Morning mate...what can I do for ya?"

"You must be Bill."

"Yup. Who wants to know?"

"I'm Seth Martin, new in town, and I'm looking for a place to stay for a few nights."

"You'd better come on in. Follow me. We'll talk in the kitchen."

The furnishings were simple but tasteful. Everything looked incongruous next to its owner.

"This business keeps me really busy, ya know, and it's a real bitch trying to run it on my own. Making a bloody cake just now and cooking lobsters for room number four's lunch. Still got two rooms to clean up and get ready, laundry to do, and the town's electric bills to get out." They walked into a steamy kitchen where an overpowering smell of fish filled the air. Bill continued, "People just don't realize what's involved here. Er, ah...what did ya say your name was?" He pulled out a chair for Seth.

"Seth, Seth Martin. Looking for a room. You got any available?"

"No. You're out of luck. In fact, two folks came off the ferry this morning and took my last one. Couple of creeps they are! I looked all over trying to find them at the wharf but couldn't find 'em anywhere. Turns out they went off to do a bit of sightseeing first...can ya believe it? I'll probably have space in a week if you're still around and interested."

Seth replied he would keep looking and might call back in a week's time if he had no luck. Then, risking further dialogue, he decided to ask where he could find Captain JB Thompson or Captain Ronnie Moody.

"I saw Ronnie go to haul this morning; don't know about JB. Might be home or over at Orran."

Placing three lobsters into the steaming pot, Bill went on to explain there would soon be a big shindig on Orran Island, one of those events that brought the rich folks over for a few days of partying, socializing, and figuring out how they could make even more money.

"JB usually helps out by taking people and junk over from Sandaray to Orran. He might be out there now."

Bill gestured to the corner of the room, "There's a phone over there and a phone book on the table. Call him up. I got to get to pickin' these lobsters now and getting the rest of the damn lunch going."

Seth dialed JB's number and a smooth female voice answered, "Thompson's."

"Hello, my name is Seth Martin, may I speak with Captain Thompson, please?"

"I'm sorry, but he's gone to haul and won't be back until about five. Would you like to leave a message?"

"Yes. I've heard he's looking for a sternman, and I'd like to talk to him about it."

"I see…have you any experience?"

"Yes, some. I went with Charlie MacBride on the mainland for a while. But," he added, "I learn quickly."

"Can you come down this evening after dinner?"

"Sure. What time is best and where exactly are you?"

The honey-textured voice went on to explain the best chance of catching him would probably be around seven o'clock, after dinner and before he retired to bed. She proceeded to give him directions.

"We're opposite the church. It shouldn't be difficult to find us. It's a pretty small place!"

"Thank you, Mrs. Thompson, I'll be there at seven."

"You're welcome. But it's not Mrs. Thompson, it's Mrs. Wilson. I'm JB's daughter. See you tonight."

"Sure thing, and thank you again."

Seth noted JB's and Ronnie's phone numbers on a scrap of paper and stuffed it in his pocket. Turning back to Bill, he asked, "You wouldn't happen to have a map of the island, would you?"

Bill put a half-picked lobster down, wiped his hands on the towel, and went into the entranceway. "This do ya?" he asked, proudly handing Seth a professionally printed sheet of shiny paper with a detailed map on one side and names, addresses, and telephone numbers on the other. "It took me a lot of work to put this together, but folks really like having it. It even shows most of the trails."

Seth thanked Bill, reiterating he would probably call about a room in a couple of days. Bill went back to preparing lunch.

* * *

Map in hand, Seth set out to explore more of the island and perhaps locate the house across from the church. The well-kept properties certainly contrasted sharply with the fish houses and industry around the harbor. *Lobstering must pay well*, he considered.

He walked northeast toward the airport but turned back once he realized the time, quarter past twelve. He acknowledged how absorbed he had become in his new surroundings, but, motivated by a desire to learn more of what work might be available, he retraced his steps to Port MacKenzie.

Emma's Café seemed the most sensible place to base himself. Once again, he took a seat at the counter as Emma appeared with a tray of food for three folks at one of the tables. As she made her way back, she looked at Seth and, with a big smile, said, "Oh, hello, it's you, er…something or other Martin. Guess good ol' Bill was full up, right? And now you're tired and hungry, and it's past your lunch time…so, what can I get you? Want coffee?"

"Yes, please, to the coffee, and how about a grilled ham and cheese sandwich?"

"Comin' right up."

As he ate, Seth decided he should see if anyone might be around at Thompson's or Moody's fish house. If that failed, talk to whoever might be down there, and find out what living and working on the island would be like. The altitude of Emma's Café afforded an excellent view of almost every building around the harbor, and Emma appeared more than happy to point out who owned which fish house.

* * *

Finding both Thompson's and Moody's fish houses proved easy…Ronnie's by itself down at the very end, and JB's beside the power pole with the big transformer. By the looks of things, both fishermen were quite successful at what they did. Each had neatly stacked, spare traps in good condition, and buoys freshly painted and ready for the water. Peering through their workshop windows told a slightly different story. He saw a careful, neat worker at JB's and a hurried one at Ronnie's. JB's dock looked spotless, whereas Ronnie's, like several others, bore the remnants of projects past and half-finished jobs.

As he walked, his feeling of being watched returned, making him nervous. *It's only curious natives,* he thought. *No one knows you're here.*

He stopped, momentarily distracted by two boys sitting on one of the jetties. He wondered how different his own life would have been if he had been brought up in a place like this. "Shit!" he said out loud, checking his watch, annoyed he had let time slip away. Emma's place closed at five. If he wanted to survive until it opened in the morning, he should get another bite.

He found the energy to run most of the way up the hill, all the while hoping the café would still be open. He arrived, and luckily, she had not yet locked the door. He entered to find the place deserted…no customers and no Emma. "Hello," he quietly called. No reply. "Hello," he repeated with more volume, "anyone here?"

"Yes, yes, yes," came a harassed reply from the back. "I'm coming, I'll be right there." Within seconds, Emma appeared in the doorway, looking upset and angry. "Oh, you again, want another coffee?"

"Yes please, if it's not too much trouble," Seth said, trying not to cause further aggravation. "Is everything okay?"

"Sure," she replied matter-of-factly, adding, after a pause, "I mean…hell no, definitely not, things are *not* okay!" Shoving a mug of coffee in the microwave, she elaborated. "It's the damn computer. Every week, I send an order in to D. R. Fox. They're good, and I can get anything if I send it in by email, except not today, though. Ooooh no, not today!

"Today the G.D. computer has it in for me, and after all the work of putting a big order together, it won't let me send anything, no matter what I do. I've tried everything!" She slammed open the stainless steel hood covering the sandwich-making area. "I'm going to take the damn machine down to the shore and let the fish have a go at it. Bet you're hungry now. How does a cold roast beef sandwich sound? Might even have some coleslaw left to go with it."

"That sounds terrible…er…I mean, terrible about the computer trouble and great to the sandwich."

The microwave bell rang, and a steaming cup of coffee appeared in front of Seth. "I've had a computer or two in my time. Want to let me have a look at it? Maybe I can fix it for you."

"I suppose it won't do any harm," she said, putting a thick roast beef sandwich and a dish of slaw down in front of him. "You know about computers then?"

"Umm, some," he said, his words blurred by the sandwich.

After ten minutes of comfortable feeding and watering, Emma led him to the back room, where he soon found himself seated in front of a fairly new computer surrounded by chaos. He cautioned himself not to move anything since it would certainly upset the organization only she understood.

"Where's your order?" he asked.

"Here, I'll show you." As she leaned over him to reach the mouse, her hair gently brushed his cheek, subtly reminding him of a time, indeed a life now past. A nice feeling, but he put it aside.

She opened the browser and selected "MMIC.com." Moving closer and reaching around him, she then typed in her address: "EmmaCafe@MMIC.com," followed by her password. After a couple of successful clicks, she pointed aggressively at the screen, leaving a greasy imprint of her forefinger, and explained, "This is what I'm trying to send, but the creepy, dumb, stupid, little mind-of-its-own machine won't do it. Have a look at it, see what you can do. As for me, I'm going back out to clean up the shop."

Seth worked like a pro, his fingers flashing over the keys, never touching the mouse. In a few minutes, he sat back and watched as a special program did its work. Noticing one particular issue in the growing list at the foot of the screen, Seth bolted to attention. *Son of a bitch! This is the same Chinese root-kit that gave everyone in the government fits five years ago!* Quickly, he removed the antique malware and invoked programs to clean and repair the trouble. As they did their work, he got up and went out front, remarking to himself that at least he hadn't lost his touch.

Out in the café, he found Emma sweeping the floor.

"Can I help you clean up?" he asked, surprising her.

"No, just get that darned machine working," she replied. "Any good news yet?"

"Oh, it'll be fine shortly. I found a problem and have a fix working. It'll take about ten minutes."

"You really found the trouble?"

"I certainly hope so."

"Well, then, here you go," she said, tossing him a soggy rag smelling of chlorine, "you can disinfect the tables."

"Sure." He set about wiping down the tabletops. "How come you don't stay open for dinner?"

"Most customers just come in for breakfast and lunch, and that's really about all we can handle. But I'm fortunate. I have a part-time helper, Mandy Sharpe. She's been a godsend and the reason I can stay open most of the day. A lot of the fishermen here are regulars. I open for them at four every morning, but by evening, they're all at home, and only the occasional tourist comes around then."

"Tables are all done, I'll go check your machine," Seth said.

He returned almost immediately. "You had a lousy virus and one particularly nasty bit of malware messing things up, but it looks like they're all gone, at least for now. Come and try sending your order again."

"Okay, I'm coming."

Emma sat at the desk and clasped her hands in front of her as if mentally sending a message to the machine it had better

14

behave. Then almost ceremoniously, she grasped the mouse and opened the browser, while Seth stood behind, carefully watching every move. "So far so good," she said, logging into her email account. She found the order under "Drafts."

"Better check it's just what you want."

She began going through it line by line and, having verified it, went on to recheck the address.

Finally, she moved the pointer over the "send" button, stopped, and looked up at Seth. "Well, here goes."

Click. They waited. Nothing happened. Then, just as always in the past, the message disappeared, and a box appeared, saying, "Your email has been sent."

"There you go. Bob's your uncle!" said Seth, instinctively patting her on the shoulder in celebration.

"It worked!" she exclaimed. "You're a genius. But I don't get it, who's Bob?"

"Just an old expression my dad used, meaning everything is all right."

"Thank you so much! The sandwich is definitely on the house."

* * *

The walk to JB's took longer than expected, making him five minutes late for the seven o'clock appointment. Using Mrs. Wilson's directions and Bill Harris's map, he had no trouble finding the church and JB's home, an old Cape Cod–style house surrounded by a white picket fence. He made his way up the steps to the porch, knocked twice, and waited.

Wearing the merest touch of blue eyeshadow, pale pink lipstick, and dressed in a stylish cream linen trouser suit, Mrs. Daniel R. Wilson oozed charm and self-confidence. "You must be Seth Martin. Please come in," she said, extending a warm smile and an elegantly manicured hand.

Her voice was unmistakable…and she didn't look much like his idea of a fisherman's wife!

"I'm Linda, JB's daughter. The Mrs. JB Thompson you referred to on the phone was my mother. She passed away ten years ago."

"Oh, I'm very sorry."

"Thank you, Seth. Now how about a coffee? I have a fresh pot on."

"Coffee would be great. Thank you."

He followed her into the kitchen, admiring her long, glossy, chocolate-colored tresses and seductive gait. She placed two delicate china cups of coffee on what must have been the old Thompson family table, a massive, solid oak affair that seated ten and had no doubt seen a lot of action. "None for Captain Thompson?" Seth remarked.

"Well, I'm sorry to disappoint, but it's just me for now. Dad got in from hauling a bit early today, but there were eight people wanting to get to Orran Island, so he came home, had a quick bite, and went straight back out. He didn't say what time he'd be back, but he did say to tell you if you're interested in work, you should show up at his fish house at four thirty in the morning, and he'll talk to you then."

"Well, please tell him I'll be there," Seth answered, rising from the table. With his mind now focused on the impropriety of the situation, he added, "I won't hold you up any longer. Thanks for your hospitality."

He also realized if he had to be up at four thirty, he needed to find somewhere to sleep.

"No need to rush," Linda said. "You know they roll up the sidewalks on Sandaray at six p.m., and besides, you haven't finished your coffee."

Chapter Two

Just after four in the morning, with an overcast sky hiding the stars and the waning moon, lights were starting to come on around the shore of Port MacKenzie announcing the beginning of a new workday.

In Emma's Café, several sternmen crowded around two tables and chatted about their exploits from the night before, waking up, if not sobering up, with strong coffee while eating he-man breakfasts.

On a bench outside the ferry terminal, the buzz of his wristwatch alarm abruptly woke Seth. "Oooee," he spoke out loud, raking stiff fingers through his dark, unruly hair and rubbing the sleep from his still tired eyes. *Better get my act together.*

He could see JB's fish house across the harbor, a single floodlight illuminating the dock in front. Unlike most of the others, no light showed in either the upper-floor apartment or the workshop below. Keeping an eye on the floodlight, he carefully picked his way along the south shore. As he did, he spotted a figure emerging from beyond JB's building.

Dressed in waterproof coveralls—commonly called oilskins—and rubber boots, the stocky figure looked to be about five feet, eight inches tall. Almost certainly his prospective new employer.

* * *

JB's life revolved around the sea, just as his father's and grandfather's had before him. His weathered face reflected a lifetime of hard work, and he bore the look of a man with a deep understanding of, and respect for, both the weather and the ocean. His hands told a story of years of hard manual labor, doing what he did almost every day of his life: lobster fishing. Only the worst unpredicted weather, the most debilitating illness, or the direst emergency ever kept him from the work that provided a living for himself, his wife, Martha, and their daughter, Linda.

He watched intently as Seth emerged from the darkness, tiptoeing confidently over the large boulders and climbing up onto the dock. From years of experience, JB immediately began to form an impression of his potential new helper...a little cautious perhaps but generally strong willed and self-confident.

"You must be Captain Thompson," Seth offered.

"I am."

They shook hands and studied each other closely. The captain sensed a different sort of newcomer, a man from far beyond the normal circle of fishing people he had worked with and known for years. Not really a man of the sea nor one of the drifters he had met so often, but a real outsider. A serious, youngish man with some unstated reason for being on Sandaray. This all gave JB a troubling impression and raised a red flag in his mind.

"Linda told me you came by last evening; sorry I missed you. She said you were looking to stern out here. How much experience have you had?"

"I went with Charlie MacBride for two weeks earlier this year, not as third man, just me and Charlie. I learned a lot...I can do the job."

JB scanned Seth's lean six-foot one-inch frame, from his bushy beard, dark, straggly hair and well-developed but untanned arms, right down to his "not really the best footwear for this kind of work" boots. "Well, you look like you could handle going third man okay, which is what I had in mind for today, but that ain't happening. Last night, Jason called to say he needed to go into town with Dick Walsh. Good old Jase has been going with a girl over there, and I guess his wife found out and is after him. So no second man today. Since there are only a hundred traps to haul this morning, I thought just you and I could handle it. I'll take it easy on you. You okay with that?"

"No problem," Seth replied with more confidence than he felt.

"There are a couple of rules, mind you. First, I run this boat, not you or anyone else in the back, remember that. Second, if I ever catch you doing anything with drugs, you're done right then…and I mean done forever as far as I'm concerned. And there's no smoking here either. I hate the smell of that shit, and it makes me cough. Understand?"

"Yes, sir."

"You got any oilskins?

"No, sir."

"Okay. I have an old set onboard, but you got to get a decent set if you're serious about lobstering. Ask Carrie this afternoon. We're going over to their boat *Clacken* to sell our catch. She usually has 'em."

"Thanks, I will."

JB went to the fish house door and held it open. "You can store your bag in here for the time being."

"Great. Thanks again."

Without wasting another minute, the two men were down the ladder and seated in the small skiff JB used to get to his boat. The four-horsepower Suzuki started instantly and powered them steadily across the harbor through the maze of buoys, boats, and floating platforms. From time to time, a voice could be heard, or a light seen, but mostly they were alone in the eerie half-light.

Soon they were aboard the thirty-eight-foot *Linda-T*, a typical Maine lobster boat, built for business with a 350-horsepower engine. Like almost every other modern Maine lobster boat, *Linda-T* had been made mostly of fiberglass, with the notable exception of her deck. For this JB had insisted on wood because its softness made standing long hours much more comfortable.

JB slowly but expertly guided the *Linda-T* into the open waters of the Atlantic. A slight offshore breeze but no swell, made for a smooth ride. "Pretty standard layout as you can see," JB said, turning to point with a gaff, "bait box there, lobster tank there, and oh, by the way, do you have a good sharp knife on you?"

"Er, ah. Actually, no."

"Well, I always keep one in the stern. I'll show you where." JB pulled the throttle to idle, put the boat in neutral, and walked aft—Seth followed.

"Right, here it is, and don't forget it…it can save your life. If you ever shove a trap overboard and then get the rope wrapped around your leg, you'll be pulled to the bottom in seconds, you'd better believe it. Don't matter how strong you are, even a single trap will pull like a ton of bricks. Two lessons here: first, don't ever let that happen, and second, if it does, have a sharp knife handy, and use it quick."

In about twenty minutes, JB had maneuvered the boat alongside the first yellow-and-green buoy, and their work began. Commercial lobster fishing required a well-disciplined team and a routine: ropes go here, buoys go there, lobsters get measured this way, banded that way, and so forth. No improvisation, just the timesaving efficiency and safety of standardized work. JB snagged the buoy and ran the rope up over a large pulley and onto the hydraulic hauler. When the trap appeared, he grabbed it and swung it onto the gunwale rails.

"Now pay attention: see the way this lid is tied? That's the way I want them all tied. The measure is over here, use it, and don't guess about their size. I don't want any illegals in the tank. Bands are over here. Finally, always put new bait in, and tie it like this, see?"

Seth watched carefully and soon got right in the flow of things.

JB kept a close eye on him, noticing everything he did. From time to time, he would make a comment or offer a suggestion, but overall, he seemed quite pleased. By ten thirty, they were done: one hundred traps had been emptied of their catch, rebaited, and replaced on the ocean floor, and *Linda-T* was headed back to Sandaray.

As instructed, Seth grabbed the broom and hose and began sweeping the shrimp, small crabs, sea fleas, and other unwanted residents of the hauled traps down the deck to the open scuppers through which they returned to the sea. With the work area spic and span, he moved the day's catch from the water-filled holding tank to large plastic crates. The mouth of the harbor came into view as he finished.

Like most fishermen in remote places, JB accumulated several days' catch and stored the precious little "bugs," as they were commonly called, in crates floating below the surface of the harbor and tethered to the same mooring as their boats. This kept the catch in its natural environment until enough lobsters had accumulated to justify a trip to the mainland or some local buyer. Today JB would be buying bait and selling several days' catch to a buyer in the harbor at nearby Orran Island.

The engine slowed as they entered the harbor at Port MacKenzie. "Take the hook, and get your butt up on the bow," JB directed.

Using the gaff, Seth caught the large mooring rope and tugged it on deck. He freed the line to the skiff and carefully secured the big rope to the bow cleat. He then passed the skiff line to JB, went back to double check the security of the mooring line, and made his way back to the main deck.

"Nice job," JB commented.

Using the hydraulic hauler, JB pulled the floating crates up the side of the boat one at a time. Seth slid them aft along the gunwale. One by one, he stacked them in rows two or three high on the deck. By the time they were all loaded, there were five stacks of two and one stack of three, neatly secured in the rear of the boat. As a rough guess, there would be about 1,300 pounds of lobsters.

Soon they were underway again, this time headed for nearby Orran Island. Seth sat on the engine cover and, for the first time since he had arrived, felt relaxed. "Really nice boat you have," he said.

"Umm, yeah," JB responded, then changing the subject, added, "You seem to know how to handle yourself, but you don't look to me much like the average 'running away,' 'confused,' 'all messed up,' 'in deep trouble' young person who usually makes his or her way out here looking for work. I'm not trying to pry, but you'd better tell me if you're in any trouble with the law."

Seth felt his color rise as memories of the intense six-month-long investigation flashed through his mind. Forcing a smile to cover his embarrassment, he responded, "No, err…no, absolutely no trouble with the law."

"Mind telling me where you're from and why you're here?"

"I come from rural Virginia, went to college in Virginia," Seth said slowly, trying to think of a way to get out of the discussion. The words of Sir Walter Scott's famous poem suddenly flashed into his head, *Oh, what a tangled web we weave when first we practice to deceive!*

As he paused, the radio crackled, "*Linda-T, Linda-T,* you on here, JB?" Picking up the microphone from its perch, JB responded, "Yep, *Clacken*. Got thirteen crates for you, be there in about five minutes."

Saved by the bell, Seth mused, mightily relieved.

The harbor at Orran Island appeared large, well protected, and surrounded on three sides by rising woodland. Apart from the occasional curious traveler and *Clacken II*, it only served those who lived there. This included five fishermen, who lived on the island only when lobstering, and six multibillionaires who lived there anytime they wanted. As *Linda-T* entered the harbor, a forty-five-foot sailboat and two gleaming white, very well-polished oceangoing motor yachts came into view. Closer to the mouth of the harbor sat *Clacken II,* a sixty-five-foot wooden boat made for the job of buying lobsters and selling bait.

As JB pulled *Linda-T* close, a woman, decked out in orange oilskins and wellies, came to the side and threw him a line. "Afternoon, handsome," she said with a big grin and a distinct down east accent.

"Afternoon yourself, beautiful," he responded as he made the line fast to the hydraulic hauler.

"Seth, grab the line astern, and tie it to the farthest aft cleat."

"Need anything but bait, JB?" she asked.

"Actually, yes. Would you happen to have a set of oilskins for young Seth here?"

"Frank," she shouted, "we got any large oilskins on board?"

"I'll check," a man's voice responded.

"So you're Seth. I'm Carrie," she said as she threw the line from the boom above.

Seth nodded, muttered a hello, and grabbed the line like he knew what he should do with it. He fastened it to the first crate, and in no time at all, thirteen crates were on *Clacken II*'s deck. Carrie sorted and weighed the catch with incredible speed as Seth watched, amazed at her skill and dexterity.

Frank appeared, "Here, see if these'll fit you," he called out as he threw a package to Seth. In seconds, Seth appeared decked out like a proper fisherman, confident he would be visible for miles in any emergency.

Soon all the transfers were complete. The lobsters were aboard *Clacken II*, and the accounting papers, money, bait, empty crates, and oilskins were aboard *Linda-T*. With the workday almost done, they started back to Sandaray.

About ten minutes out of Orran, JB looked at Seth and said, "Look, I don't know what you're up to, but as long as you keep it clean, I'll take you on. You get seventeen percent before bait and fuel. I presume you don't have a license, but you can go on mine. If you need a place to stay, I'll rent you the apartment over my fish house for four hundred bucks a month. Jason has already moved out. I'll show you around as soon as we get back. You look like you could really use a shower. Do we have a deal?"

"Yes, sir, we do." Seth heaved a huge sigh of relief as they shook hands to seal the agreement.

Having safely moored *Linda-T*, the two men made their way in companionable silence back to the dock and to JB's fish house. JB led the way up an outside wooden stairway to a small porch on the upper floor. As he opened the door, the friendly odor of old wood struck them both, triggering a flood of memories for JB. With a nostalgic sigh he said, "When Martha and I were first married, I picked her up right here and carried her through this doorway." And then, his voice cracking with emotion, he added, "She wasn't heavy at all, she...." His voice trailed off, and he couldn't go on. Silence followed as they moved inside. Then he continued, "Well, this is it. Our first home, that big place up the island was just a dream then... seems a lifetime ago now."

The apartment was compact and functional. JB pointed out the usual facilities: gas stove, refrigerator, and clothes washer. Several shelves above the counter were loaded with pots, pans, and crockery.

An archway led to the largest room in the place, the living room. "Very nice view," Seth exclaimed as he looked out over the harbor toward the ferry terminal. He located *Linda-T* as she lay on her mooring. The place might seem old-fashioned to some but perfectly acceptable to him, and *hey,* he thought, *folks would pay a million bucks for a view like this on the mainland.* The wall to the right had a small window that looked down the row of other fish houses, while the other side wall had a door to the bedroom. There were lots of photographs of life on Sandaray, all arranged with great care. *Hmm, definitely a woman's touch.*

"This is perfect," remarked Seth, following JB toward the bedroom.

Before they entered, one particular picture caught Seth's eye. It drew his attention, not because of its subject matter but because of its location, right up against the doorframe. An awkward place for a painting of its size. Seth pointed at the painting. Then, with a questioning look, turned his gaze on JB.

"I know, it's a funny place to hang a picture." JB offered. Seth waited for additional explanation.

"I hung it there when we moved out thirty-six years ago, and wouldn't you know, not a single person since has ever asked why."

"Okay, Captain," piped up Seth, "why is that lovely picture hanging in such a daft location there by the door?"

"Well, I'll tell ya. But first, you have to remove it from the wall."

Seth carefully took down the painting to reveal a ragged hole the size of a saucer. Judging by the grime and the cobwebs, it had been there for many years. "Oh, I see," Seth said with surprise and wonder.

"It's almost as old as the building," JB continued, "and made by a man driven by a fit of rage…my rage and this fist."

Wow, Seth thought, *I didn't have this guy down as a loose cannon or a fit-of-rage type.*

"So what brought that on," Seth asked. "What made you do it?"

"Martha and I were having an er…ah…disagreement of some sort. I don't remember what prompted it anymore, but we were both right, and our heels were dug in. Neither would give, frustration grew, she went into the bedroom and locked the door, loaded my shotgun and got ready to use it. I pounded my fist into the wall, vowing that no locked door or wall would keep me out!

"In the end I took my bleeding fist out on the porch where Martha soon joined me and, thankfully, things calmed down. We left the hole there to remind us to listen, understand, compromise, and forgive. It's helped me many times over the years."

As they looked at the rest of the apartment Seth's thoughts returned to the lesson surrounding the fist hole, his mind recalling events two years earlier. *And I wouldn't be here at all if my so-called colleague had only lived by that philosophy.*

The tour of the apartment had provided a remarkably interesting insight into his new employer, and he wondered if there might come a time when he could share his own life-changing experience with someone. *Not now, however.*

* * *

JB took two keys out of his pocket and offered them to Seth. "The other one is for the shop downstairs. If you want to use the phone, you pay for it, and you pay for the gas, I buy the electric.

Linda does all the books, so pay her the rent each month. Get yourself cleaned up, settled in, and be ready to go to work the day after tomorrow. I'll see you then at four thirty."

Chapter Three

By the time the brisk westerly wind had joined the heat of the sun to free the island from a dense morning fog, most fishermen were away and well into their workday. At Emma's Café, the only customer, Kenny, remained immersed in last week's newspaper while nursing a half cup of cold coffee.

With Mandy cleaning up from a busy morning, Emma could find no excuse for not tackling her deskwork. "I'll be in the back for a while, Mandy," she said as she made her way to the cubbyhole she called the office. She found a place to set her mug among the mountain of papers, slumped down on the chair, and sighed loudly. "I really hate all this desk shit!"

She stared at the computer for a moment and then flipped the switch. As the machine sprang to life, thoughts of the newcomer who saved its very life sprang to mind. *An outsider came in here last week and in no time managed to fix this darned machine. No charge, no "you need a new this or that," no nothing, except for a computer that worked. Damned remarkable and unusual, and a really nice guy in the bargain...could have had me in a heartbeat.* But he'd left over five days ago and she had seen neither hide nor hair of him since. Maybe she'd never see him again, as frequently happened with new sternmen on Sandaray.

With the promise of a better day, Emma pushed back on her chair and decided to take a short walk. *Who knows who I'll run into?* she mused, "Back in thirty minutes, just need some fresh air," she shouted to Mandy, slipping on her Bean boots and heading briskly out the door.

She walked up the hill toward the center of the island, enjoying the clean, fresh air and the sparkling view provided by the lush, newly washed greenery. As she approached the brow of the hill, a car passed, splashing her with water from a pothole. She jumped out of the way but not fast enough. "Touristers! Can't live with 'em and can't live without 'em," she muttered under her breath while checking her trousers. As she continued, the air and the exercise became more and more invigorating, and her mood began to lift.

Walking briskly, not paying attention to her location or the time, Emma realized she had almost reached Bill's B&B. She had been gone for over twenty minutes and would have to run to get back in time for the lunch crowd. As she began to jog, a vehicle without a muffler approached from behind. When abeam of her, the driver shut off the engine and stopped.

"Bonjour, Emma. How are you this fine day?" schmoozed Bill Harris.

Oh, shit, what a time to run into him. I wonder what he's up to. "Good morning, Bill. I'm fine, thanks. How've you been?"

"Oh, fine. Busy, you know. Say, I need to talk to you. Have you got a couple of minutes?"

"Tell you what, I'll give you two minutes, maybe two minutes and thirty seconds, if you drive me down to the café. I'm late to help Mandy."

"Okay, jump in."

The broken-out windows, together with the missing muffler, made riding in Bill's truck like being inside a bass drum. Emma sat back, gazing at this man who had once shared her bed. *Just think, if we hadn't been in that bar at the same time, we would never have met, and I would never have come to Sandaray. On the other hand, I would never have learned about making marital decisions based on character rather than chemistry...a tough lesson indeed.* The roar of the engine stopped as they arrived at the café.

"I've been thinking of offering your Mandy a job as a cook at the B&B. Do you mind, Emma?"

Why, you son of a bitch, she thought, that's a really rotten trick. Poaching my staff!

"Oh, have you?" she said with mock surprise.

"Yes, but only on weekends, of course. She works for you four days a week, doesn't she? It would give her some nice extra income, and it would be perfect for me."

I wonder what he means by perfect for him. "Well, that decision is up to Mandy, of course. But just don't you screw with her, Bill Harris. She's a fine woman and a really good worker."

"Moi? Mess with your employee?"

"Yes, *you*! don't mess with her, or I'll come after you with both barrels."

"You've already done that once, dear. I'll be good, truly. I'm a changed man, and I really need help with the cooking, particularly on weekends."

"Well, go on in, order something, and you two can talk over in Kenny's corner. Don't you dare lure her out here into this disgusting truck, understand?"

Emma and Bill entered the café, Bill making a beeline for Kenny's seat.

"Cup of coffee, please Mandy, and two minutes of your precious time if you please."

Emma pulled Mandy to one side and whispered, "Just listen to old lover-boy but don't commit to anything. I'll fill you in later when he's gone."

As the café got busy, Emma did her best to keep her eyes and ears on Mandy and Bill, but she couldn't make out what they were saying, and Mandy's body language gave nothing away. After a few minutes, Bill got up, gestured, as if blowing a kiss to Emma, and left. *Creep,* Emma thought as she prepared a sandwich. *I wonder what kind of a line he gave her.*

Around two thirty came a welcome lull. The two women moved near the window where they could see everything going on and talked quickly. "He wants me to cook at the B&B on the weekends, three meals both days. That's a lot of work, but he is offering twenty bucks an hour, and there will likely be good tips."

"That's a hell of a lot of work," Emma replied. "Where is he going to be all this time? He has that weird guy Harold helping cook breakfast during the week. Heck, if you take this deal, he'll hardly be doing anything."

"Oh, Emma, be a little kinder to your ex. He has laundry to do every day and rooms to make up and all the rest."

"Yes, I know. But that's way too much for you…you need some time to yourself. You should tell him you'll do breakfast and lunch, or lunch and dinner, but not all three. If the place is full, you would meet yourself coming back, and it could be a real killer."

"I agree. Maybe just breakfast and lunch would be best. After all, I don't have a clue about making some of that stuff he serves, like snails."

"Snails are easy, but your point is valid. Bill, of course, is a really good chef, and he'd teach you. That could be the biggest plus to the job." *But that better be all he teaches you!* "Please think hard about this Mandy."

"I will," she answered, hanging up her apron. "You know, the two-meal thing might just work fine. I think I can do it all,

31

and the extra money would be nice. But I'll sleep on it and call him tomorrow."

"Good plan. See you in the morning Mandy," Emma sighed, weary from work and the anxiety brought on by her ex potentially stealing her staff.

Around four thirty, when the last customer had left and with the good chance no one else would come in before closing time, Emma began setting up the tables, sweeping, mopping, and cleaning up the counter and food preparation area. As she did so, an intense, almost painful wave of loneliness swept over her, perhaps prompted by the beautiful day or, more likely, her chance meeting with Bill. It was the first time she had seen him in months, but the scars of an unhappy marriage were still raw even after all this time. Or maybe she just felt very alone and wanted not to be.

At ten to five, she turned the sign around to "Closed," locked the door, and went through to the back. She rinsed out her coffee mug, filled it with red wine, and flopped on the easy chair. Soon, between sips of wine, her thoughts became focused on Bill and their early relationship. It had all started with such promise back in Massachusetts in the late '90s. After a whirlwind romance, they had married on Sandaray and spent the next four years transforming Captain DeVoe's old home into a modern Bed and Breakfast. It became a highly successful business, but constant bickering and relentless hard work had cost them their marriage.

She looked into her empty mug and thought of her life… also empty. She looked around the room and it too seemed empty, until she glanced at her computer. *Emma Harris*, she mused, *you are a complete fantasist. He's never going to look at a frumpy exhausted waitress. Mind you, he has been very kind and helpful. Maybe I should make a bit more effort with my hair or something.*

32

Gradually the emptiness subsided as a plan formed and a feeling of self-worth began to return. "Get your ass out of this chair and get yourself something to eat, you idiot!" she said out loud, rising to her feet. "Long day ahead and you need to build in extra time in the bathroom." She padded back to the kitchen and, within a few minutes, headed upstairs clutching a sandwich and another mug of wine.

Emma's large apartment above the café occupied the same square footage as the restaurant below. The biggest area was the well-appointed living room. She put her food on the table by the sofa, turned on the TV, and changed into pajamas. The six o'clock news started, and as the talking heads related the latest troubles, disasters, and problems on the mainland, Emma sipped her wine, ate her dinner, and thought about Seth.

The news soon gave way to a program about elephant poaching in Africa, not a subject she wanted to consider while eating, so she pressed the "off" button and continued her musings. *Did he get a job with JB or Ronnie? It would be nice if he stayed around for a while. I'd sure like to see a lot more of him.*

Chapter Four

It had been a rough day on the water, one of those days when every move Seth made and every action he took seemed specifically opposed by the rolling, pitching, or bouncing of the boat. It had been the kind of day when he took extra care checking his feet for rope loops and the survival knife for quick access, before pushing any trap overboard. He had no excess mental capacity that would allow his mind to wander, even a little, as the job and survival demanded his total attention.

It took what felt like twice the normal time to haul the day's allotted traps, stow the lobsters, and head back home. But when his cleanup duties were complete, Seth worked his way forward and stood near JB. Finally, he had time to look around and reflect on the sea, the combination of awesome power and incredible beauty that surrounded them. A place that made them and their vessel totally insignificant, he realized, and could swallow them up in an instant if it wanted to.

"How many keepers were there in the last string of traps?" asked JB.

"Eight."

"How about the one before?"

"Twelve and two crabs, which I threw back."

"Twenty years ago, old Sam Young used to go with me. He would always know how we were doing, never missed a count, always paying attention. Haven't had anyone since Sam who could remember so well. You must like numbers and details; that's a good thing in this business."

Remembering a life now past, Seth replied he always liked to keep his mind busy with some mental puzzle or other exercise, reasoning an exercised mind meant a healthy mind. But there the conversation ended, giving way to wind, engine noise, and the pounding waves.

Soon they were on dry land, the day's work complete. As they walked down the dock toward the fish house, JB said they wouldn't be leaving the next day until about nine thirty because he had a job to do for his daughter. Then, to Seth's surprise, he added, "Why don't you come over for dinner tonight? You can have a lie-in in the morning."

Seth accepted, happy at the prospect of having a break from the humdrum regularity of his own basic cooking.

"Five thirty, okay?"

"I'll be there."

Up in his apartment, Seth went into the living room to unwind and digest the events of the day. He stood alone gazing out the window, thankful for the peace and quiet. He watched the ferry and wondered if he would ever get over that eerie feeling of being hunted by visitors from his past.

Suddenly his body instinctively tightened as he watched two men dressed in business suits walk down the ramp. *Dear God, are they looking for me? What if…?* His heart pounded but soon calmed as the harbor master appeared and escorted them to the terminal. "Be still, memories," he muttered to himself, "No one will find you here."

The shower felt good, as did the fresh clothes and even the thirty-minute walk up the island to JB's house. Seth looked forward to an evening with his boss, some time to talk without the dominance of their work environment, an opportunity to get to know this man better, and indeed, absorb some more of the wisdom the years of experience had given him.

Seth arrived at the house as the chimes of the old grandfather clock inside signaled the half hour. He knocked gently on the door, feeling good about his promptness but a bit nervous, as this would be their first social encounter. Then came the second surprise of the day as JB's extremely attractive daughter, Linda, opened the door. She sported a tailored white cotton shirt and expensive denims, tucked into knee-high leather boots. Wisps of glossy brown hair escaped from a red scrunchy, framing her beautiful face and mischievous eyes.

"Well hello, Seth. Good evening. Please go right on through," she said, ushering him into the house. "Dad's in the next room. I'll be along in a moment."

Momentarily speechless, he finally found his tongue, "Linda! Err, hello! What a delightful surprise. I wasn't expecting to see you again so soon."

"Well, I'm not sure Dad's cooking would have impressed his new stern man, so I thought I'd cook for you both tonight—welcome you properly to the island. Go on now, Dad's expecting you."

"Good evening, Seth, and welcome to our home. Are you a drinker?" JB asked, producing a large bottle of Johnny Walker Black Label. "I have some great scotch here if you'd like some."

"Sounds good," Seth replied, watching the old man arrange three crystal glasses and carefully pour very generous measures. Leaving a glass for Linda, he motioned toward the leather recliners and invited Seth to make himself at home. Soon Linda joined them to enjoy the strong, smooth, and peaty drink.

"Seems like the storm that blew us all around this morning has decided to leave," Seth offered, breaking the somewhat awkward silence. This prompted JB to begin a discourse on the current weather pattern, the position and pressure of the latest low, the type and movement of a nearby front, and other details that it seemed only a professional weather forecaster would understand.

Like all good fishermen, JB constantly, perhaps unconsciously, paid close attention to the weather conditions. Seth listened until Linda interrupted, chuckling, and adding, "Weather is Dad's life, you know. He studies it—the water, the tide, the wind—and he does it all day, every day. He should be the guy on TV!"

Fact is, Seth thought, *this old man wouldn't have survived fifty years fishing out there if he hadn't been totally in tune with the elements.*

A timer rang, prompting Linda to get up and tell the other two to drink up as dinner would be on the table in just a minute. Whiskey in hand, she headed off to the kitchen. As she passed him, Seth took in the musky perfume scent that lingered in her wake. It gave him a wonderful feeling he instantly knew he shouldn't have. He took another sip of whiskey and, trying to direct his thoughts elsewhere, turned to JB and asked about the photograph of the *Linda-T* hanging on the wall.

"It's me, winning a lobster boat race in Rockland," JB began, but before he had time to get into the story, Linda's voice came from the kitchen.

"Come on, you two, dinner's ready."

The meal consisted of a perfectly prepared lasagna, crusty French bread, and green salad. JB and Seth drank Coke, and Linda had a glass of wine. "A toast to the new sternman," Linda said, raising her glass. "Welcome, Seth!"

As the meal proceeded, the conversation stayed on things relative to Sandaray, its history, and the unique challenges and rewards of living in such an isolated place. Seth listened politely, casting occasional glances in Linda's direction. She wore the practiced expression of someone who had heard her father in full flow on many occasions. Then, in a brief lull, she seized the opportunity to shift the conversation to something more immediate that currently dominated her thoughts, the major gathering to be held on nearby Orran Island toward the end of the following month.

As Seth knew nothing of this "gathering," Linda started with a brief explanation. "Orran Island is unique. In the nineteenth and early twentieth centuries, the island had a thriving farming community of around twenty families who had lived and worked there for generations, pretty much cut off from the rest of the world. In the mid-1950s, the remaining depleted population left the island for good, relocating to the neighboring island of Sandaray where life's conveniences, and the mainland, were much more readily available."

Eager to rejoin the conversation, JB regaled how Orran had remained uninhabited for the next fifteen years, being visited only by fishermen, adventurous tourists, and the occasional opportunistic thief. Until, that is, a highly successful English billionaire, one Sir Reginald Wilson, the man who eventually became Linda's father-in-law, bought almost the entire island. Sir Reginald had initially made his fortune developing property in postwar Britain but had moved to the States after meeting and marrying American socialite Elizabeth Carter.

Following the unexpected arrival of their only child, Daniel, in 1967, Sir Reginald began his search for a new home, a place to raise Daniel away from the hustle and bustle of eastern Connecticut. He found the perfect place on the beautiful island of Orran.

Within a year, he had built a contemporary, energy-efficient, and totally self-contained house. But by the late 1980s, following his wife's untimely death, he relinquished his near-total ownership of the island by selling off land to five business friends looking for similar getaway places. Within five years, each of the new owners, despite the logistic difficulties of building in such a remote location, had constructed lavish, luxury vacation homes.

While the development of Orran had been initially unpopular with Sandaray islanders, they soon realized there were significant economic gains to be had in transporting people to and from the island and providing vital services. As JB pointed out, it provided employment opportunities for islanders like Bill Harris's father, who worked as a full-time caretaker for the Wilson family.

Soon a tradition began in which all six families held a major annual gathering on Orran, where, together with selected friends, they partied, socialized, and generally unwound for three or four days each summer. As the years passed, the annual meetings became more and more business oriented. This year, Sir Reginald would play host to the group, a role he relished. Fortunately for him, but less fortunate for Linda, Sir Reginald proved to be a very persuasive and a skilled delegator so, rather than pay a party planner, he recruited Linda and his son to organize the whole affair.

"We gotta go to the mainland to pick up all the fancy stuff for this party. We're heading over there first thing, which is why you get to sleep in."

"Do you need me to help out?" Seth asked with some enthusiasm, but silently hoping the answer would be "no."

"No, but thanks anyway. Linda's coming along and says she and Dan can handle everything by themselves, so you can stay in bed."

After dessert, JB and Seth adjourned to the living room for coffee. Taking full advantage of the relaxed atmosphere, JB asked the question Seth had been hoping to avoid: "So Seth, what were you doing before you came out to Sandaray?"

Taking a moment to consider his response, Seth gave what he hoped would be an acceptable, if vague, answer: "I had a few jobs in the city but fancied a change of scenery, so I headed north and ended up in Maine to try my hand at lobster fishing." Eager to redirect the conversation, he returned a similar question to JB: "And have you been on Sandaray all your life?"

JB, always happy to point out the uniqueness of the island's culture, told the story of how, despite being the son of a Sandaray fisherman, he would never be accepted as a "native" since he had been born in the state of Rhode Island. The fact he came here when he was seven days old made no difference.

Unusual social structure, Seth thought.

Casual but interesting conversation continued until around eight thirty, which Seth recalled would normally be JB's bedtime. He politely thanked Linda for preparing an excellent supper and both of them for their generous and enjoyable hospitality. As he walked toward the door, JB reminded him about the arrangements for the morning.

"It'll be about high tide when I get back, so to save a bit of time, I'll meet you over at the ferry wharf. Be there at nine."

Seth extended his hand to the captain and turned to Linda. For a brief, awkward moment he considered, but rejected, a farewell hug, despite the recurrence of the emotion he'd felt earlier.

Back at the fish house, Seth poured himself a large glass of red wine and flopped on the couch in front of the TV. He mindlessly flipped through the channels for several minutes, settling eventually on the Al Jazeera News channel as a way of distracting himself from some very exciting but dangerous thoughts.

Chapter Five

Since his workdays now started so early, having a lie-in was an unexpected treat. It was bright outside and the sound of the wind was strangely comforting. He smiled. *What a change from the crazy rush-hour chaos of the Washington Beltway.*

He looked at the clock. 5:30 a.m. *Bummer!*

Pulling the covers up to his face, he snuggled back into a comfortable position and closed his eyes, hopeful of sleep returning. But his mind remained busy, full of images and thoughts from the previous evening. It had been so long since he'd felt the stirrings brought on by an attractive woman. But Linda…a married woman and his boss's daughter to boot. Hey, he didn't need that kind of complication.

Now with his mind fully awake making him too wired to get any more sleep, he threw off the covers. "Just get up, you lazy bum," he ordered himself, forcing his feet to the floor and his body upright, "and stop filling your head with things that don't belong there." In a moment, the cold, wooden floor under his feet quickened his step to the bathroom, where a shower completed his total return to reality. He decided to get out of the apartment and head for Emma's and a hot breakfast.

In the café, he picked a seat at the counter, which gave him a good view of the harbor and the ability to spot an early arrival of the *Linda-T*. Several people were talking or eating, and Kenny was giving a creatively embellished version of a recent lobster war to anyone who would listen.

Mandy greeted him with a bright "Good morning, Seth," a hot cup of coffee, and a cheery smile. Soon he was enjoying sausage, eggs, and home fries, while keeping one eye on the activity in the harbor and what looked like an increasingly stiff northerly wind.

When he had finished his meal, he headed toward the ferry wharf, realizing the northerly wind might well shorten JB's trip from Orran making him earlier than planned. He carefully scanned the harbor, identifying each boat in sight. No sign of the *Linda-T*, at least none yet. At the very end of the wharf, exactly where the *Linda-T* would be docking, he spotted a young boy, his legs dangling over the edge and his mind apparently engrossed by some sort of handheld electronic game. Seth walked over. "Hi, there. What're you up to?" No response. Seth went closer, looking over the young boy's shoulder. "Mind if I watch?" he asked.

Seth got a lackluster "okay" and a mumbled comment about how there wasn't much to watch as "I just can't get out of here, I'm totally stuck."

"What does 'stuck' mean?" Seth asked as he sat down next to the boy.

"It means I can't find my way out of this place," he answered, pointing at the screen. "I've got to get out of this ravine before nighttime because the Mobs will come after me, and if I die, I'll lose all my items!"

"What kind of items?"

"Well, stuff like iron ore, diamonds, food, and wood."

"What do you need all those things for?"

"I need the food and wood to stay alive, the iron ore to make weapons and tools, and the diamonds to buy armor to protect me from the Mobs. If I die, I'll respawn and lose all my items and have to start again. I need to figure out how to get more blocks, so I can climb back up to the top of the ravine."

"Hmm," said Seth. "You could glitch your way out."

That got the boy's total attention. "What?"

"Try this: surround yourself with iron blocks and press yourself against the wall. That will give you X-ray vision."

"Yeah, right, I know—"

"You'll see there's a cavity behind the wall and a rocky slope beyond that. Use your pickax to chip through, and then you can crawl up the rocks to get out."

The boy looked at him in amazement. "How do you know this stuff?" No response. The boy followed Seth's instructions and within seconds, found himself at the top of the ravine. He shook his head in disbelief. Again, he ventured, "How did you know?"

But the sound of JB's air horn preempted Seth's answer. "Good luck, young man," he called, turning swiftly and sprinting across the wharf to take his place on the deck of the *Linda-T*.

JB greeted him with barely a grunt and a nod of hello, quickly guiding the *Linda-T* out of the harbor and into the open sea. As Seth grappled to get into his oilskins, he looked back and waved, but the young boy remained lost in the mysteries of the game. Seth busied himself getting ready for the day's work, as his mind filled with things of which the young man had no concept… *the guts of the computer game, the coded commands, algorithms, objects, procedures, subroutines, and the machinery that brought it all together to both entertain and fascinate young people.*

He had to get his mind on something else. So with a curiosity to find out more about the forthcoming extravaganza on Orran, he went forward, stood next to JB, and asked how things had gone on the early morning delivery trip.

Apparently suffering from overexposure to everything concerning the upcoming event, JB sidestepped the issue, brusquely reminding Seth they needed more bait bagged and this looked like a good time to get it done. Continuing to show his state of general agitation, he grumbled that, while some people were having a lie-in, he had been loading two bushels of fresh bait aboard, and Seth could make himself useful by stuffing it into bait bags. The workday had begun but gotten off to a rocky start. JB appeared out of sorts, and Seth's thoughts were now drifting back into exciting but very troubling waters.

Traveling to the southeast, they were soon well out of sight of the islands with the sea getting rougher, the wind stronger, and the ocean deeper.

"You want to save crabs today?" Seth asked.

"Hell, no. No one wants them anymore; throw the damn things back."

By two o'clock, with the wind gusting to around thirty knots, they were both relieved when only one more string remained to haul before heading to the northwest and home. Seth stood banding a lobster when a voice crackled over the VHF radio: "Mayday, Mayday, Mayday! This is the *Jasper*. We're about thirty miles southeast of Sandaray, just north of Milton's Ledge. We have a fire in the engine room and...." The radio went chillingly silent.

JB grabbed the microphone and called, "*Jasper, Jasper, Jasper!* This is *Linda-T*. What is your heading, Jamie?" No answer. Yelling to Seth to forget the traps and get the glasses on the horizon, JB turned the *Linda-T* east-southeast and pushed the throttle full open. As Seth asked what kind of boat they were looking for, JB shouted, "It's Jamie Lewis, *Jasper*...they're on fire, somewhere out this way. She's a sixty-five-foot dragger, lots of rigging."

Despite the pitching of the boat, Seth glued himself to the binoculars and as carefully as he could scanned the horizon. One minute, he thought he'd spotted something, but the next, nothing in sight. "Look at ten o'clock," JB shouted, "I think I see something."

"Yes, *yes*! Got it. I think it's a boat…now about eleven o'clock… looks like she might be smoking too."

"Give me them glasses," barked JB. Immediately, he felt certain his friend Jamie had gotten into big trouble.

* * *

On board the sixty-five-foot scallop dragger, FV *Jasper*, the crew had been securing the gear and cleaning up at the end of three and a half days of constant hard work. The weather had been cooperative and the sea generous, yielding 103 forty-pound bags of scallops, all of which had been shucked and carefully packed in ice for the ten-hour journey to the mainland. With an exhausted crew, Captain Jamie Lewis had set a course north by northwest to Rockland and, taking the first watch himself, instructed the others to go below and get some rest.

As Jamie fought his own exhaustion, the radio chatter between fishing boats in the area confirmed a rapid deterioration of the weather. *The last thing they needed.* And when a quick calculation showed it would only add about forty minutes to the total trip, he immediately changed course to make for the safe harbor at Sandaray. He fought sleep by not using the auto pilot and by forcing himself to continually check all the engine and navigation gauges.

Time dragged on at a snail's pace, but they continued to make headway. Suddenly the engine RPM indicator showed zero without the slightest variation in engine noise. *Damn fuse must have blown again. I'll just go stick a new one in.* He engaged the autopilot and made his way aft. When he opened the engine room hatch, a thick, acrid wall of smoke peppered with bright flames confronted him. In an instant, everything changed.

Unbeknownst to *Jasper's* crew, only the first few words of their Mayday call had been transmitted due to the electrical failure. But the *Linda-T* had heard the abbreviated call and soon had them in sight, slamming through the waves toward them as fast as they could.

* * *

As radar on the *Linda-T* showed five miles to the *Jasper*, the Coast Guard called, saying a Dolphin helicopter had heard the abbreviated Mayday call and changed course in their direction. JB responded giving their GPS location.

What's happening on the Jasper? JB wondered. *Anyone injured? Have they got the fire under control? Did they still have power to steer in this increasingly difficult sea?* Only two facts were certain: they had no communication, and smoke still billowed from the ship. At least he could see they were still afloat. JB kept all the throttle that the rough sea would allow, while staying glued to the binoculars. With every passing minute, he could see a little more detail but no movement on her deck. He noticed their life raft missing from its usual place above the wheelhouse. *Had they abandoned ship?* Seconds later, he saw a figure emerge, vigorously waving a jacket. He breathed a sigh of relief but had no way to respond. For the moment, JB stayed focused on keeping the Coast Guard informed and planning how to best maneuver so either he or Seth could board.

JB planned to sail alongside *Jasper* in the most sheltered condition possible. Heading northeast, and with the waves and the wind as they were, boarding would need to be on her port side aft of the wheelhouse. Handling *Linda-T* in these conditions made his decision clear: Seth would have to try and jump onto the boat. It would be a tricky maneuver. "Seth, you're gonna have to get aboard. I hope you're okay with that." Seth's response came firmly and without hesitation. "No problem, Captain."

* * *

Seth had no thought of not going, but only of the unwritten law of the sea that drives all seamen to help others in distress. He knew he could neither manage the *Linda-T* in this situation nor let the old man try to jump. He had watched on TV as harbor pilots boarded large ships from small boats. Surely, it couldn't be that difficult, but, on the other hand, the TV pictures never showed waves and wind like they had, and the pilots were trained and experienced in doing that sort of thing.

JB would be sure to get him into the best possible position to board, but he would only have one chance to get it right. And, unlike the TV shows, there would be none of those nice-to-have extras, like lines, ladders, and helpers…or rehearsals. They each knew one thing for certain: they would both give it their very best shot.

Seth got into a survival suit and stuffed the portable VHF radio and a flashlight in the pockets. He grabbed the fire extinguisher, making sure the safety pin had been well seated, and laid it on the starboard side under the gunwale. He thought he had everything ready until the ever-watchful JB pointed a commanding finger at their first-aid kit. Seth took it and laid it near the readied fire extinguisher. JB motioned for Seth to come close.

"This may get tricky," JB began. "*Jasper*'s deck is a bit higher than our gunwales. We'll approach her port side from the stern, staying in her lea. I'll get you as close as possible, and we may even touch. As we close in, toss everything over, then try to grab the safety rail or else dive through an open place. Watch for a moment and go when we're rising and they're falling. When you think it's best, jump quickly to get as much of yourself on board as possible. Once you've made it, I'll move back and stay at a safe distance. Use the radio to call me right away to make sure it still works." By the time all had been prepared, the *Jasper* sat less than a mile away.

As the distance between the two vessels decreased, the size of the waves seemed to increase. In no time, they were a mere hundred feet apart. "Get your butt up there," JB shouted. "I'll hand you the stuff."

Seth obeyed and, in a moment, stood on the starboard gunwale, fire extinguisher and first-aid kit firmly in his right hand, his left hand solidly gripping the handrail above the house. Fifty feet, twenty, ten. The two vessels were now pitching violently in different directions. Seth tried to study the rhythm.

When the ships were about five feet apart, he threw the first-aid kit and watched it skid to a safe spot. With about the same distance separating them, he heaved the fire extinguisher but watched in horror as its handle caught the rail, flipping it instantly into the boiling sea. JB slowed the *Linda-T*, letting her drift astern a few feet. Seth waited for what seemed like an eternity. Then he saw his chance. As the *Linda-T* surged upward almost touching the other boat, Seth propelled himself forward with all the energy he could muster. He landed heavily on the deck, safe and still in one piece. Looking back, he gave JB a thumbs-up, collected the first-aid kit, and started forward.

Beside the wheelhouse door a man lay motionless, covered by a blanket. Nearby a bulky life raft sprawled awkwardly on a pile of fishing gear. The wheelhouse door swung open.

"My God, I'm glad to see you guys. I'm Keith." The man's relief was palpable. "We've got a major problem here and two men injured …"

"I'm Seth. Let me just make sure we have radio contact." He pulled the portable radio from his pocket. "Linda-T, you read me okay, JB?"

"Loud and clear, Seth."

Turning back to Keith, Seth quickly shook hands. "What's the story?" he asked.

"The fire is in the engine room. All the electrics are out, but the engine is still running okay. The skipper and the other two are down there." Keith added that John, who had been thrown off the roof of the wheelhouse while freeing the life raft, looked close to death. "We straightened him out, covered him up, and left him 'coz there wasn't much else we could do. I think he's in a really bad way, though. A spike has punctured his right side. The bloody thing pulled out when we rolled him off the pile of gear. His breathing is really strange, and he's got a very rapid pulse."

"I'll see if I can do anything for him."

As Seth turned to leave, he used the portable radio to relate what he knew to JB.

John's breathing did indeed appear very labored and shallow. Seth could see the bloody pin nearby and the spot where it had punctured his survival suit. Using scissors, he peeled back the layers to expose the wound. It spluttered and sucked in, indicating that his chest cavity had been punctured and a lung may have collapsed. "Keith," he shouted, "do you have any small plastic tubing? Something a quarter inch or so in diameter."

Soon Keith appeared with a short length of 3/8-inch plastic tubing. Seth cleaned it with the alcohol wipes and carefully inserted it into the oozing wound, sealing around it with gauze and tape. He began to suck on the tube, pinching it off tightly between breaths, every suck improving John's breathing. After a few minutes, he stopped, watched carefully, waited, and then removed the tubing, taking great care to seal the hole quickly with strips of tape. John, now breathing much more easily, moaned and opened his eyes.

"Which way to the engine room?" Seth asked. Keith pointed. Seth grabbed a fire extinguisher and headed for the starboard side. The heavy smoke belching from the engine room partially concealed a man lying on the deck and another crouching over him.

"Okay. What's happening, how can I help?"

Seth listened as the man explained how they had found his buddy Shorty unconscious in the engine room. "The skipper is in there now trying to fight the fire. Best we both stay here till he comes out; ya can't see nothing inside. Shorty fell against the red-hot exhaust manifold, caught himself with his hand, it's a real mess. Ya got anything to bandage it? Oh, I'm Lucas by the way."

"Seth. Off the *Linda-T.*"

Kneeling by Shorty's side, Seth looked at his burned right hand. Its appearance, together with the fact Shorty did not seem to be in much pain, led Seth to believe he had a third-degree burn. Seth reasoned a burn like this needed a doctor's attention and the most they could do would be to protect it until he got to a hospital. Taking charge of the captain's safety rope, Seth sent Lucas off in search of a clean plastic bag.

But before Lucas returned, the skipper emerged from the smoky hatch with a rag tied over his face. Between bouts of coughing, he introduced himself as Jamie and proceeded to explain what had happened. "A high-pressure hydraulic leak started fires all over the place. I've stopped the leak but this extinguisher has run out. Who are you?"

Seth thrust another fire extinguisher toward him and said, "Here, take this one. I'm Seth, JB's sternman."

"Thanks. This'll take care of all the other little fires but I'm gonna need some heavy plastic and small rope—there's a pinhole hydraulic leak. I tied my coat sleeve around it for the moment." Seth watched Jamie disappear back into the smoke just as Lucas arrived with some plastic storage bags.

Handing the safety rope back, Seth proceeded to put Shorty's burned hand carefully into one of the bags while relating what Jamie had said about the hydraulic leak. As he secured it with tape, he listened as Lucas explained how the skipper had discovered the fire. They were interrupted by a crackle from Seth's radio. "FV *Jasper*, this is Coast Guard Helicopter 60432. We have you in sight and will be overhead in two minutes."

"Roger, understand." *Thank goodness. Better let Keith know.*

Minutes later, in the wheelhouse, Seth and Keith watched as the huge helicopter hovered overhead. The noise became deafening and the wind so intense it began to slide John across the slippery deck. Seth rushed out and grabbed John's survival suit while holding onto the wheelhouse door. In a few seconds, a medic from the chopper joined him, and the two men dragged John into the relatively windless area behind the wheelhouse door.

The ear-splitting sound of the aircraft lessened a bit as it moved aft and off to the side of *Jasper*. Seth summarized the situation: "There's a fire in the engine room. One crewman there can walk but has a severely burned hand. Two probably suffering from smoke inhalation. John here has a puncture wound on his right side and may have a broken arm." The medic looked quickly at John, then took out his radio and asked for a stretcher. "We'll get him up first. Do you know the status of the fire?"

"They were making progress but are out of fire extinguishers."

"432, send a couple of fire extinguishers with the stretcher," the medic shouted into his radio.

The throbbing sound of the chopper's blades increased as it moved closer, and soon a stretcher lay on the deck not more than six feet from John. Seth grabbed the extinguishers.

"Get the guy with the burn over here. He can go next," the medic shouted to Seth over the roar.

"Will do. Be right back."

* * *

Leaving Lucas to get Shorty over to the wheelhouse, Jamie grabbed a rope and plastic bag and motioned to Seth, "Now all we have to do is stop the hydraulic leak before all the fluid is gone and we lose rudder control."

The scene inside the engine room looked grim. There were smoldering cables and charred wires everywhere. Nothing seemed to have escaped the fire, but in the middle of it all, the old reliable Volvo diesel engine kept running. "Follow me," Jamie said, "the trouble is on the other side. Be careful where you put your hands." *Boy, are we lucky none of our fuel lines burned through!*

On the starboard side of the engine, Jamie's coat marked the location of the pinhole leak in the high-pressure hydraulic line. "Here's the plan," Jamie began. "I'll remove the jacket and you slide that bag down the hose over the leak. While you're holding it, I'll tie the rope around it and, if we can find any, we'll put an outer bandage of duct tape over the whole thing."

"Okay. Let's do it."

In the end, both men were soaked in hydraulic fluid, but the hose repair held.

Back on deck, Lucas and Keith waited as they evacuated John. Soon the thumping and the roar of the helicopter increased as the stretcher returned to the deck. This time, the medic strapped Shorty in and clipped a line to his own harness. In a moment, they were both on board. Rescue helicopter 60432 then departed for the mainland, leaving Jamie, Keith, Lucas and Seth in relative quiet.

"There's one more thing that we really need to do," Jamie said, turning to Keith. "I'll take the wheel while you locate the spare five-gallon bucket of hydraulic fluid. I'm sure the reservoir will take it all."

* * *

During the next few minutes, Seth used the portable radio to update JB on what had occurred, then suggested he leave their radio with Jamie. With the fire out and the situation stable, he felt he could make his way back to the *Linda-T*.

JB closed in just as before, and in one swift movement, Seth returned to where it had all begun.

The two boats set off slowly toward Sandaray and were eventually joined by a Coast Guard escort ship that ultimately stayed with *Jasper* all the way to Rockland.

Onboard the *Linda-T*, Seth stood next to his captain and related all that had happened in great detail. Then, as on every other day when they hauled, he went aft and got things ready for their return to port. *Not really your average day of lobster fishing,* he mused.

As they glided past the ferry wharf, Seth thought of the beginning of this day and the young boy attempting to overcome the trials and tribulations of a computer game. *I wonder if the Mobs got him!*

Chapter Six

The following Wednesday, JB had no plans to haul, so Seth walked up to Emma's Café for a late breakfast. As he entered, he spotted Ronnie Moody sitting alone at one table, a tourist couple studying a map at another, and Kenny holding down his usual seat at the end of the counter.

Kenny looked up from his newspaper and motioned for Seth to sit next to him. As Mandy appeared with her usual cheery "hello" and a steaming cup of coffee, a very excited Kenny thrust the newspaper into Seth's hands. "Look here," he said, his scarred, arthritic finger resting on the bold headline, "Lobster boat aids distressed dragger." "That's JB Thompson and you, ain't it?" At which point Kenny launched into a full-blown summary of the article. As he neared the end, and in an elevated tone primarily for the benefit of the tourists, he added, "And it says John Hajula would most likely be dead if it weren't for the swift action of you guys. You two are real heroes!"

As casually as he could, Seth sipped his coffee and glanced at the paper, his mind and heart racing. He really didn't want any publicity, not now, not ever. *Five months of daily harassment by the news media was more than enough to last me a lifetime.*

"Come on, Kenny, what do you want, my autograph or something?" he said flippantly. "You know the way of the sea, don't you? JB, me, you, Ronnie over there, all of us know that if someone needs help, and you're there, you help. No debate, just people helping each other."

Ronnie had been listening quietly to the exchange, and as he picked up his jacket to leave, he turned to Seth and said, "You boys did well. Those guys were very lucky you were nearby."

Kenny went back to his newspaper, and Seth sighed with relief, happy the "hero" hype had dissipated, or so he thought.

"Regular breakfast, please, Mandy."

"Coming right up, Mr. Hero!"

As Mandy refilled his coffee mug, Seth turned to Kenny, asking him what he had been up to lately.

Now such a question would normally open Kenny's verbal sluice gate, yielding the latest island gossip, but today, the newspaper account of *Jasper*'s troubles had taken Kenny back to his youth. He began talking of the dramas in which he himself had been involved. Things had been tougher back then before modern-day navigation systems and rescue choppers, and yet, to Kenny, it had been, somehow, a much better time.

In his parents' time, there had been little emphasis on lobster fishing. Oh yes, every family had built a few traps and a small boat for fin-fishing near the shore, but a good life meant farming: a few chickens, sheep, or pigs, and land to cultivate. No tractors either, just oxen. For most, a trip to the mainland occurred once a year, not once a week. They were all hard workers, indeed their collective survival depended on it.

"When me and my brother were kids, we had to walk to the town well to bring water. Now I have indoor plumbing, color TV, and the internet!"

Seth pondered the life of the old man and considered how dramatically the world had changed with the passing of just one generation.

"What about now, Kenny? What are you going to do this winter?"

Kenny proudly replied that he had a basement full of firewood, a tank full of oil, a freezer full of grub, a new TV, and some carefully stashed whiskey. "I'm looking forward to the cold weather and not so many people being here." And, smiling at Mandy as she delivered Seth's breakfast, he added, "Plus, I get to have beautiful girls like Mandy all to myself."

"Ooo, you old charmer," Mandy retorted as she waved her dish cloth affectionately in his direction.

"So you're planning on staying here this winter, Mandy?" Seth asked.

"Really depends on whether Emma stays open or not."

Seth considered this for a moment. Surviving the long, dark days of winter without Emma and Mandy's hearty breakfasts and good company was not a pleasant prospect. He really hoped she would not choose to shut up shop.

Pushing ten dollars across the counter to pay for his meal, Seth asked Mandy to add in the cost of a newspaper. It had been a thought-provoking hour at Emma's in more ways than one, and besides, he really wanted to read what they'd said about him.

He walked slowly down the road from the café enjoying the warm sun and the luxury of not being in a hurry. He sure as hell hoped they had not used his name. Standing in the middle of the road, and oblivious to everything else around him, he read the whole story. It spoke in glowing terms of the heroic efforts made by the crew of FV *Linda-T*, her captain, JB Thompson, and crewman, Seth Martin. *Shit!* He supposed it was inevitable he would be named; after all, it would not have made much of a story without details of their collective efforts. But the publicity—any publicity—was unwelcome. *I could be in big trouble now.* His mind went into overdrive. *Maybe I should leave. I could leave after JB's taken up his gear for the winter. I'll be out of a job then anyway.*

He folded the paper and continued down the road musing over several possibilities until a car horn blew him right back to reality. Looking around, he saw JB's truck with Linda at the wheel. She stopped and, with a big smile, asked if he fancied going to the mainland. With the last load of party goodies finally ready, JB had agreed to a pickup and delivery operation, as long as he had time to look at some new hydraulic gadget he wanted to purchase.

Seth liked Linda. How could he pass up an opportunity to get away for a few hours and enjoy a rather attractive distraction from weightier matters. He could also stop by the big grocery store.

* * *

Three and a half hours later, they docked at Johnson's Marina, a place where JB's family had done business for more than two generations. To no one's surprise, JB, feeling like part of the Johnson family, skillfully weaseled the *Linda-T* into the handiest loading spot on the floating dock. A man in a well-used, greasy flannel shirt greeted JB, helped him secure the boat, and asked if they needed anything. JB replied they would be gone for an hour or so and asked the man if he would fill both fuel tanks while they were away. Having shut down the big engine, JB wasted no time in heading off to look at some replacement hydraulic fixtures. Seth and Linda set out for the grocery store in her fancy, red Range Rover, which enjoyed privileged parking in one of the larger boat sheds.

For all his adult life, Seth had lived and worked in the city, but now, after just a few months in the semi-isolation of Sandaray, the noises, paved streets, crowds, cars, traffic lights, even the odor of this place seemed strangely surreal. He realized he had not only escaped the slings and arrows of the past year, but he had also left behind a number of familiar pleasures, like shopping in a mammoth supermarket.

He looked up and down the aisles. There seemed to be more people in Shaw's than the entire population of Sandaray. Linda disappeared toward the gourmet food section, while Seth sought out more mundane consumables. Soon, with very little effort, he had filled a basket with everything on his list.

Joining a checkout line, he searched for Linda and spotted her three lines away and almost finished. With one person still ahead of him, he thought, *Perfect timing.* While he waited, he studied Linda, admiring her impeccable posture, lovely figure, and silky hair. He continued watching as she picked up her bag of purchases and started toward the exit.

The automatic door swung open and a blond, good-looking man in his mid-thirties, rushed over, calling her name. They embraced, spoke for a moment quietly, and then parted. A strange feeling of jealousy stirred in Seth's gut—prompted, no doubt, by the more than just friendly greeting he had observed.

"That'll be thirty-two eighty-six, please," the checkout lady said, bringing Seth back to the reality of the groceries. He felt his color rise as he handed her the money. He had been completely lost in thoughts and images of Linda. *Watch yourself. Remember, she's a married lady and your boss's daughter.*

In the parking lot, Linda held the car's rear hatch open. Seth quickly stored his groceries and jumped into the front seat. With no mention of her handsome friend, they headed back to the marina.

It didn't take long to load their things into the boat. As they did, Seth noticed three large boxes had been carefully secured aft of the bait box. "Is that your party stuff?" he questioned.

"Yes. Johnson's men must have loaded it while we were away; nothing really heavy, just delicate, expensive decorations that can get messed up quite easily."

Linda returned the Range Rover to its parking spot and, on the way back, met her father coming out of the marina office. Eager to get underway, he asked, "We got everything Linda?"

"Yes, but well, err…can we wait just a minute, Dad? Oh, and by the way, did you get your hydraulic thing-a-ma-jig?"

"They showed me two, but I'm not sure which one I want. I'll study the specifications and give them an order by phone in a day or so. Come on, let's get going. I've had enough of this town and all these people."

"Hang on Dad. I need to tell you something."

Of all the people in the world, no one, except Linda, could have delayed the captain's departure. "What on earth is it?" he asked, starting up the engine.

"I ran into Scott Young in Shaw's," she explained. "He'll be down in a few minutes to take some pictures for a follow-up article he's doing about the *Jasper* incident. I didn't think you'd mind."

JB grumbled something about not wanting to be photographed, and Seth kept out of the conversation and well out of the way.

Scott duly arrived, camera in hand. "Be quick now, Scott, the tide won't wait."

Scott took several pictures of JB.

"That's enough, Scott."

"Oh, just one more JB, please? How about one with your sternman? Get him over here."

"Okay, but just one, and that's it. Come on, Seth."

Before they knew it, JB had steered Seth into the wheelhouse where Scott proceeded to snap the pair of them three times. Finally, he turned the camera to get two candid shots of Linda as she sat on the engine box.

"Thanks a lot guys! Have a safe trip home," he called, jumping up onto the dock and sprinting away in search of the next big story.

Seth didn't like the whole thing, not one bit. His earlier anxiety returned as he considered the possible implications of Scott's photographs. *If one of those pictures shows up in the national papers, it might well put me on a very slippery slope.* However, what was done was done. He had work to do now. Without a word, he went forward and undid the bow line.

By sunset, Linda and her delicate cargo had been safely deposited on Orran Island and the boat taken back to her mooring. JB headed home to bed, and Seth sat in his living room with a glass of whiskey, pondering the effect of not just one *Jasper* article but a second that might contain his picture.

Chapter Seven

A few white cotton-ball cumulus clouds lay on the horizon to the west, while a brilliant sun lingered low through the haze in the east. Linda stood watching it all through the window of her father-in-law's island retreat, sipping coffee from a delicate china cup and contemplating the events soon to begin.

Her husband, Dan, sat at the breakfast table, reading the latest news on his iPad while muttering about the current price of oil and the continuing troubles in the Middle East. From her vantage point, Linda watched the *Clacken II*, moored in the harbor as its crew loaded bait onto a local lobster boat. Several other working boats were busily coming or going, corpuscles in the lifeblood of the fishing industry, indeed the entire world economy. This was *her* heritage, a life focused on fishing, family, and survival. However, since marrying Dan, she had been absorbed into another culture, a complex and sophisticated world of excesses focused on business, profits, growth, and relationships. As she had many times before, Linda wondered where she belonged—in both, or perhaps neither.

As she watched, a much larger vessel entered the harbor and caught her eye. She immediately recognized the seventy-five-foot, gleaming white, oceangoing yacht *Stella*, the pride, joy, and home away from home of Mr. and Mrs. Hector Fernandez. Flying the Spanish flag, *Stella* had become a frequent visitor to

Orran and often brought friends, colleagues, or associates to visit or do business at the Fernandez's luxury home on the far western tip of the island. "Dan," Linda exclaimed, "Hector and Helen have arrived. I hope we see something of them before the group gathers on Friday evening."

"Great. I hope they haven't brought more guests than they have room for. Remember the mess two years ago?"

"I certainly do. And I also hope no uninvited newspaper weirdos show up like that Reuters guy who came to the door, seriously asking how to find the Orran Hilton." They both chuckled as they remembered what had almost become an embarrassing event. Linda sighed, put down the coffee cup, picked up her notebook and cell phone, and left to begin the day's work. The first of the party guests had arrived.

By Thursday afternoon, two more shiny, sleek yachts had moored in the harbor. Other guests who were flying into Sandaray would be ferried over by lobstermen. In just one day's time, all fifty-three guests would gather in Sir Reginald's house for the formal welcome dinner.

* * *

Back on Sandaray, Seth busied himself in the workshop below his living space, preparing traps with his newly learned skills. The sharp trill of the phone on the wall got his complete attention. He answered, "Seth Martin."

"Linda just called to ask if you could come and help out with the dinner Friday evening and the party on Saturday. Apparently, one of her hired helpers just canceled."

"Ah, JB! Yes, right, and err…what kind of hired helper am I going to be?" He was nervous about more possible exposure to the news media. JB, Mistaking the reason for Seth's hesitancy, replied, "Don't worry, you'll get paid and she has a place arranged for you to say." JB waited while Seth considered the proposal. "Well, okay, I'll do it. Suppose I'll be mostly in the kitchen. It shouldn't be too complicated, and I can always use the extra cash. How do I get there?"

"Good. Ronnie Moody says he can take you over tomorrow morning around nine. I'll be going over on Saturday morning to deliver the band for the big party—but mostly to help Danny Rogers install new rudder hydraulics in his boat. I'll be staying with Danny and Celia overnight so you can come back with me and the band on Sunday morning."

Despite his paranoia about attracting media attention, Seth was more than a little curious about what six billionaires did when they got together on an island in the middle of nowhere. "I'll be out with Ronnie at nine then. Will I see you at the party, JB?" he responded.

"No way!"

* * *

The *Fair Morn*, normally crewed by three, had only her skipper, Ronnie Moody, at the helm that morning, and in around twenty minutes, Seth, along with a load of groceries and two cooks, had been efficiently deposited on Orran Island.

Built on the side of a hill overlooking the harbor, Sir Reginald's island getaway appeared unconventional in several ways. It was essentially an upside-down house with a large multi-purpose living space on the first floor and eight guest suites, all with superb views of the island, below. It presented a huge, curved facade mostly of glass and towered over the harbor like a medieval castle.

Seth headed up the hill until he reached a sign indicating the entrance to the property. He followed the driveway to the rear of the upper level and headed for the impressive, heavy, solid oak double doors.

Just as he reached for the bell pull, Linda opened the door and greeted him. "Hello, Seth. Welcome and thanks for coming to help on such short notice. Please come in, and I'll show you around." They entered a massive, wood-paneled antechamber furnished with paintings, sculptures, and a huge, colorful, wire-and-metal Alexander Calder mobile overhead. Moving into the main body of the house, he could see how strategically placed pieces of furniture could easily define the space so that a group of fifty people could gather for dinner as comfortably as two.

"We've started reconfiguring the place for tonight's formal dinner," Linda said as she guided him around. At a stairway, she added, "I was able to find all the temporary staff rooms in other houses, but, ended up one short…And you drew the short straw. The guest bedrooms are all down here…come on, I'll show you yours." They descended into a huge, carpeted, beautifully decorated hall that ran the whole length of the house, connecting all eight suites. She stopped outside a door marked ANDREW CARNEGIE—*hmmm, interesting touch*—and pushed it open.

"Wow, some short straw! Are all the rooms down here like this?" Seth asked with genuine curiosity. He imagined it would not have looked out of place in a fancy five-star hotel.

"Just about," Linda replied. Then changing the subject, "What kind of work clothes have you brought?"

Seth replied he had brought two clean shirts and an extra pair of jeans in case his got soaked washing dishes.

"No tux?" she asked.

"I need a tux? Err…no, no tux."

"Okay, that's kinda what I expected. Come with me. I think I can fix you right up." Linda led Seth down the corridor to the room with NIKOLA TESLA carved into its door. "This is our room.

64

Dan is just about your size, and I think you might be able to get into one of his tuxes. Come on in." The same five-star opulence greeted him, along with a large quantity of high-class luggage. Linda rooted through a suitcase and came up with a dress shirt. "Here's a start," she said, tossing him the shirt, "try this on."

Seth pulled his PROPERTY OF STARFLEET ACADEMY ATHLETIC DEPARTMENT sweatshirt up over his head, bringing with it his undershirt and revealing his well-developed muscular arms and chest. Linda's gaze went back to the suitcase where she found a black tuxedo jacket. She turned and, for a split second, had a heart-stopping fantasy as she imagined his chest pressing against her naked breasts and his powerful arms around her. She looked away but tossed him the jacket.

"The shirt looks fine, but you'll need some links and studs," she said in a croaky voice. Seth slipped into the jacket.

"That looks just great. Now try these trousers."

But there the good fits ended. Seth held the trousers to his waist and observed their hems on the floor. "Just hold it right there," Linda directed as she gathered up some pins from a small sewing kit and knelt beside him. Carefully she turned the pant legs up and pinned them. "I'll have these tacked in a jiffy, but I don't see any way you're going to be able to use Dan's shoes. I'll make the trousers a bit long to hide as much as possible of your tennis shoes."

* * *

Linda instructed Seth to leave all the stuff with her and said she would put everything on his bed when she had finished with the trousers. "When you put them on, just be careful you don't tear out the tacks. You'll have them back by about four o'clock, but right now, I need to get you upstairs to Emily."

The intimacy of the fitting over, they quickly headed to the kitchen, where a graying, slightly rotund, middle-aged lady was dumping a box of lettuce heads into a sink. "Emily," Linda said, "this is Seth. Seth, this is Emily Harris. Emily oversees everything up here, and you'll be working for her. When she says, 'Jump,' your only response is to ask, 'How high?' See you both later."

Under Emily's watchful eye and direction, the dining area soon took shape. The arrangement of tables and of course, the exact seating, had been carefully and politically engineered by Sir Reginald and Linda. Finally, after laying out the freshly polished silverware, they carefully placed gold-embossed place name cards.

"Sounds like a cliché, but have we met some place before, Emily?" Seth asked.

"No, but we both live on Sandaray, so our paths must have crossed somewhere along the way. Perhaps it's the family resemblance to my cheapskate brother Bill. He's the guy who runs the overpriced B&B up at DeVoe's old mansion."

"Oh yes, I met Bill my very first day on the island. He has a nice-looking place."

"Nice, my foot! Ten years ago, he and his then-wife worked round the clock to put the old place into really fine order. Eventually she left him and, since then, the place has just gone down in quality and up in price."

"But it has a super location and really beautiful views."

"Yup, I'll go along with that all right. You know, on a clear day, you can even see it from here."

Soon they found themselves working on the last remaining table, and as they drew close, he asked impishly, "Where are you going to put my name tag?"

Her response was quiet and serious, "It's already in place, right next to the sink in the kitchen." They both laughed.

With the room all set up, Seth followed Emily to the kitchen where she explained, "Your job is to make sure everyone has as much wine and water as they require." She showed him the cases and the cooler as she reminded him of the cardinal rule. "Don't spill any wine on either a guest or the carpet. Now go get yourself dressed. The group will be arriving in ten minutes."

The dinner proved a formal affair with ladies dressed in evening gowns and the men in tuxedos or evening coats with black ties.

By five o'clock, the entire group had assembled in Sir Reginald's great room, enjoying themselves and filling the place with mostly business-related conversation. Emily directed Seth to make a few rounds with a tray of assorted appetizers, a duty he found much more difficult than he had imagined, and another brand-new experience for him. Concentrating on not dropping anything, he constantly scanned the room, intrigued by the average appearance of these unusually rich and powerful people.

Heading back to the kitchen with his empty tray, he glimpsed a familiar face, Scott Young. *So this is Scott's gig. Wonder what he'll be reporting this year?* he mused.

When he got back to the kitchen, his senses were affronted by a wall of heat and a cacophony of chatter interspersed with barked orders and clattering pots and pans. It seemed organized chaos prevailed as the serving hour approached.

At exactly seven o'clock, a bell sounded, and Sir Reginald welcomed everyone, inviting them to take their assigned seats.

Serving began with Seth and the waiters scuttling in and out of the kitchen under Emily's watchful eye. Her efficiency and effectiveness reminded him of a good football coach.

The volume of drink consumed surprised Seth. He had emptied nine bottles of red wine and two bottles of sparkling water even before the main course. As he came back on a second refill round, he noticed a piece of paper bearing the words 'For Seth Martin' next to Scott Young's wine glass. Seth filled Scott's glass and casually pocketed the note as Scott remained deep in conversation with an attractive Chinese lady about the changing distribution of sea ice.

Back in the kitchen, Seth read the note: "Very much want to speak to you about the *Jasper* incident. May we meet tonight?" Seth's heart raced. *What else did Scott want to know? What had he found out?* Various thoughts sprang to mind, but curiosity won out, so he penned an answer: "Okay. Come to the ANDREW CARNEGIE room at midnight."

* * *

The banquet continued until everyone appeared contentedly full, at which point their host rose and went to the podium. He gave recognition to the major guests and a sincere welcome to all. After a humorous interjection and compliments to the kitchen staff, he described his business objective for this year's gathering. At his seat, Scott pushed his tiny recorder closer to the edge of the table.

By eleven forty, the leftover food had been stored away, the dishes washed, the work surfaces scrubbed, and most of the staff dismissed. Emily watched as Seth finished mopping the floor, keen to get the job done but not overly anxious about returning to his room.

"You're a damn good worker, Mr. Seth Martin! Maybe we should open a place on Sandaray together."

Seth smiled and said he would think about it.

Bidding her good-night, he threw his soiled apron into the clothes bin, and headed slowly for ANDREW CARNEGIE. His mind could not have been further from opening a restaurant.

He traded all the bits and pieces of Dan's tux for his own, much more comfortable pants and then stood by the window reviewing all that had happened. *Perhaps my life is getting ready to take another 90-degree turn or maybe a really big 180-degree one.* Scott knocked at 12:05. *Suppose I'm about to find out.*

"Hello, Scott. Come on in."

They shook hands and walked toward the window. Looking out over the lights of the harbor and momentarily lost in thought, Seth commented, "This is one really peaceful and beautiful place. Funny, the formality of the gathering and particularly Sir Reg's speech back there seem out of place."

"Indeed. Look, thanks for agreeing to see me, Seth." Scott moved over to one of the ample easy chairs. "I know it's late, so I'll get right to the point."

Scott began by telling Seth he knew the doctor on duty in the emergency room the night the Coast Guard brought John Hajula in from the *Jasper*. "He told me by the time he released Hajula to the ICU, he felt certain of two things. First, his patient would have been dead if it hadn't been for the immediate treatment he'd been given, and second, whoever had provided that treatment knew exactly what to do and how to do it. Most normal, well-intentioned people would probably have bandaged the bloody lacerations on his head, raised his feet, and covered him with a blanket to prevent shock. They would never have noticed the small, sucking wound under his survival suit, which would likely have killed him even before the Coast Guard got there."

Seth said nothing.

"That discussion made me very curious about you," Scott went on, looking straight at Seth. "Would the average, relatively young sternman have known what to do? Would he have the training to save a man's life with that kind of a wound?" Scott explained these questions had continued to bother him, so he had started searching through the national news databases for pictures of people named Seth Martin, who might also happen to be a medic. Surprisingly, no one of that name and profession showed up. "For some reason, I just couldn't give up the search, and what do you know…?"

A wave of panic washed over Seth, and he felt a sudden burning in his neck and cheeks.

"I think I've found out who you are."

Seth sank back into the chair. *Shit! These news guys just never give up.*

"You're Seth Morrison, MD, Harvard Medical School, 2002, aren't you? Funny the similarity in names, don't you think?" Scott got up from his chair and walked toward the window. "It really took a lot of looking and comparing pictures. You didn't have a beard back then, but I know it's you. All the pieces fit together. I reckon you moved from Michigan, and you're the so-called euthanasia doctor from Marquette who mysteriously disappeared from the news and, some believe, from the face of the earth, about six months ago."

Seth began breathing again but couldn't speak, so he put on his best "guess-I've-been-found-out" look and waited. Unsure where the conversation might head next, one thing remained certain…he could never admit he had been through very specialized field emergency medical training.

"Well," asked Scott insistently, "are you Dr. Seth Morrison?"

For another long moment, Seth remained silent, then quietly asked, "And what are you going to do if I say I am?"

Scott immediately replied, "Publish a follow-up article expanding on the original, of course. It would have new, exciting, and verified facts about what really went on that day. That's what our readers want. It would make a blockbuster story, no doubt be picked up by the national wire services, and very possibly lead to a third article."

"So then what happens to the doctor?"

"Look, I have an ethical obligation to report the facts, all the facts. It's not for me to make any moral judgments or to have the slightest bit of emotional involvement. The original story elevated a regular sternman to hero status, while in truth I believe it should have told the story of a doctor fulfilling his sworn duty to save another man's life, Hajula's, in this case."

Seth thought, *In for a penny, in for a pound.* Looking straight at Scott, he retorted, "Let me ask you, Mr. Young, have you ever considered what it would be like to be old, past those rewarding years of doing and giving, only to find out the pain in your chest signaled the beginning of the end. And the end would involve an incurable disease and suffering for two or three agonizing, worthless years?"

"You *are* Morrison, aren't you?" Scott exclaimed, jumping to his feet.

"I didn't say that. I just wonder how your ethics make you feel about throwing someone to the sharks when his only crime is helping folks do what they truly want. Is it not their right to choose when they want to end their lives, regardless of the written law?"

"Guess there is another side to it, but we *are* a country of laws, and such a thing is against the law in the state of Michigan."

"Yes, we're a country of laws all right, laws that deny a person the right to choose ending their life with dignity and professional assistance, but still legally allow them to end it by drinking a bottle of rat poison or blowing their brains out with a shotgun."

Silence.

Eventually, Seth spoke again. "To answer your original question, I have to say, no, I am not Dr. Seth Morrison from Michigan, but I hope you let him live in peace wherever he is. Now, if you really want to make a name for yourself, you'll learn all you can about the plan Sir Reginald laid out this evening. It will surely be a blockbuster story capturing the interest of millions way beyond the northeast fishing community."

"You're one hell of a fellow, Seth Martin or Morrison or whatever your name is. Here's my card, and if you ever have a free moment in town, look me up. I'll buy you lunch, show you some pictures, even the one from Michigan. I'm still sure it's you." As they shook hands at the door, Scott added, "And don't worry, I won't write any more about Hajula and the *Jasper* or 'Dr. Death,' for that matter. Even though it would've made a helluva story. Are you sure you're not…?"

"Just leave it, okay?" Seth pretty much got the last word.

"Okay, okay, I got it!" Scott held up both hands in surrender and bid Seth good-night.

Walking back to the window, he stood for a while digesting the bizarre conversation with Scott Young. He hadn't seen that coming! *Perhaps I should have gone along with the Dr. Death charade. A lot easier to explain than the truth.*

Chapter Eight

An otherworldly site greeted Seth as he drew back his curtains. Fog had begun to form over the water, diffusing the sun's rays as they crept slowly down the hills on the northwest side of the harbor.

Only after showering, shaving and completely dressing, did he notice the time. *Shit, it's only quarter to six. I'm really early, but maybe not too early to gin up a cup of coffee in the kitchen.* And so, he started for the stairs.

Halfway up, he could hear the muffled voices of people talking. Then, as he approached the top, he stopped, curious about the nature of a discussion at this ungodly hour.

"Damn, Reg, you've nailed it again. This is just the thing for the future. I would sign up right now except for one detail: security. When dealing with small things of great value, security goes to the top of my list."

"Agreed. And since we've now outlined the technical piece, I think we go no further until we have a world-class security man on board. This has been a very productive meeting, but I suggest we adjourn now and pick it up again later in the day. Let me know of any security prospects you can think of. I for one am ready to move."

"How about a guy with twenty years' high-level experience in CIA security? His letter arrived just before I left."

"Do you have his CV with you?"

"No, but it's very impressive. I'll see if Jessie can email it over."

Seth froze. *How many people could fit* that *description?*

Chairs scraped as the group disbanded. Seth took his cue to continue casually up the stairs, trying to look like just another helper headed for the kitchen. He glanced at the group as he passed, but of the five he only recognized Sir Reginald.

With his heart racing, he entered the kitchen to find Emily perusing several pieces of paper over a cup of coffee.

"Good morning, Seth."

"Morning, boss. It's early. I thought you'd still be in the sack. Can I help with something?"

"Get yourself a cup of coffee and sit down here. I have your day all planned, but there's no immediate rush because, as you may have seen, some of the eagles are still hatching their eggs out there."

"Yes, but I just noticed them spreading their wings as if to fly away."

"It's about time; they've been hatching there all night."

Seth got coffee as Emily outlined the day's events. The morning would be filled with converting last night's banquet area into a dance floor edged with small tables, along with the construction of a stage. The afternoon would involve getting her nephew and his band set up. Then the party would start.

"When the guests arrive in the evening, your job will be to circulate, getting whatever folks want, staying bone-dry sober, and paying very good attention to everything going on."

"Got it...and are you part of your nephew's band?"

"No, not at all," Emily responded with a throaty laugh. "I just play the CD machine. The band is quite good though, you'll really enjoy them. Pete plays the sax."

"Well, I look forward to hearing him. Do most folks dance, or does it tend to be all shop talk?"

"Oh they definitely enjoy the music and dancing but you're right, they do spend most of their time talking shop. Every one of them is in one spotlight or another, so coming here, even for just a day, gives them a real break as well as providing an opportunity to discuss business matters openly.

"Every year," Emily continued, "a major new project of some sort gets conceived. Right here! Three years ago, for example, Wilson Engineering didn't even exist, but today, it employs over twelve thousand people and is listed on the New York Stock Exchange. Now that's a big deal!"

This again impressed Seth, since his vision of parties attended by the uber-wealthy had always been one of drunken orgies where the whiskey flowed freely, the nut dishes were filled with little blue pills, and thoughts concerning conception had nothing to do with business.

"Of course, I'm not saying someone won't get a bit tipsy, try to pick a fight, or chat up the wrong woman," Emily added, "but it's also why Mr. Price always lends us two of the security people who travel with him. These guys are big, strong, and very watchful. They're my buddies, and they keep the peace.

"You'll meet Douglas and Caroline Price as well. They're nice folks. Their place is just across the road a bit north of here. Now get your butt out of here, Mr. Seth, and help the others roll those big carpets. We'll have brunch for all us kitchen folks around eleven."

The work had been easy, and the day passed quickly.

With the great room conversion almost complete, Seth took a moment to glance out the window where he spotted the *Linda-T* offloading people and goods at the dock. "Emily," he called across the room, "the band is here."

"Great. Go down there with Sir Reg's Gator and help them get their gear up here."

"Will do."

* * *

The group of six musicians called themselves "Searsport." Each loved music of all kinds but, as a group, they played mostly rock-and-roll and swing. For this gathering, their emphasis would be on swing from the mid-twentieth century.

Seth met them, and in less than an hour, all their equipment had been set up, and a sound check completed. The saxophone player, noticing his aunt near the kitchen door, waved a hello, blew her a kiss, and then greeted her with a few bars of the jazz classic "Emily." Everyone in the huge room stopped and listened. Emily smiled broadly, waved, and applauded.

By seven o'clock, Seth was dressed to the nines in Dan's tuxedo and his own tennis shoes. Most of the guests had arrived and were milling around the bar area making small talk. But, in a very short time, the champagne began flowing copiously, the dance floor became packed with couples, and the party was in full swing.

Tray in hand, Seth circulated and, as Emily had predicted, found most people simply having a good time reconnecting with friends and acquaintances. Conversations touched on everything from politics to religion but frequently found their way back to the common denominator of business.

Near the dance floor, Sir Reginald's son Dan and his wife, Linda, silently sipped their drinks. When the clarinet player took center stage and began a slow, romantic Benny Goodman favorite, the floor again filled quickly. Even at a distance, Seth could sense Linda's disappointment as Dan made no move to ask her to dance. Instead, he seemed happy just to sit and ogle the young lady in the spotlight. Her musical abilities were obvious and her looks stunning to boot. Still, these were no excuse for Dan's lack of consideration.

Seth continued to watch and, as the piece finished, Dan sprang to his feet, shouting an embarrassing "Bravo!" and applauding way too long. He remained standing as the band began their next piece, then sat for the rest of the set, rarely having the clarinet player out of his sight.

When they stopped for a break, Dan headed over to their table, without a word to Linda. Loudly and pretentiously, he introduced himself. "Hi, folks. I'm Dan Wilson." Turning toward the clarinetist, he continued, "Say, I really enjoyed your solo piece…you play superbly. Would you care to join us for a few minutes?" He motioned toward Linda with one hand, and gently eased back her chair as she readily accepted the invitation.

"Let me get you a drink," he gushed, steering her toward their table and waving to attract a waiter's attention.

The dark-haired beauty looked from Dan to Linda. "Hi. I'm Julia."

"Linda Wilson," Linda said, extending her hand, "and I'm with him. I really enjoyed your music too. How long have you been playing?"

"Since first grade, all through school, and now a bit over two years with this band. It's a pleasure to meet you both." A bottle of champagne appeared out of nowhere. "Got any requests?"

As they talked, Dan drank, scrutinizing Julia for an embarrassingly long time, his gaze fluctuating between her finely chiseled features and her compact but alluring cleavage.

"Doesn't make any difference to me as long as we hear more from you," Dan enthused.

Linda could see Dan had a request in mind, all right. And judging by his actions, not a very subtle one.

Julia rejoined the band, and soon they were back on stage, starting their next set. A dejected Linda looked around the room, spotted Seth, and waved him over.

"Good evening, Linda. May I bring you something?"

"Yes," came the decisive response, "bring us another bottle of the Perrier-Jouët." *And some cyanide pills for my oversexed old man*, she thought morosely.

"Right away."

She knew what Dan wanted all too well, but even she could not believe how forward he had just been. So when he jumped to his feet at the end of the next set, inviting Julia to join them again, she considered her best exit strategy.

As they approached the table, she rose and, casting a scornful glance in Dan's direction, gathered up her purse, glass, and the champagne bottle, and headed for the bar.

Dan seemed unperturbed by his wife's departure and summoned another bottle of champagne for his new companion.

"Let's drink to the band and its extraordinarily talented clarinetist!" he whispered, handing her a glass.

"Dan, I love champagne, but I can't have any just now," Julia explained. "It has a terrible effect on my clarinet."

"I'll keep a bottle cold for when you're finished, how about then?"

"You're on!"

* * *

By the time midnight arrived, the crowd had begun to thin out. Seth observed Linda from across the room as he cleared glasses. She sat alone at the bar, glass in hand, listening to the music. He wondered why she wasn't on the dance floor in Dan's arms. A beautiful, sexy woman sitting all alone. There had to be something wrong with Dan to leave her and chase the clarinetist.

78

The party went on, but for some, business discussions continued, and as Seth made his way from table to table, he caught snippets of a conversation that included two of the men he had overheard from the top of the stairway earlier in the day. Certain phrases piqued his interest. Phrases alluding to government-level computer hacking, such as, "remember what…did to Sony," and "… don't forget how Russia and China…" coupled quickly with, "I'll be with you if you guarantee the necessary security…" He wondered what they were really talking about.

A man in full highland dress motioned to Seth with an empty glass. As Seth moved to serve him, he realized he had also seen this man in the early hours. Seth waited. The man was in full flow. "…there'll be a meeting next week in London with a retired US government security expert, some guy called Henderson. It sounds like he's the right man for the job…." Seth froze. *Holy Shit! It **was** him they were talking about this morning. I don't believe it. These guys move fast. It's got to be the same Edwin Henderson. This is terrible!*

"Ah, here's the waiter. Five whiskeys please." Seth hoped no-one had noticed the wave of panic which had momentarily swept over him.

By two fifteen in the morning, the cleanup had been completed, and Emily had dispatched her staff to their beds. Seth made his way back to his room, fully aware that, in just seven hours and forty-five minutes, JB and the *Linda-T* would be leaving for Sandaray. *Better get everything together tonight and be ready to just roll out of bed and run to the dock*, he thought as he pushed the door open.

Though it was pitch black, Seth could sense a presence. Letting the door swing, he stopped, all his senses tuned, searching the darkness. His hand found the light switch and flipped it on. His eyes were drawn to a figure sitting on a chair by the table.

She held a champagne flute, her blouse partially unbuttoned, and her hair ruffled as though fingers had been run through it multiple times. A bottle stood on the table. "Helloooo, Seth."

"Linda…are you okay?"

She got up, clearly on the verge of collapse, and came over, putting her arms around his neck. She pressed her body against his. "Want me?" she said in a very low tone.

Seth held her arms. "Let me take you back to your room, Linda."

His offer produced instant and uncontrollable sobbing. "I can't go back there. He's locked the door and is probably in there right now, fucking the clarinet floozy!"

Seth pulled the covers down on his bed. "Okay then, crawl in here."

"You do want me, don't you?" she said, fumbling with the remaining buttons on her blouse.

"What I want is for you to get some sleep." Seth muttered gently. As he propelled her awkwardly onto the bed, she grasped at him.

"Seth, I need you. Come on. No-one will know."

Somehow, he managed to extricate himself and slide her legs under the sheets.

"You sleep here, and I'll go down to the boat. We leave in just a few hours anyway."

"But it's cold there. I'll make it nice and warm for you here… come on now. You know you want to crawl in here…you know you wanna be with me."

By this time, her efforts to entice him into the bed had made her naked from the waist up. They had also made it almost impossible for her to keep her eyes open. Seth pulled the covers over her, easing her down to a comfortable sleeping position. He tucked her in securely and stopped just to look.

"You're a really nice person and a beautiful woman. There's no way you deserve what that son of a bitch did to you tonight."

But she didn't hear him because drink, the late hour, and the comfort of the bed had finally brought deep sleep.

Seth changed back into his regular attire, leaving the borrowed items on the opposite side of the bed from the sleeping Linda. He stuffed everything else in a bag and went over to her. He watched for a few minutes, studying the beauty of her face, then knowing she had fallen into deep sleep, leaned over and gently kissed her lips, whispering, "Good night, lovely Linda. Sleep well."

At three in the morning, Seth crawled into the bunk aboard the *Linda-T*.

* * *

"What the hell ya doing here?" exclaimed JB.

Seth rubbed his eyes, yawned, and answered, "We got done really late, so I just brought my stuff here, knowing it would be the only way I'd be sure not to miss you."

"Crazy boy," JB responded. "I brought a thermos of hot coffee. It's above; go get yourself a cup."

Soon the band members and their gear showed up. The clarinet player was the last to arrive once again, looking particularly frazzled.

At ten o'clock sharp, the *Linda-T* pulled out of Orran harbor, bound for Sandaray.

The weather proved perfect, and in no time at all, JB's passengers were back on dry land and in Bill Harris's truck bound for the airport.

Soon, with the boat moored for the day, JB and Seth made their way back to the fish house. They parted at the steps to the apartment, understanding the next day's work would start about the same time the party day had ended.

Chapter Nine

For Seth, life soon returned to normal, and the unique weekend experience on Orran faded into a bizarre dream. His days were once again filled with the routines and hard work of lobster fishing. He and JB had become an efficient and effective team, and when things fell smoothly into place, he experienced a very pleasant sense of accomplishment. At the end of one of those days, he decided to sit for a while on the wharf and watch the ferry dock, savoring the inner feeling of contentment. Life was good.

The passengers looked like the usual mix of tourists and islanders, and he smiled recalling the day he first set foot on the island. He wondered if any of these folks had come for the same reason he had.

Caught up in his musings, a sharp jolt brought him back into the moment as he spotted someone familiar. *Shit! No way! It can't be him.* Seth strained to see better, but the man had disappeared. *Surely it can't be him...can it? I've got to get a better look.*

He rushed into the fish house, knowing JB kept a pair of binoculars on the bench. Positioning himself under the open steps to the apartment, he scanned the line of people. *Damn! Looks like I lost him.* He shifted his position slightly, but still no sign of the man. Breaking his cover, he darted farther along the dock and turned left up into the woodland behind the fish houses.

At the top of the embankment, he crouched behind a tree and watched. Several people entered Emma's Café. Others carried on toward the shop. Some made for their vehicles.

Then suddenly, there he was. *God, it is him.* His pulse raced. He was almost 100 percent certain but needed to see the face full-on. He waited. *Turn round you bastard. Let me get a proper look at you.* The man stopped, glanced at his watch then looked to the left, directly at Seth. *Shit, he's seen me.*

Instinctively Seth ducked down. He took a minute to compose himself, then raised the glasses again. Now he had a very clear view. It was *not* him.

He almost dropped the binoculars, as a huge wave of relief washed over him. His nemesis had not followed him to Sandaray. He was safe…at least for now. He leaned back against a tree trunk and considered what he would have done if he had been right.

Back at the fish house, Seth poured himself a stiff whiskey. Although Scott Young's curiosity had been real, it had proven nothing and left Seth's deception secure. But if today's encounter had been real, the same deception would have been shattered forever. How long could he keep up the pretense? Should he think about readdressing the past?

* * *

Summer had flashed by in an instant, and soon the trees took on their autumn hues. The days were getting shorter and colder, and the sea unleashed its fury more frequently.

One Tuesday in mid-October, JB announced he had decided not to fish through the winter. It had been a good season, but his arthritis was making the job twice as difficult. He wasn't getting any younger, and a winter at sea was really no longer an option. In addition, his sister had once again invited him to winter over at her home on the Gulf Coast of Texas. This year he had accepted and now planned to haul out his gear, close up the house, and head for Texas on December 15th.

Seth considered how the decision would affect him, recognizing life on this little island would be totally different in just a few short weeks. Indeed, these months on Sandaray, and his experience on Orran were beginning to change the way he looked at his future and—particularly—his past.

For the first time in nearly a year, he found himself questioning the decision to pursue this totally new life in semi-isolation. The man who had gotten off the ferry and nearly scared him to death, the snippets of conversations he had overheard on Orran, the name 'Edwin Henderson'—all these things made it clear he had some difficult decisions ahead.

* * *

One Sunday, with no work to be done, Seth lay in bed, listening to the wind whip past the side of the fish house. He needed to focus on a way forward. Logic dictated he should write down all the pros and cons of staying or going back, consider them carefully, and come up with a sensible plan. But first, nourishment.

* * *

A big smile spread across Emma's face and her eyes lit up with warm emotion. "Hey, Seth! Haven't seen you in ages. How ya doing?"

"Doing okay, thanks, Emma." He paused before continuing. "But seems like we've been out to haul or up to our ears with other stuff every day for the last three months, and there just hasn't been time to come in and have one of your terrific meals."

"Well, then," she said, meeting his eyes, "you're here now. What can I get you?"

"Just the usual please, Emma."

A hot coffee and large plate of eggs, ham, and fried potatoes arrived almost immediately. "Here ya go, stranger!"

"Looks wonderful. Thank you, Emma." Then, in a more serious tone, he asked, "Emma, are you going to stay open all winter?"

"Great question!" She drew up a stool and, taking a sip of coffee, went on to explain how the past winter she had stayed open, but while the locals had done their best to frequent the café, it had literally taken all of her savings just to survive till spring.

"The real trouble," she continued, "starts just after Christmas, when more than half the fishermen are gone, and the tourist count goes to zero. The truth is, I love this place best then, but those two big freezers and the stove keep the electric and gas bills coming in even on the days when there isn't a single customer. It would actually be more economical for me to close up shop."

"Yes, I suppose."

"What about JB," she asked. "Is he going to haul all winter like last year? Just think, it would be a wonderful opportunity to learn how much fun it is to work totally frozen all day, every day!"

Seth chuckled. "No such luck. I'm afraid I'm going to miss that particular learning experience this year. He says he's going to Texas on December fifteenth."

"And what will you do then?"

"Still looking at options, I guess. Part of it depends on what there is to do around here in the winter. JB says I can continue to stay in the apartment over his fish house if I want, and that's certainly good. Guess time will tell."

* * *

Walking down to the harbor, Seth suddenly realized there was something different about Emma. She had seemed genuinely pleased to see him. That definitely wasn't it. No, if he was not mistaken, she had colored her hair! He shook his head, smiling to himself.

At the foot of the fish house steps, he paused recalling their conversation. He really needed to weigh up his options very carefully.

On the positive side, he had been on the island for several months, enjoying the place, the work, and the people. He had a comfortable place to live and a fairly healthy stash of money tucked behind the painting by the bedroom door. There would almost certainly be odd jobs he could pick up to keep himself busy. If he stayed permanently, his long-term objective would be to fish full-time with his own boat and his own sternman. The downside of staying, however, was a gnawing feeling of guilt about leaving a situation unresolved. He well knew it would continue to eat away at him for a very long time.

The following Tuesday brought stunningly beautiful weather, so, taking advantage of the warmth, Seth decided to repair half a dozen damaged traps out on the dock.

As he got his tools and the traps out of the shop, he stopped to watch the ferry dock. It was strange to see only two trucks, one van, and an SUV drive off, followed by just two foot passengers. One truck carried building supplies, the other food for both Emma's Café and the store.

Four people rode in the SUV, which disappeared up the hill, and the two on foot were met about mid-wharf by Bill Harris. *Amazing how only a few weeks ago, every ferry came over packed. Fall here on Sandaray is certainly different, and winter will be even more so.*

As he worked, the sound of Bill's vehicle got louder and louder, making Seth wish again he would get a muffler for the old thing and return peace and quiet to the island. In the opinion of some islanders, he kept it that way intentionally to create a rugged, isolated, out-of-the-mainstream image for his guests. Seth and most of the others thought it more reflective of miserly Bill's idiocy. As it approached the path to the fish house, the noise stopped, and Seth looked up.

86

Bill jumped out, waved, and started jogging down. "Morning, Seth. JB around?"

Seth answered in the negative.

Bill stopped and, between gasps, asked, "Do you have any lobsters? I've got a load of guests for tonight, and it would solve my supper plans."

"We have a few," Seth answered, using the island jargon for "we've got plenty," and quickly adding Bill knew how it worked, so he would have to ask JB first.

Changing tack, Bill then asked what Seth's plans were for the coming months. He had heard about JB's plans to spend the winter in Texas with his sister.

"Guess I'm going to stay right here and pick up whatever work I can."

"Great. I have some work I can put your way if you're interested. Come over for a chat sometime."

"Oh, okay. JB leaves mid-December. I'll be over sometime before then."

"Look forward to it."

Thoroughly enjoying the sunshine and the light breeze, Seth had repaired three of the damaged traps when JB arrived.

"Morning, Seth. Sure is a nice day."

"You bet. Did Harris find you?"

"Yes, he wants some lobsters. I'll get 'em for him. I want to go out and check the boat anyway." Seth went back to work as JB took the skiff out to the *Linda-T*.

* * *

Almost three weeks later, on what the old folks called Armistice Day but the young folks knew as Veterans Day, Seth's phone rang. As on the other rare occasions when this had happened, the sharp intrusive trill startled him. He ran to the kitchen.

"This is Seth Martin."

"Want to go to town tomorrow?" JB's unidentified but familiar voice asked.

"Sure. It's supposed to be a really nice day. I'll bring my camera and get your picture."

"You know damn well about me and pictures. But you can take some of Linda. We'll be picking her up at Orran, so she can do some Thanksgiving shopping in town. I'll be down about six thirty. We need to load those sixteen crates of lobsters and take them to Frank on the *Clacken* first."

"Great, I'll be ready."

* * *

As forecasted, the next day began with storybook-perfect weather. The glass-like water in the harbor only being disturbed by the wake of an occasional departing boat. Seth stood on the end of the dock, drinking in the scene and wondering if any place he had ever lived before could provide such a peaceful and beautiful sight. JB's voice broke his reverie.

"Morning, young man. Beautiful day. You all ready to go?"

"Yes Sir"

Twenty-five minutes later, the two had loaded their things. The sixteen crates of lobsters were securely aboard, and the *Linda-T* headed north, along the west coast of Sandaray, toward Orran Island. Seth stood on the starboard side, camera in hand, snapping pictures from their uncommonly close vantage point. *Everything we pass looks different from the way it does on land.*

Soon they glided into Orran harbor and tied up alongside the *Clacken II.*

"Good morning, handsome," Carrie said, handing JB a mug of hot coffee. "Kinda late for you guys to be showing up here.

What's the matter, couldn't you get your butts out of the sack this morning?"

"Ain't going to haul this morning...at least, not going to haul lobsters anyway. I'm taking Linda into town to get a turkey and all sorts of other stuff for Thanksgiving."

"Lucky Linda, eh?" she replied as she turned to begin sorting, counting, and weighing the catch that Frank and Seth were hauling aboard.

In a short time, they were almost done. Frank came over, handing JB a check and an envelope containing cash for Seth. They could see Linda waiting on the pier, so JB secured the papers, started the engine, and said his goodbyes, while Seth undid the mooring lines. As they started for the pier, Carrie's parting words drifted over the water: "Don't forget, boys, the day before Thanksgiving will be our last day out here for the season."

In minutes, Linda boarded, and they were on their way to the mainland, JB at the wheel, Linda taking in the scenery, and Seth straightening up the back deck, securing things just in case the sea decided to bounce them around a little.

* * *

Seth came forward and stood next to Linda. "Haven't seen you since the big bash out here. How're you doing, Linda?"

"Doing fine, thanks. Busy. You know how it is. How about you? Dad says he's been keeping you jumping."

"Well, yes. But I'm sure you know he's decided to haul out in December and spend the winter with your aunt in Texas. The way I see it, he's trying to give all the lobsters an extra opportunity of seeing the inside of one of his traps before he leaves. We've been out almost every day. Are you and Dan staying out on Orran now?"

Linda explained Dan had been spending nearly all his time at his father's place, and she had been going out there one or two days

89

a week to bring him food, do the laundry, straighten up, and the like. She then added Dan had been working nonstop on a new business his father had started up, staying there for privacy and secrecy.

Wonder if all that has something to do with the clarinet player from the party? Better stay away from that subject, Seth thought.

"You know next Thursday is Thanksgiving, Seth—"

"Gosh, the year is certainly rocketing by, isn't it?" he interrupted, unsure of where this might be leading. "Here, would you like some coffee?" he continued, fumbling in his bag for the thermos and a cup.

She nodded. He poured, looked up, and met her eyes.

"Would you like to join us for Thanksgiving dinner?"

He hesitated, torn between saying yes, at the risk of being some sort of referee between her and Dan, and saying no and missing out on her beautiful and very enticing company. He felt his color rise at the thought of being close to her for even a few short hours. "Thanksgiving dinner is usually just a family gathering, but if you're sure you don't mind an outsider tagging along, I'd be delighted to come."

They passed the remainder of the journey in companionable silence, standing a respectable distance apart at the stern. Seth could not help casting furtive, admiring glances in her direction, and twice, he felt sure her eyes had been scrutinizing him too, rather intently. He felt like a foolish teenager with a crush. As long as he stuck with fantasizing, he would be okay.

* * *

The shopping trip proved to be a relaxing and enjoyable interlude in what had otherwise been just another long, hard week. And fortuitously, they were able to finish early on the Saturday affording Seth the opportunity to call on Bill Harris.

Stepping up onto the large porch of DeVoe Lodge, Seth paused to drink in the view. As in a Thomas Cole painting, the crisp, clear fall morning and the mansion looked majestic. *Old Captain what's-his-name picked a perfect spot to build this house. Just as Bill picked the perfect house to turn into a B&B.* The large brass parrot knocker announced Seth's arrival, and soon he sat in the kitchen across from Bill, sipping a cup of coffee.

Bill got right to the point, explaining the whole place needed a major overhaul. This winter he wanted to get it done with the objective of turning it into a high-end, luxury guest house for more discerning clients. The January 2nd ferry had been already booked to bring two trucks of new fixtures and fittings. A team from the mainland, with experience in renovation, would fly out each Monday, returning Friday. They needed a helper, however, a gofer to work with them. Seth, he believed, fit the bill to a tee. A grand reopening would take place on March 12th. "Like any project out here, there'll be unknowns, but JB says you're good in a crisis and can certainly do the job. I'll pay you fifteen bucks an hour."

Seth considered his offer and decided he would take it. But thinking he had a good bargaining position, replied, "I'll do it, but how about twenty?"

"How about fifteen and lunch every day?" countered Bill.

"Lunch and dinner would be okay."

"Okay then. It's a deal. My last guests depart on the same January second ferry, so how about starting then?"

"Sure, that'll be great."

Then, slipping into an unusually nostalgic mode and almost reluctant to let him go, Bill added, "This place has needed a good fixing and cleaning up for some time. The big thing missing, of course, is Emma's touch. God, she's good with all the interior design stuff, and a damn hard worker as well."

"Don't worry, Bill, we'll get it all done," Seth said, trying to sound reassuring.

As Seth started for the front door, he wondered if the new rebranding included the purchase of a luxury taxi to ferry his "more discerning" guests around the island!

So that's it, Seth thought. *The die is cast...you've committed to a job, and who knows, it may even turn out to be a good learning experience.*

* * *

The three days leading up to the Thanksgiving holiday were the same as all the other normal hauling days, except on the Tuesday when JB decided to take up twenty of his seven hundred traps. By three thirty, JB's dock held a pile of buoys, ready to be cleaned and painted, and two neat stacks of traps, one ready for the next year, the other needing repairs. Both men had the same thought: *Only six hundred and eighty to go.*

On Wednesday, JB and Seth went to Orran to sell the week's catch and say farewell to Frank and Carrie. It gave Seth a funny, almost out-of-place feeling, as he knew he would genuinely miss the routines of fishing. For these seven months, he had lived a comfortable, stable existence, one which had provided a much-needed release from the stresses, problems, and pains of his life before. Although this solid stability had returned a wonderful feeling of self-worth, it remained tainted. The past had a nasty habit of breaking through into his present, reminding him of its existence and unfinished business.

As they approached the stairs leading to Seth's apartment, JB told him he would come by in his truck to pick him up promptly at quarter to two the next day, adding with a laugh, "You'd better not smell like bait, either."

Chapter Ten

Seth stood by the fish house door, armed with a small, luxury box of chocolates. As he waited for his lift, his mind replayed both the recent trip to the mainland and events of his last night on Orran. He had to get those thoughts out of his head to survive today's intimate family gathering. Instead, he must focus on the "thanks" part of Thanksgiving and on the memories of such gatherings from his childhood.

The last seven months of his life had been like no other… complicated, and at times difficult, but generally productive, and for this, Seth gave sincere thanks.

The sound of JB's horn brought him back to reality. The time had come to leave.

* * *

Linda and Dan's house, situated on a prominent rise, had spectacular views across the ocean from two sides. On a good day, Orran Island became clearly visible, some six miles to the northeast, while to the northwest, there were occasional glimpses of the mainland hills many miles away. Behind their house, a small lawn separated them from the dense spruce forest that dominated most of the island.

Dan watched the truck pull up and, as the two men approached, he opened the front door and extended his hand to JB. "Welcome, JB. Happy Thanksgiving. Come on in." Linda appeared from behind him, hugged her father tightly, and lovingly kissed his cheek. Dan nodded the briefest of acknowledgments to Seth and proceeded to steer the group through to the living room. Linda gently touched Seth's arm, "Welcome. I'm delighted you could join us." Despite Linda's kind words, Seth felt distinctly unwelcome.

In the living room, Seth stood for a moment taking in the opulence of the room, his gaze stopping to study the fine oil portrait of Linda hanging over the fireplace. He found himself transfixed by the way the artist had captured her expressive eyes, though he regretted her somewhat melancholy expression.

Linda's movement at the door diverted his attention, and he turned to face her. Those same dark eyes stared back at him now, but this time with genuine warmth. She smiled and turned to her husband. "Dan, get everyone a drink please."

As Dan headed over to the cabinet, Seth quietly intercepted Linda and presented his gift. She looked radiant in a figure-hugging, red velvet dress, her hair pinned high with soft tendrils framing her face, and again he found it impossible to look away. "Thank you, Seth. Now go back through and join the others. I'll be a little while in the kitchen."

Seth took his seat at one end of the sofa and watched as Dan produced a whiskey on the rocks for JB and, almost as an afterthought, asked Seth what his drink preference would be.

"I'll have the same as JB please, only neat."

Dan set about pouring Seth's drink, silently questioning how a sternman would even know the meaning of the word *neat*.

Soon the TV came on, with an early but traditional football matchup from Detroit. The favored Houston Texans versus the

Detroit Lions. "Yuck, this is probably going to be a one-sided massacre," Dan muttered as he began fiddling with the switches on his video player.

Not particularly interested in watching anything on TV, Seth rose and made his way to the kitchen.

"Wonderful smells coming from this room," he said. "I think Dan's putting on a recording of this morning's New York parade. Have you got time to see some of the world-famous floats and big balloons?"

"Thank you for the thought, but no, dinner is just about ready."

"Oh. Well then, is there anything I can do to help?"

"Sure, you can drain those potatoes while I finish this sauce."

Soon the carefully decorated table was adorned with a mountain of food, the centerpiece being a perfectly roasted, stuffed turkey waiting to be carved. Motioning to the unlit candles, Linda tossed Seth a box of matches, then turned and rang their antique bronze dinner bell, inviting all to the Thanksgiving dinner table.

As they ate, the lighthearted conversation gradually gave way to more serious subjects. Dan officiously tapped his wine glass. "Before we get any further into the meal, I must make an announcement, and it's very apt considering what day this is." Politely putting down their cutlery, all turned their eyes to Dan. "Father has decided to make me an office manager in London! I start work on January first. Something special to give thanks for, don't you think?!"

An awkward silence followed as the stunned guests glanced from one to the other. Dan seemed oblivious and carried on, "Amazing isn't it. Finally, a real step up the old corporate ladder!" He looked across at his wife, her steely glare speaking words her lips dared not utter.

After what seemed like an eternity, JB broke the icy silence with the obvious. "Well, Dan, tell us more."

In his typically arrogant style, Dan began a long explanation of how the new company his father had just started would be based in Brussels, with offices in numerous places, including London. The London office would be headed by Bob Blackstock, Sir Reginald's current operations chief in New York, along with some hotshot, ex-US government guy who would head security. Bob would be replaced in New York by the director of logistics in Dubai, who, in turn, would be—

"Holy cow," JB interrupted, "just skip the rest of the dominos and get down to the one with your name on it. What does this all mean for you and Linda?"

Dan carried on in a wave of naïve enthusiasm, as Linda looked daggers at him down the table. It quickly became obvious to everyone that she had been totally in the dark about any of this...until now. He planned to leave in early December, find a new home, and be ready to start work full-time in January. Linda would follow as soon as she had closed up their place on Sandaray.

Linda finally exploded. "You son of a bitch! You've said nothing to me about moving. You've just gone and done it all on your own, right down to the final detail...*again!*" She stood up, hands on hips, face flushed with anger, and eyes trained on her husband. "Don't you think I should have been consulted in this process? Don't I get a vote for once? Doesn't all we have here mean anything to you?"

"Oh, Linda, cool down. You've certainly been uppermost in my thoughts all through this. Please, just sit down, relax, and hear me out. After all, it's Thanksgiving, and once you have the whole story, you'll agree this news is really something to give thanks for."

Reluctantly, she sat down surreptitiously sliding Seth's whiskey glass close. She could barely listen as Dan rattled on about this new venture, and after just a minute or so, she downed all of Seth's whiskey in one gulp. Dan droned on. *Who is he trying to convince?* She attempted to listen as he boasted about how this opportunity finally would launch him up the corporate ladder. *I know where I'd like to launch him,* she thought.

Linda folded her napkin carefully, neatly placing it next to her plate and, without a word, began clearing the dishes. Seth rose to help her.

The arrival of pumpkin pie and hot coffee finally interrupted an awkward silence, and gradually, muted conversation resumed.

* * *

In an attempt to divert attention away from his announcement, Dan asked JB if he had any firm plans for the trip to Texas.

"Yep. All figured out," he responded, adding he had already purchased an airline ticket and would be departing from Portland on the morning of December 15th. "All of which means I must be closed up, packed, and in Portland, ready to go by the evening of December fourteenth." He stopped abruptly and, focusing his attention on his daughter, added he had been counting on her and Dan to look after his house during the winter.

"I'm sure all these things can be worked out," Dan said, quickly changing the subject and adding patronizingly, "Linda, this has been an outstanding meal. Thank you very much for doing all the superb cooking. We can clean up later, but for now, why don't we all go into the living room and have a nice cognac to top it all off?" Dan steered JB through to the other room, while Seth began clearing the table. Linda remained seated, seething over the news, her pie untouched.

* * *

Soon the afternoon gathering ended. JB and Seth left, thanking Linda and Dan for a lovely meal and a nice afternoon. Linda gave her father a long hug, then lingered in the doorway, waving until his truck disappeared down the road. She closed the door slowly and headed back to the kitchen. Dan emerged from the living room with two glasses and stood behind his wife. "How about a cognac?" She gave no response as she continued cleaning the remaining dishes. After a few moments, Dan put the glasses on the counter and held her shoulders, trying to gently turn her toward him. But she twisted out of his grasp and, with tears welling up in her eyes, mumbled a barely audible, "How could you do such a thing?" She closed the dishwasher and walked down the hall to the guest bedroom. He heard the door close and lock.

Chapter Eleven

The next morning, while he was getting breakfast, the shrill bell of the telephone startled Seth so much he almost dumped the hot oatmeal on the floor.

"This is Seth Martin," he said, slightly breathless but listening carefully.

"They're giving northeast forty by mid-morning, so we're staying put today."

I wonder if he ever identifies himself when he makes a call?

"I'm going down to check the boat, and I'd like to stop by for a minute, okay?"

"Sure, the coffee is hot."

"Good, be there shortly."

A blast of cold air accompanied JB as he entered the kitchen, reminding Seth winter would soon be here. He poured two mugs of hot coffee, and the two sat at the kitchen table.

Direct as ever, JB asked what Seth's plans were for the coming months and whether he would still be there in the spring. Seth told him about the work he had lined up, helping Bill Harris with the remodeling of DeVoe Lodge.

"Think it'll keep you here all winter?"

"Well, if the work runs out, I'm sure I'll stay put at least until you get back. I don't have any other plans at the moment and kinda hoped you might take me on again come April. If anything changes, I'll certainly let you know."

"Thanks for telling me. I doubt you'd find a sternman on any of these islands, even on the mainland, who'd make such a commitment," JB said in a very serious tone. "You've turned out to be a fine worker. I'm impressed with how quickly you've learned and become comfortable in the back of the boat, and believe you me, I have seen some who spent much more time back there and never became as effective."

Then, looking Seth directly in the eye, he changed the subject. "But you just came here right out of nowhere, and I'm still trying to figure you out. Are you sure you ain't going to run away from here, the way you were most likely running away from something when you came here?"

Seth felt his color rise. Relating any part of his past would probably start him down one of those irreversible slippery slopes which, at this point, he really wanted to avoid. He took a few moments to get his thoughts together. JB had been kind and, apart from asking if he had been in trouble with the law, never brought up any personal questions despite his obvious and quite natural curiosity.

Seth knew JB had accepted him "as is," with the only important thing being how well he worked and followed the rules, rules that defined red lines never to be crossed. Could JB now be digging into the past because of something he had been told or found out? Seth decided to open up a little.

"I really appreciate you not prying into my past. I will be here all winter and probably all year, but there are bothersome issues remaining from before my time in Maine. Nothing, mind you, involving the law or anyone coming here looking for me."

"Not even a very curious newspaper guy like Scott Young? I've heard he did some research on you that got him very interested."

"hmm…well, I guess he has. He did corner me while we were over at the gathering, but I'll tell you, he just put two and two together and got twenty-two instead of four. Apparently, a doctor disappeared a few months ago up in Michigan. He'd been in some sort of newsworthy trouble involving euthanasia. The guy must look a bit like me, and after the publicity of the *Jasper* incident, Scott Young became convinced it must be me." Seth paused. "Not only am I definitely not a doctor, but I've never been to Michigan!"

JB studied Seth for a long moment, mentally searching for signs of deception. He knew Scott and his background as an intense and tenacious, former Washington, DC, newspaper reporter, and he knew Scott wouldn't have pursued Seth if there hadn't been some real substance to his suspicions. But nothing had come of it, and JB soon relaxed his thoughts, accepting the story and changing the subject to his upcoming schedule.

"Tomorrow will be really lousy again, but it should clear by Monday, making it possible to haul all six hundred and eighty by Thursday at the latest. We'll let them sit until the following week. Then, with luck and fair weather, we can get the whole batch on the dock before the tenth, and I'm off. Oh, and by the way, there's one more thing. I'm sure you remember the little bombshell Dan dropped at Thanksgiving dinner. Well, I don't know much about what they're up to, but I do know he leaves for London next Friday, and Linda will follow three weeks later, so they can have Christmas together. All of which leaves me with no one to check on the house; would you mind doing it?"

"Sure, be happy to. I'll need a briefing and some instructions on what to do. And I'll need to know what to do with my rent payments. When are you planning to be back?"

"Some time around mid-March, but it ain't firm yet. I'll let you know when it is. Come by one afternoon next week. It'll only take ten minutes to show you what's what. And regarding the rent, just hold on to it till I get back."

JB reached in his pocket and produced a key attached to a small steel gear. He laid it on the table, together with a slip of paper. "Here's my sister's phone number; call her if you need to get hold of me. Her name is Ethel Griffin." JB put his coat on and, thanking Seth once more, headed down to check on his boat.

* * *

Over the coming weeks, Seth noticed several stunning changes as winter approached. Although the work remained essentially the same, it seemed everything had become colder, wetter, and took twice as long to get done. Perhaps the most striking and surprising of these happened one day when he decided to go to Emma's for breakfast. Arriving, he found the place totally empty except for Kenny, who had almost become part of the furniture.

"Morning, Kenny, what you up to?" Seth took the stool next to the one reserved for Kenny's paper.

"I see the piles of JB's traps getting larger each day," an unusually morose Kenny mumbled. "Must be nearly all hauled out and getting set to go visit his sister Ethel in Texas. Nice to have something to look forward to, a bit of sunshine. What're you doin' for the winter?"

Before Seth could answer, Emma appeared with a steaming mug, and turning toward Kenny, answered, "I'll bet you a gallon of lobster stew to a buck young Seth will be staying right here all winter."

Seth nodded in agreement, adding, "Yep, I'm going to be right here working on Bill's remodeling project and learning the finer points of staying warm."

"Well, you won't be learning any of them finer points here on these stools after next Tuesday," Kenny blurted out in town-crier fashion, as he jabbed his thumb in Emma's direction. "Emma's closing up for the winter, ya know, and won't be back till April!"

"Mid-March," Emma quickly corrected him, glancing toward Seth.

In all honesty, Seth could see why she had chosen not to stick around, but selfishly, he couldn't help feeling extremely disappointed. Emma went on to explain how her parents had wanted her to return home every winter for several years. This year, not only had her grim memory of the previous winter brought her to this final decision, but also her determination to finally grant her parents their wish. She would shut up shop and be on next week's ferry.

Seth ate his breakfast, contemplating Emma's decision to close for the winter. He would miss her excellent cooking. Indeed, he would miss her company as well, Mandy's, too, and even Kenny's. It would be a long haul until mid-March.

With his meal finished, he walked down to the end of the counter where Emma worked preparing things for lunch. "I hope you have a great Christmas, Emma, and a Happy New Year way up there in Jefferson Creek ski country." Adding, in as bright a tone as he could muster, "And be very careful on the slopes. I don't want you to break anything."

He paid for the breakfast, and then, impulsively he took her hand over the counter and said quietly, "Stay well, Emma, and hurry back." They shook hands, and he turned to leave, pausing only briefly to say farewell to Kenny.

This is going to be another different kind of existence. I'm not going to let this get to me. I have work to do, books to read, walks to take. Heck, this winter is going to be one long vacation!

Back at the fish house, he gathered tools and began the arduous task of inspecting, repairing, and returning all JB's traps to good-as-new status. As he began, he mentally did the math: *JB leaves on December fourteenth and returns on March fifteenth. Let's see...ninety-one days, and there are somewhere near eight hundred twenty traps here to be worked on. Well, ninety-one is about one hundred, and eight hundred twenty is about eight hundred, so eight hundred divided by one hundred is eight per day. Definitely a piece of cake.* But so far, his count for the day remained zero. Total done: zero.

* * *

Five days later, as the first rays of the sun filtered through a gray, watery sky, Seth spotted the headlights of a vehicle making its way down the ferry wharf. He went to the window and watched as JB headed for Kenny's almost leak-proof skiff, the only one in the harbor with oars, "borrowed" it, and rowed out to *Linda-T.* Seth watched him start the engine and then head back to the wharf, skiff in tow. *Damn,* Seth thought, *this is the fourteenth, and he is leaving for his Texas trip right now. I forgot all about the date!* He jumped into his boots, grabbed his coat, and headed out, hoping he would get down there before JB left.

* * *

At the end of the wharf, Linda handed bags and boxes down to her father and, when they were all safely loaded, descended the ladder to say goodbye. JB took her hand to help her aboard, then hugged her as only a loving father could. "I'm really gonna miss you, baby... you be very careful over there." With a heavy heart, JB genuinely worried about what his only child might be getting into. While she had grown to be her own woman—energetic, intelligent, self-sufficient, and as fiercely independent as any Sandaray fisherman—he had grave concerns about this

London venture. Dan worried him as well, big-time. Reluctantly, he released his embrace. "Get yourself home now. I don't want to miss the tide."

Linda kissed his cheek and offered the usual reassurances, despite her own inner misgivings about Dan's new job and the idea of moving to another country. Barely holding back tears, she climbed up onto the wharf.

As she did so, Seth, who had been running full tilt toward them, arrived at her side and between gasps for air shouted, "Hey, I didn't realize the time! You look like you're all ready to leave; can I come down for a moment?"

"Sure, undo the bow line on your way."

Seth duly did as instructed and then, after jumping onto the deck, extended his hand, wishing JB a safe trip and a good, warm vacation.

Looking straight at him, JB replied, "Now you take good care of yourself, young fella. I hope you survive the winter and will still be here when I get back. You're a damn good sternman!"

"No worries, Captain. I'll be here, your traps will be ready, and your house will be warm. Travel safe."

Seth jumped to the ladder as the untethered *Linda-T* drifted slowly away from the dock. He stood with Linda, waving and watching as JB headed out of the harbor.

Want a ride anywhere?" Linda snuffled, turning to him and wiping her eyes with an embroidered cotton handkerchief.

"Sure. Home?"

* * *

In less than a minute, the truck stopped at the path leading behind the row of fish houses. He turned to face her. "When do you have to leave? Are you going to spend Christmas with Dan in England, or will you be here?"

"We'll have Christmas over there. I leave next Monday, and the flight from Boston is Tuesday night."

"Oh, okay. Well, if I don't see you, I sure hope you have a safe trip, and everything works out for both of you."

"Thank you, Seth. You take good care, too."

Without lingering further, he got out but stood watching until the truck disappeared past Emma's Café, his head filled with a tumult of thoughts, stirred by the look in her still teary eyes. *JB is not the only one who's going to miss you, lovely Linda.*

As he walked the short distance back to the fish house, his thoughts drifted from Linda to the people and events he had been trying so hard to forget. He wondered if his worries about Sir Reginald's new London security man were real, and even more, he wondered if this would open a very dangerous can of worms.

* * *

The weather deteriorated over the next couple of days, making trap work difficult and leaving Seth well behind his "eight per day" objective. In a very short time, the TV had become his almost constant companion. *What a change,* he thought, *and only two days after JB's departure.*

On Sunday evening, a wind of at least thirty miles per hour, a temperature near freezing, and rain made even the thought of being outside send shivers through Seth. And, although the stove kept the apartment warm, he wrapped a blanket around himself as he settled onto the couch to watch TV. Soon, with his mind consumed by an action-packed thriller, he heard but didn't react to a knock on the door. The second knock, a bit more forceful, brought him back to reality, and he jumped to see who in the world it could be out there on a night like this.

As he turned the handle, a huge blast of cold air forced the door open and thrust a hooded figure into the room. Completely surprised, he leaned his weight against the door to close it. "Wow!" he exclaimed, as he looked around to greet his visitor.

"Wow, indeed!" said Linda, placing a large box on the table and shaking off the hood of her parka.

"Linda! What the heck are you doing here? Don't you leave tomorrow?" Trying to get his thoughts together, Seth stood for a moment while Linda struggled with the bulky parka. He quickly moved to help her, his mind searching for some sort of explanation. As he hung the dripping coat on a hook by the door, she started taking things out of the box, saying she had prepared a pot of lobster stew and brought it over as a thank-you gift for looking after her the night of the party on Orran.

"I've also brought one of Dan's expensive bottles of wine in the hope I can share it with you over dinner. Didn't fancy dining alone on my last night."

Reeling from the happenings of the last few minutes, Seth managed to put the pot of stew on the stove and uncork the 1982 Margaux.

As they ate, Linda reminisced at length about her early life on Sandaray and how much the island and things in general had changed. The conversation remained light and pleasant as Seth successfully kept the focus on her past, to avoid any potentially tricky questions about his. When they had eaten, he cleared the dishes and asked if she would like coffee. "There's still wine in the bottle…let's take it in the living room and see what's going on in the harbor."

Following behind Linda, Seth switched off the kitchen light, putting both rooms in total darkness. Through the picture window, a strangely abstract and alluring view became visible as the harbor buoy rose, fell, and flashed in the fog. For a long moment they both stared out, mesmerized by the scene. Eventually Seth switched on a small table lamp.

He watched as Linda surveyed the room. He guessed it was some time since she had last been in there. She was probably also curious to see what he'd done—if anything—with the place. and to see what kind of temporary home Seth had made of it. Walking over to the picture by the bedroom door, she stopped and remarked, "Do you know the story about why this picture is here?" Now lost in childhood memories, she continued, almost to herself, "It happened before my time. Dad got into a row with Mom, who locked herself in the bedroom. He made a hole with his fist, trying to get in. For some reason, he never repaired it but hung a picture there instead. Neither of them ever spoke about it. Strange."

"I do know some of the story from your dad. I'd wondered about repairing it, but I've kinda got used to seeing it there." *It's also extremely useful*, he mused.

They sat side by side on the couch. He passed Linda her glass of wine and touching it with his, said, "To Linda. Here's to your new life in London. May it bring you the happiness you deserve." They drank.

"Ever been to London before?" he asked.

"Never, how about you?"

Lying, he answered, "No, never, but I've heard there's lots of neat things to do there. You excited about going?"

"Yeah, in a way. It'll be really different. What are you gonna do with yourself all winter?"

"Your dad's traps are first. In the beginning, I planned to do eight per day which would have them all done by his return on March fifteenth, but since then, Bill Harris has offered me a job starting in January, so I have to increase the pace. It's a lot of work, but I'll be done by the end of the year.

"What's Bill lined up for you?"

"He's getting some mainland professionals in to renovate the whole place, and I'll be their gofer. I'm looking forward to learning from them."

An awkward, lengthy silence followed. They looked at each other.

Without a word, Seth put his arm gently behind her neck, his hand softly nudging her shoulder toward him. She placed her glass next to his and slipped one arm behind him. Their eyes locked. He gently caressed her cheek, and then their lips met, softly at first, then with growing intensity. His hungry tongue parted her moist, welcoming lips, sending thrilling tingles through her whole body. His heart pounded like a jackhammer as he savoured the deliciously sweet, musky taste. Then, without warning, she pulled away, leaving him momentarily disoriented and confused.

"Are you sure about this, Seth?"

She knew. She must have sensed it. His whole world being torn between reason and emotion. He took her face in his hands and gently pulled her close until the tips of their noses touched.

"It's just us Linda…no one needs to know anything."

Muscular arms pulled her in tightly; there were no questions now. They kissed again, this time with an increased urgency, a desire heightened by months of pent-up emotions and liberated by fine wine.

He tried to rein himself in to prolong the delightful sensations, but with no success. His hands moved up inside her blouse. The luxurious feel of her smooth, silky skin heightened his emotions.

As he unhooked her bra and began to caress her breasts, she let out a long, low moan. Soon he had discarded his own cloths and let himself submit to her teasing caresses. Bolts of electricity shot through his entire body. He lifted her blouse and gently sucked her hardening nipples. Raw animal instinct took over and in no time, they were moving together rhythmically, reaching heights of mutual ecstasy in seconds. Time and the universe became meaningless…they were as one together, rising over the summit, soaring into the vast unknown. Never in their lives had either experienced such complete and exquisite fulfillment.

* * *

They lay spent in each other's arms. No words seemed appropriate. Eventually Seth got up and offered her his hand. Taking it, she eased herself off the sofa, and he drew her to him again, this time more tenderly.

"We should get dressed. It's getting chilly in here."

As they both gathered and put on their clothes, he asked if she wanted an after-dinner coffee now.

"Actually, I think I should go home. Early start in the morning."

He went to the kitchen and took her parka from the hook. Fighting a powerful urge to slip his arms around her once again, he instead helped her on with the coat. Then, remembering her dishes, he put the stew pot and pie plate back in her box. "I'll carry these out for you." Again, a blast of cold, wet air met them. Linda followed him carefully down the steps to her truck. Soaked and shivering, Seth opened the driver's door and put the dishes on the bench seat. Linda got in, turned, and looked at him. Without any words, they kissed briefly, and she drove away.

Seth slept longer than usual the next day and lay in bed, thinking back on the previous evening, as well as his life in general. What had he been thinking? What an idiot, messing around with a married woman, and his boss's daughter to boot. And what would happen next? He hadn't thought about that. Would he end up having to run away from the place he had run away to? Twice now in twelve months, he had made a really bad call. The first time, his reasoning had been irrational, driven by fear and stress. This time, it had been completely hormone-driven but equally irrational.

With the weather improved, he resumed work on the traps at first light and found the monotony a welcome distraction from other thoughts.

Mid-morning, a Cessna 208 flew low over the harbor, making its final approach. Linda would soon be departing for the long trip to London. *Be well, travel safely, and please, for God's sake, keep our secret, Linda. I just hope to goodness you're not pregnant, otherwise, I'm one dead sternman!*

In less than an hour, the plane departed, leaving Seth wondering if he would ever see her again.

* * *

The weather remained settled, so Seth applied himself diligently to trap work, knowing in two weeks, he would be spending most days working at Bill's. Despite keeping busy, his loneliness grew more intense. More and more, his mind turned to thoughts of the past. His separation from it had been total and absolute, but facts remained facts.

As predicted, Christmas brought a few returning residents, some summer people, and even a handful of tourists. As families got on with their celebrations, Seth found himself alone with trap work, television, and a simple Christmas meal consisting of a small chicken and a handful of brussels sprouts. He sat at his kitchen table, eating, drinking wine, and thinking. The seeds of change were starting to germinate.

Chapter Twelve

The ferry terminal bustled with activity most of the year. Now, in the depths of winter, things were very different, so when a pickup truck rattled up to the building, it caught Seth's attention. He stopped his trap repair and watched as a tall figure emerged, walked to the large bulletin board, and carefully attached a sheet of paper so big it appeared to cover most of the other notices. Seconds later, the truck left, and silence returned. Mildly curious, Seth decided to take a break.

He put down his tools and started along the path, wondering what the notice said. *All ferries canceled until April due to lack of interest,* he considered wryly, or maybe a photograph of another drunk fisherman mooning an unsuspecting group of tourists. Whatever had been posted, it felt good just to stretch his legs and get away for a bit. Arriving, he found neither of his way-out speculations to be correct. Instead, the paper announced from now until March 15th, the Island Store would only open on Monday, Wednesday, and Friday and only between 10:00 a.m. and 2:00 p.m. No more café and now, less than half a store. *Well,* Seth thought *today is Friday and just past ten, so there's no time like the present to go get some groceries.*

* * *

Franklin Spencer stood six feet, four inches tall and weighed 198 pounds, just as he had in his high school days. Back then, his lanky frame had earned him the nickname "BP" for Bean Pole. It stuck and now had been used by so many for so long, that most thought BP were his initials. As Seth approached, he found BP in his usual spot, reading the newspaper behind the very same counter where his great-great grandfather had sat back in 1887 when the store first opened.

BP put down the paper and greeted Seth warmly. "Merry Christmas, Mr. Seth Martin, What ya up to these lovely cold days?"

"Oh, not a whole lot. Just getting JB's traps ready for spring. Saw your notice; how come the change in store hours?"

"Well, there just ain't enough folks to justify it this winter. But the real reason is the wife and me have decided to finish writing our book on the history of Sandaray. We've been working on it for six years."

"No kidding?" Seth responded with genuine surprise.

As Seth wandered off to look for canned fruit, BP moved from his till to the post office counter in the corner to sort through a pile of undelivered mail.

"Hey, almost forgot, you got a letter!" Waving a small white envelope in the air, he added excitedly, "Here ya go."

Seth headed to the counter and BP, scarcely able to contain his curiosity about its sender, handed him the envelope. "Must be your first one. Wonder who it's from?"

Hiding his own surprise and cautious excitement, Seth casually examined the envelope addressed to Mr. Seth Martin, c/o General Delivery, Sandaray, Maine. How odd. A piece of mail, no return address on the envelope, no way of reading the off-island postmark, so no idea where it might have come from. He casually placed it in his jacket pocket.

"Well ain't ya goin' ta read it?" BP asked, boiling over with an interest which, days earlier, had almost brought him to the point of steaming it open.

"I'll check it out later…just need to get a few more things."

BP seethed silently as Seth got the other items he needed, paid the bill, and left for home. "And a Happy New Year to you too," BP muttered sarcastically, turning to reimmerse himself in the news and gossip of the week-old newspaper.

* * *

As Seth walked, he imagined BP's upset: *Things like a mystery letter are big in this isolated place. But if this one has anything to do with recent events or even my past, I don't want the whole island knowing about it.*

Turning his own mind to the letter, he tried to figure who could possibly have sent it and why. *Obviously not someone from around here. Everyone knows where I live. And no one from here would send me a letter anyway. Hmm…maybe someone got my name out of Scott Young's article. That's the only possibility. No one knows I'm here.*

By the time he got home, he too had become desperate to discover who had sent him a letter. Carefully running his penknife along the crease, he removed a Christmas card with a lovely Currier and Ives winter scene on the front. Inside he found a short, handwritten note:

> M,
> Merry Christmas and my sincere compliments for your heroic, lifesaving actions earlier this year aboard the Jasper fishing vessel. This world needs more people like you and your captain!
> C

PS if you're the man I believe you are, bring the file to room 303 at 4:00 p.m., I have news.

He read the note, read it again, and then, leaving the groceries, walked into the living room to sit and think. The cryptic postscript clearly identified the sender as Cheryl Murphy, a colleague and close friend from his past. If either wanted to talk, vent, or just get away from their work for a while, they would signal such desire with a code and meet in the cafeteria fifteen minutes before the stated time.

He believed she knew a lot about the events leading up to his departure. She cared about him and always kept her eyes and ears open. Her saying "I have news" surely referred to much more than a report of the local weather. He sat for a long moment, staring but not seeing, as his mind filled with memories consciously suppressed for many months. Soon a partial return to reality motivated him to go back to the kitchen and put the groceries away.

But Cheryl's unexpected communication had revived those intermittently nagging thoughts. Suddenly, everything had changed.

In the years immediately before coming to Sandaray, his life had been interesting, challenging, and fulfilling. He had worked hard and done significant things well. He had made good friends, loved intensely, and indeed, nearly married. But events and the power of incredibly influential people had caused his life to spiral out of control, ultimately reducing him to the point of having a lone objective: survival.

Although it was painful to dredge up those memories, Seth's mental outlook had clearly changed. Here, in a new environment, around people who accepted him and made no judgments without facts, his thinking had become more rational, bringing him to the conclusion that his original departure may have been a mistake. Nevertheless, he could still vividly remember the day when he could take no more, and there had genuinely been only one course of action: to disappear, perhaps to the other side of the world, perhaps permanently.

He had thought running away would be the answer, but it hadn't changed what had happened. *They were wrong to do what they did. But I was weak. They forced me to cave in, and I did.*

He shuddered, realizing the time had come for those events to be brought to a proper conclusion, for justice to be meted out, and for his own innocence to be proven.

This new, much simpler existence had become very satisfying, making the past too easy to sideline. But only a few months ago, Scott Young had suspected, investigated, and almost found him out. Similarly, his friend Cheryl, after only a year, had found the proverbial needle in a haystack and written to him. Now, as he thought rationally, this charade had never really been a viable option. It had become crystal clear he needed to address what had happened and prove his innocence by exposing those who had actually committed the crime. He quickly penned a short note to Cheryl:

C,
Can't meet you for coffee but would love to see you and chat. If you can come up with a reason to go to New England, let me know when and where, and I will meet you. I hope to get access to a computer soon, and if I do, will send an email to your old address. Hope you and John are both well.
All the best,
M

As he sealed the note and addressed it to the old post office box he hoped still belonged to her, the shrill ring of the telephone brought him back to the reality of Sandaray and the work he had to get done.

"Seth Martin," he answered.

"The ferry's all set for next Wednesday, and the boys will be in on the plane around zero-nine-hundred," an unidentified voice stated (obviously an island thing). *Kinda sounds like BP.* "There will be a pickup truck, and you need to drive it off the boat," he continued. *Ah-ha! Bill Harris.*

Bill proceeded to explain that a "massively big" truck from Collins Lumber, along with his mainland Ford F250 pickup, both loaded to the gills with stuff for the renovation, would be coming on the Wednesday morning ferry. Time would be tight, however, as the lumber truck had to return on the same boat. Bill's pickup would be driverless, having been driven on by the lumber company, so it would need someone to drive it off. And the guy from Collins had never been to the island before, so he would need someone to guide the truck up to the lodge. It would be Seth's job to drive the pickup, with its quirky clutch (as Bill put it), and show the lumber truck the way up to the lodge. Meanwhile, Bill would transport the last of his guests to the outgoing ferry.

"Sounds like a plan. I'll make sure to be there in good time," Seth responded, duly marking the date on the kitchen calendar.

Over the coming days, Seth busied himself preparing more traps, the stacks of "ready" traps growing rapidly larger than the stacks of those waiting. How quickly things had changed! Instead of wondering how he would ever find enough things to keep himself busy over the winter, he now pictured himself with no spare time at all.

New Year's Eve came and went, with Seth going to bed not long after the fireworks went off in London. By the end of the first day of the new year, the last traps were finished.

* * *

The Wednesday ferry arrived right on time, with the large Collins Lumber Company truck parked amidships and Bill's Ford pickup just in front. Seth found the keys and headed straight up to the lodge with the truck following.

In no time at all, Seth had joined the others, and pandemonium ensued as the big offload began.

Bill kept out of the way until they were done. Then, in his usual brusque way, he hustled his last four guests and their luggage into his pickup and, followed by the empty Collins truck, headed down to the ferry.

They all breathed a collective sigh of relief.

Seth spoke first, "Hi, I'm Seth."

"Ken."

"Jake."

"George."

Everyone shook hands.

The hasty offload left things strewn over the lawn and driveway in total disarray. But the experienced foreman, George, soon had the group efficiently moving it all into the house, placing it in perfect project order.

Bill returned later in the afternoon and gathered everyone around the kitchen table to discuss the work schedule. "Now, George says, you will be done on March fifteenth," he began, pointing to the calendar, "so, having great confidence in you guys, I've booked two couples in for April second."

"Ain't a problem," George said slowly, grinning like a Cheshire cat. "We'll have at least two bedrooms done and maybe even one of the bathrooms." Everyone except Bill chuckled. George then got to the business of laying out the details of what he referred to as their "order of battle."

Soon Bill and Seth were alone as the others busied themselves settling into their accommodations. Bill started getting dinner ready, and Seth retreated to a chair beside the stove, his mind drifting back to Cheryl and her note. The beginnings of a plan began to take shape.

To address what had happened, he reasoned, would require help, and, after some careful thought, he decided to approach Scott Young. Scott, obviously a very aggressive and energetic investigative reporter, had the additional advantage of ten years working in the hectic political environment of Washington, DC. His tenacity had been obvious from his actions after the *Jasper* incident and had left Seth with the impression he could keep a secret. Now Seth needed to contact him without everyone finding out why.

Seth decided to take advantage of his current position and ask Bill if he could use his computer. "Sure," came the response, "as long as you don't do it while you're on the clock."

Later, in the evening, he showed Seth how to bring his computer to life. Within ten minutes, Seth had created a new email account and sent two messages he hoped would get the ball rolling. The first one went to Scott.

> Hello Scott,
> If this has reached the Scott Young who covered the *Jasper* incident earlier this year, please reply, as I would like to speak with you.
> Many thanks,
> Seth Martin

Next, he wrote to his friend Cheryl Murphy.

C,

Now I have access to the internet, so if my memory
is correct about your address, this should reach you.
Please respond, as I am eager to hear your news.

All the best,

M

The next four evenings yielded no email replies, but surprisingly, at lunch on Monday, Scott's newspaper became the topic of the conversation. It all started when Bill tapped his coffee mug with a knife and, in a very officious manner, announced he had pulled off "the advertising coup of the century!" Their ongoing renovation work would become the subject of at least two articles in the local newspaper, both with pictures, under the general subject heading of historic preservation.

"This is an old historic place, and what you guys are doing is more restoration than renovation. The history buffs will love it. They'll read about the restoration and its famous sea captain owner and come flocking over here by the thousands! It'll be the best and busiest B&B in the North Atlantic!" he said with great pride.

"I guess you've just answered the question about replacing the bloody crown molding in the bedrooms then," Jake interjected with a note of resignation.

"And I suppose that also ends the discussion about not replacing the widow's walk," George added.

"You bet. When you're done, I expect if old DeVoe himself were here, he'd feel right at home—except, of course, for those few minor changes, like the lighting, plumbing, heating, insulation, appliances, TV, Wi-Fi, and the like," Bill responded.

Seth listened to the banter, but his thoughts flashed elsewhere as he considered whom the *Chronicle* might dispatch to do the story. Sending Scott Young could be perfect for him as well as Bill; he had to check this out quickly.

As their lunch ended, Seth turned to Bill and asked if he could briefly borrow the truck to go back to his apartment. "Sure," Bill answered.

Just four minutes later, Seth dialed the *Chronicle's* number from his kitchen phone.

"*Chronicle* newsroom, Mary Hicks speaking."

"Hello. Can I reach Scott Young on this number?"

"Certainly. Who may I say is calling?"

"Seth Martin."

"Just a minute, please."

Scott came on the line. "Well, hello, Mr. Seth Martin. How's life on Sandaray Island treating you?"

"I'm fine, thanks. It's been a cold but busy time. Oh, Happy New Year, by the way."

Seth then got right to the point. "I hear your paper is sending someone out here to do two articles on the restoration of Captain DeVoe's mansion. Is there any chance the writer might be you?"

"As far as I know, no one's yet been assigned, but I generally do the island stories. Let's see, might this have anything to do with our friend Dr. Seth Morrison? I got your email by the way."

"Okay. Good. And it might be to do with him, at least if such an answer will get you out here. I need your help. Help that might even pay off for you with a big story."

"Well, then, Doctor, I'll do my very best to get the assignment."

"Thanks, I hope I see you soon. Bye for now."

* * *

At his desk, Scott pondered the short conversation. Ever since the *Jasper* incident, Seth had remained an object of Scott's curiosity. Hours of research had brought him to the tentative but vehemently denied conclusion that Dr. Seth Morrison, the runaway from Michigan, and not Mr. Seth Martin, had saved Hajula. Scott felt the tingle of excitement that only occurred when a significant story, one perhaps of national interest, felt close.

Suddenly, obsessed with getting the DeVoe Lodge story, he got up and made a beeline for the editor's office, intent on convincing her to give him the assignment. After all, the islands were his beat, and the renovation of Captain DeVoe's nineteenth-century mansion certainly fit. As he approached, he met her coming out as though the fire alarm had just gone off.

"Scott," she said in a hurried voice and without slowing her step, "I want you to do the renovation story on Sandaray. Take Jennifer Stanley with you and tell her to get lots of pictures. They're expecting you to arrive by ferry on the fifteenth. Make this a big one; there'll be follow-ups as you can imagine."

Scott had no time to reply as she made her way across the newsroom to the parking lot exit. Scott shouted a quick "no problem" and "thank you" as she rushed out the door. *Well, miracles and lightning do mix! I didn't even have to open my mouth.* He headed down the hall to find Jennifer.

* * *

The next evening, Bill Harris announced a writer and a photographer from the *Chronicle* would be arriving on the January 15th ferry and staying at least two days to document the renovation.

* * *

The initial work on the project quickly fell into a routine but turned out to be particularly painstaking as it involved the dismantling of windows, doors, and moldings that had been in place for over a century. All would be refurbished, repaired if necessary, and reinstalled. George's team were experts who worked fast. They put Seth to work carefully pulling nails, marking each wooden piece, and keeping a record of exactly where each belonged for the reconstruction. After dinner each night, Seth would log on to Bill's computer, looking for an email from Cheryl. It finally came on the tenth.

M,

Thank you for the positive response to my Christmas card. Somehow, I just knew that guy had to be you! It's been a difficult time, with no other person to talk to when I just needed to offload and no friendly, understanding shoulder to cry on when I really effed up something. As always, John has been the perfect husband. I love him dearly, but he is in HR and just can't understand the world in which you and I worked every day.

Just FYI, I'm still working in the same section, although we have moved up to the fourth floor just three below where you used to be. I even have a window now!

As you'll recall, rumors are discouraged and rarely float around the office. But three or four months ago, one made its way through our hallowed halls and is now gaining a modicum of credibility. It concerns one of your former officemates—let's just call him E. During the investigation, his name popped up frequently in the news coverage. Well, the rumor now is just out of the blue, he quit. As the story goes, he's landed a high-paying position in London, working in computer security for some Belgian company. There's also a recurring story about him being forced out with no cause, despite his longevity.

Every now and then, I would see him in the hallway or cafeteria, but I didn't really know him. They're also saying he had some troubles at home, which I can somewhat understand because of the way he used to look at me. If I hear the name of the company or any other bits about why he left, I'll send them on, since my gut feeling says you're interested.

Thank you so much for the years of coffee breaks and, of course, for your caring, comforting council, and good advice.

I hope you're well and can bring the file to room 303 at 4:00 p.m. someday soon. I miss you.

All the best,
C

Seth quickly wrote a response.

C,
Thank you for your reply. You probably have figured out my situation, but recently I have decided to begin the process of quietly gathering information to once and for all bring this whole thing to an end. E just up and quitting is, I think, a significant item to add to my set of facts. Keep your ears open and, if anything relevant comes up, please let me know.

My guess is I'll be in your area sometime this year.
Perhaps you would send me your phone number, just
in case. I can be reached on 207-555-3665.
    I sincerely hope this is a great year for you both.
    M

As the days leading up to Scott's arrival passed, Seth found himself getting more and more nervous about the whole idea of dredging up his past and sharing it with a virtual stranger. His thoughts seemed to vacillate between the contentment of his almost anonymous existence, and the agonizing realization of what might be involved in bringing the whole truth, and a conclusion, out into the open.

On the eve of Scott's arrival, the telephone rang. Expecting a curt message from Bill, Seth was surprised and delighted to discover it was Cheryl. They spoke for over an hour. As he replaced the receiver, he gave himself a lecture: *Don't let your actions be driven by the wrong emotion, as they were that night with Linda. Do the right thing now, not the easy thing. Get the evidence, and hang the bastards who railroaded you.*

Chapter Thirteen

On January 15th, just after twelve thirty, the ferry docked, bringing two cars, a grocery truck, a lumber truck, Jennifer Stanley, and Scott Young. The trip across had been uneventful, but Scott had used the time to brief Jennifer on the island's history and share stories about some of the locals.

After the cars and the trucks had rumbled off, the two passengers gathered up their things and walked down the wharf.

Like any serious photographer, Jennifer drank in the sights and sounds, while Scott scanned the area for Bill Harris. Rounding the corner of a large stack of lobster traps, they almost collided.

"Aha, Bill! Great to see you. How are you doing?"

"Oh, you know, busy, busy, busy. It's all happening! And you must be the lovely Jennifer." Jennifer suppressed a grimace but took his extended hand. "Truck's just over here. Come on. Let me take your bags."

Bouncing noisily up the island to the lodge, they were both relieved when Bill finally shut down the engine. "Leave your stuff in the back," he told them. "Regrettably, you'll be sleeping elsewhere this visit. Of course, I still have some reservations available for dates after April first if you're interested. For now, though, you're gonna have to stay up at the Wilsons' house. You'll be fine there." Glancing at each other, they got out and did as instructed.

As they walked, Bill explained their meal schedule, adding that since he needed to get dinner started, one of the guys would drive them to their lodgings. Bill led them around the side of the house to the front entrance, allowing them a glimpse of the spectacular view to the west. After entering through the massive front door and passing the wide, carved staircase, they went into the kitchen, where he proceeded to get them coffee from the very modern automatic coffee maker. "I'll just rustle up a driver for you. Be right back."

They sat quietly, sipping coffee, contemplating their unusual host, and absorbing the extreme contrasts this modernized eighteenth-century room presented compared to the rest of the house.

Bill disappeared upstairs, returning almost immediately with Seth. "Jennifer Stanley, Scott Young, this is Seth Martin." They all shook hands. Seth and Scott exchanged knowing glances, as Jennifer declared with great excitement, "You're that guy, aren't you, the guy from the *Jasper* incident, the hero Seth Martin? I remember Scott's piece about you and the incident. I'm very pleased to meet you, Mr. Seth Martin." She studied his face intently and shook his hand again.

Bill took out a house key and handed it to Scott. "Seth, drive Jennifer and Scott over to Dan and Linda's house, will you?" Turning back to Scott, he added, "I think you know the Wilsons. They're both off island just now, but they've said you can use their place. Seth, stay with our guests while they get settled, but get them back here in time for dinner."

Soon the three were on their way.

* * *

Thoughts of Linda momentarily flashed through Seth's head as they drove up the driveway. He shut the truck down and led his charges inside. As soon as he entered, he sensed her presence. *Get a grip! You're at work, remember?* He pointed out the kitchen, the living room, and the stairs. "There are two bedrooms up there. Beds should be made up. I think you'll find everything you need, but if not, just give me a shout. I'll wait in the kitchen."

They reappeared around ten minutes later, Scott preceding Jennifer down the stairs. Turning to Seth, he casually asked if they could manage time for a chat about a follow-up *Jasper* article after dinner.

"Sure," Seth replied, "how about down at my place?"

"That'd be perfect."

Seth's heart raced as they returned to Bill's truck. This is it, he thought, the point of no return. Beginning of the right ending.

* * *

With dinner over, Seth asked Bill if he could borrow the truck to take Scott to the harbor for a discussion about a third *Jasper* article.

"Sure thing, but you'd better run Jennifer up to the Wilsons' first because it'll be dark soon. And when you're done, let Scott drive the thing up there, so they can get here in time for breakfast."

A few minutes after dropping Jennifer off, Seth and Scott climbed the stairs to Seth's apartment, ears still ringing. Inside, Seth offered Scott an assortment of drinks. They both chose cognac and went into the living room.

"Well now, may I finally call you 'Doctor'?" Scott began.

"Look, Scott, let's just put this doctor thing to bed once and for all. I'm not Dr. Seth Morrison from Michigan. In fact, my medical training can be summed up in two words—'first-aid'—and I've never even had the pleasure of visiting Michigan. But I do have a past, just as you do." Seth paused, sipped his cognac, then continued, "You worked in one of the very fastest lanes a newspaper person can get into when you were a congressional correspondent in Washington, DC, and for no less than a major news network. Now that's a past worthy of note."

"I guess your homework on me is better than mine was on you. I did have a high-pressure job, right in the middle of things, for a long time." Scott went on to explain how he had been a reporter and correspondent in Washington, DC, for more than ten years. Although intense at times, the work had been both interesting and challenging. But as time passed, he had grown increasingly frustrated as news stories became more and more sensationalized and less and less about properly substantiated facts.

"So I left and took this job. It's a beautiful new world for me up here, working at the *Chronicle* for Mrs. Philbrook. Back in Washington, politics seemed to make its way into everything, but here, although each of us holds our own personal view, the word from the top is to leave all those feelings at home, dig till you find the facts, and write about them in an unbiased way. But hey, what about you? All this cloak-and-dagger stuff! You might not be Dr. Seth Morrison, but I know damned well that you're no run-of-the-mill sternman, either. Are you just getting away from something too?"

"Yes and no. Like you, my previous life was pretty full-on. Before coming here, I worked with computers, building software applications to do anything and everything imaginable. Stuff I dreamed about as a kid and studied in college. I found it exciting, rewarding, and in some cases, significant. But it became all-consuming. No work–life balance. After seven years, when my stress level got way above the red line, I had to get away and see if I could live in some totally different place, doing some totally different work."

"Interesting you would just pick up and leave, as I thought you 'techy guys' always had great jobs with huge salaries and plush working conditions. Of course, we in the media didn't pay much attention to you at all, apart from when one of you had some sort of major screw-up or cost overrun."

"Yes," Seth laughed. "It all depends on your point of view, doesn't it? Sort of like the two blind men describing an elephant. I would see the strong, sensitive creature with a friendly trunk and floppy ears, while you in the media only focused on the stuff at the other end."

Neither of them missed the imagery and accuracy of Seth's metaphor.

"You nailed it. The jobs that come in under budget with unexpected extra effectiveness never seem to make the news, do they?" On a more serious note, Scott went on, "It's very nice to know some of your pre-Sandaray life, but I'm sure there's a lot more to why you arranged this private meeting. What's up? Why the secrecy?"

"Very fair and right-to-the-point question, Scott. The answer, however, is neither short nor simple. I'll try and make it as brief as possible, but maybe you'd like another cognac first?" Without waiting for a reply, Seth brought the bottle in from the kitchen. He needed all the Dutch courage he could muster. As he refilled their empty glasses, he began describing a news story from March 8th, 2011, one that had made it to the front page of every major newspaper in the country. Highly classified government information, provided by "anonymous sources," outlined in great detail a proposed covert military operation. In those days, Washington regrettably saw many leaks of internal or classified documents; however, because of its source, *this* particular story, like none before it, sent a massive shockwave through the intelligence community.

Seth explained during the course of the investigation the origin of this information had been shown to be the presidential daily brief. This document, the PDB, contained exceptionally sensitive intelligence information for the president's eyes only. It went directly, and only, to the president.

This definitely piqued Scott's interest as Seth continued, "The contents of the PDB have always been tightly compartmentalized, carefully controlled, and uniquely protected, and yet this one item, from a PDB, mysteriously made its way into the public domain to be read by anyone. Particularly those against whom the information proposed military action. Complicating this was the fact that the total number of possible leakers could be counted on one hand." Seth paused, sipping his cognac and allowing Scott time to think. "For the rest of that year and the first weeks of the next, the FBI, CIA, and both congressional intelligence oversight committees looked into the whole case in depth. Many people were interviewed and testified under oath, but when all the dust had settled, no one could be identified as the leaker."

"Okay, unfortunate, but not such an unusual story, at least not from Washington. So where do you fit in, and where do I fit in?"

"I'm getting to it, Scott. Just let me tell you a little bit more. In Washington terms, this all happened a long time ago, and soon the incident disappeared into the annals of history. It became one more of those heinous acts perpetrated by someone who'll continue to be sought but probably never found."

Seth explained that, when he lived near Washington, most of his friends were professionals like himself, many working for the government or for government contractors. Over the years, he had become friends with several of them including one in particular, a lady who worked for the CIA. They had recently been in touch by email and phone, and in their last conversation, she had shared some inside information about a CIA employee whom many believed to be the leaker. She had told Seth this person had been reinstated to his previous, very sensitive position, but that she and many of her colleagues had remained suspicious, dubbing him "Teflon coated," "well protected" or just "a very lucky SOB." Then, only months later, out of nowhere and within three years of a cushy retirement, he apparently just up and left his secure, high-paying position. He turned in his papers and simply disappeared. No announcements, no farewell banquets, no nothing. Apparently, he had resigned, which made no sense at all. They wondered if he had been sent under deep cover, but that seemed unlikely, as he had been an overt employee. Even after his departure, the rumors persisted about him being the leaker.

Seth continued, "This news interested me. I heard both of the other suspects also returned to work at the CIA. One went back to his previous office, while the other, who'd been hounded, harassed, tried, and found guilty by the court of public opinion, was severely demoted. Something just didn't add up. The prime suspects were all CIA employees, and now the man most suspected by insiders had mysteriously disappeared. The whole thing smelled strongly of an outrageous cover-up.

"My friend thinks the investigators tried to throw the third suspect under the bus during the investigation, in an effort to divert attention from the first. And, to a degree, from the second. But in the end, the investigation closed, and still no one was any the wiser about the identity of the leaker.

"That's almost it, Scott, and, do you know, I wouldn't have given those events a second thought if I hadn't got to know the Wilsons. Sir Reginald is a world-class mover and shaker, and his daughter-in-law is a good friend of mine. Last summer, during that party on Orran Island, the name of this guy came up in connection with one of Sir Reg's business interests…the same guy my friend thought was ready to sell his country's secrets down the drain. The same guy who mysteriously disappeared. Do you see why I'm concerned?"

After listening intently, Scott recapped slowly: "So…what you're saying is, this leak investigation narrowed the field to three possible suspects. But, in the final analysis, the whole thing ended without anyone being convicted. One went back to his previous office apparently exonerated, one went back to work with a clean slate but downgraded and severely ostracized, and one went back to his old position and then suddenly and mysteriously up and vanished. He's the one your insider friends condemned as being the criminal.

"Now, because of your friendship with the Wilsons, you're worried Sir Reg might be inviting the fox into the hen house by hiring a potentially dangerous man. I remember reading about this leak at the time and vaguely recall coming to the same conclusion as you and your friends…the story just reeked of a fix. One of these guys must have been the bloody perpetrator, surely. Do you know any names? And do you have any clue why that one guy left the agency so close to retirement?"

"Well," Seth replied, "if you agree to what I'm going to ask, you'll learn his name. I've never been in the military, but I'm a citizen of this country. I love this country, and I abhor treasonous behavior. What I'd like from you is a favor. Do you think you could find out if any new facts have been uncovered since the investigation that might help prove the identity of the leaker? Maybe you could also try and find out why 'Mr. Teflon' appeared to be so well protected but then disappeared so quickly. If it turns out this guy is the leaker, Sir Reg and his new operation should be very concerned."

Seth went on to say he believed Scott's former work must

have left him with a Rolodex full of people who had their sensitive fingers firmly positioned on the pulse of 'inside' Washington. People who might have facts leading to a "guardian angel," high up in the government, able to protect "Mr. Teflon" during all these investigations.

"If you can find out anything, it might help prove the identity of the treasonous person and give you a major national news story at the same time. To dig out this sort of information is impossible for the likes of me but all in a day's work for folks like you. Your experience and particularly your Rolodex could help considerably. What do you think?"

"Wow! If you're correct about a 'guardian angel' in a case like this, it's front-page news. And if 'Mr. Teflon,' a CIA insider, turns out to be the leaker, he should definitely not be working for Sir Reg. He should be out west with Robert Hanssen, the former FBI insider. Remember him? They even made a movie about his treasonous activities. He's serving life without the possibility of parole."

The room fell silent as both men, savoring the beautifully distilled wine, considered the enormity of what Seth had divulged. Deep in thought, Scott rose, paced a bit, then walked to the window and looked out toward the harbor. "The real power in Washington is very strong, very protected, and sometimes moves in very strange ways. What you're asking will take a super-quiet and careful approach. Regardless of the outcome, if it's to succeed, nothing about this must get out, not even from this conversation, nothing. So yes, I'll make a few inquiries with my friends and see if any interesting stones have been turned over in the past couple of years. Actually, I have one good source who owes me big-time."

Seth went to the kitchen, returning with a scrap of paper and a pen. He put the paper on the table in front of Scott and wrote down a single name: "Edwin Henderson." He pushed it across to Scott, picked up his glass, and offered it silently as a toast. They stood, their glasses touched and they both finished the last of their cognac.

* * *

The following morning, a bit later than usual, Seth joined the small group sitting around Bill's kitchen table. The dishes had already been cleared, Jennifer had just left with Jake, Scott had Ken cornered for an interview, and George was putting the finishing touches to the day's work schedule. The scene appeared perfectly normal, but somehow, the memories of last night's conversation made even the physical appearance of the room strangely different.

Bill poured coffee and brought Seth a cup. "Morning Seth, looks like you had a rough night! Care to share?" Seth shook his head, ignoring the comment.

"This is going to be a busy day, buddy. Here, drink this to get ya started."

Seth thanked him, took the coffee, and listened as George briefed the team on the plans for the day.

In preparation for his interview with Scott, Bill had taken out an album of old, faded sepia photographs and was poring over pictures of the old sea captain, his beautiful wife, and the house as it had been in its heyday. Under normal circumstances, Seth would have enjoyed looking at these and listening to Bill reminisce, but today he was distracted, and his head hurt from a couple too many cognacs. Only some serious distraction would take his mind off the conversation of the previous evening and his careless hangover.

* * *

Their work on the island complete, Scott and Jennifer returned to the mainland the following morning. Jennifer absorbed herself in a Stephen King novel for the duration of the passage, while Scott mulled over the events of the past two days. With the bulk of the renovation story already written in his mind, he turned his attention to the extraordinary meeting with Seth. Seth's caring about the Wilsons and concerns about Henderson, together with the fact that three major investigations had failed to identify a treasonous leaker, all painted half a picture, definitely making the story worth exploring. If he could somehow track down and nail this leaker, he might never need to work again!

Chapter Fourteen

The biting cold February morning brought with it a light dusting of snow. Seth, having negotiated the morning off to go shopping, lay in bed, thinking about how different this past year had been.

Over a month had passed since he had last seen Linda and nearly as much time since his conversation with Scott. He wondered what had happened in their worlds, but when his thoughts turned negative—like Dan sending some goon after him for screwing Linda, or Scott calling to say none of his former colleagues had any helpful information—he bolted out of bed, dressed swiftly, and made his way up to the store.

"Good morning, Mr. Seth Martin," BP said with a smile. "I haven't seen you for a couple of weeks now. How's the job up the hill going? Oh, and I have more mail for you."

"Morning, BP. Job's going fine, thanks. Bill is on the way to giving this island a four-star guesthouse for sure. Those guys are very experienced professionals. They know what they're doing and are doing it well." Feigning lack of interest in the mail, Seth gathered up the things on his grocery list. At the counter, BP handed over the letter and started totaling up the bill.

"It must be from the Wilsons," BP said, his voice dripping

with curiosity. "Just check out the stamp; she's the queen, don't ya know?"

Seth's heart raced as he casually put the letter in his jacket pocket. He paid BP, bid him good day, and began the trek back to the harbor. *Is it from her or from him? Is she all right? Has he found out?* His step quickened and soon, back inside, with the unpacked groceries on the table, he threw off his gloves and ripped open the envelope.

The very late Christmas card showed a snowy Trafalgar Square scene on the front and a printed greeting on the inside followed by a handwritten note.

> *Merry Christmas, Seth,*
> *Sorry to be so tardy with this. I hope all is well with you and you've had a lovely Christmas. Life here has been hectic since I arrived. We are in a beautiful apartment Dan found. Sir Reg stayed here with us for a week. Dan's job is ramping up quickly, and the office is coming together rapidly. They now have six employees on board including Mr. Blackstock, the boss, Janet Williams, logistics, Ed Henderson, security, and two others I have yet to meet. What a difference it is over here! I miss Sandaray already, however, and I miss you.*
> *All the best,*
> *Linda*

He felt sick at the mention of Edwin Henderson but at least, it seemed Linda was okay. *And Dan is actually busy. First time for everything!* He put the groceries away and, grabbing the key to JB's house, set out to check it over and get to Bill's in time for lunch.

* * *

His shortcut took him up the road to Emma's Café, then north through the woods for the best part of a mile. He met no-one and the only evidence of life came from the tracks of small creatures scurrying across the forest floor. Life, for now, was good.

At Bill's kitchen table, the conversation centered on the imminent return of Jennifer Stanley. "Her plan is to fly out on Thursday, stay most of the day, and return in the afternoon," Bill announced. "George, do you think we will have anything totally completed by then?"

"Of course boss," George replied quickly, "rooms number two and four and the widow's walk will all be finished in time for her arrival."

"Is she coming alone?" Seth asked as casually as he could, hoping Scott Young might be coming with her.

"Don't really know," Bill replied. "She just said they needed some progress photos."

"Ah," interjected Jake, his thoughts running in an entirely different direction. "Now she may be coming to do progress photos of the job, but *she* is the one I'd like to photograph!" he said with a big grin.

"Keep it professional, not personal, Mr. Horny Jake," George said sternly. "Anyway, it's time to get back to work. Seth, you're with Ken in room number three."

Over the next two days, they all worked carefully yet quickly, paying particular attention to keeping things neat and tidy. Everyone had a genuine desire to put this project's best foot forward.

After dinner on Wednesday evening, Bill instructed Seth to take his truck home and go straight to the airport the next morning to collect Jennifer. *Nice thinking Bill, having transpor-*

tation waiting for a VIP. If you weren't such a cheap SOB, you'd get a muffler for the damn truck.

* * *

Seth watched closely as the Cessna 208 touched down, hoping he would see at least three heads in the cabin. But as soon as the door opened, it became apparent, Scott Young had stayed in town.

"Hi, Seth. How's my hero?" Jennifer asked, throwing her bag in the back of the truck.

"Madam, your hero is very well and happy to see you," he replied with a theatrical bow, "but where is your buddy? You know, the one with all the questions, the very sharp pencil, and the endless notepad?"

"Oh, our boss Lisa sent him off to Bar Harbor to do an interview with some guy who just won first place on a Bangor TV cooking show...the judges went ape over the way he cooked a yucky eel."

"Sounds mouthwatering!" Seth said as he fired up the truck.

Soon they were back at the lodge, where Jake happened to be in the doorway, ready to take Jennifer's bag and show her all they had done. Surprised to notice the fine quality of the workmanship, she took several closeups of the beautifully restored ceiling details, crown moldings, doors, and door hardware.

After showing off the almost completed rooms, Jake took Jennifer's hand and led her around to the alcove containing a spiral stairway to the widow's walk. "I just put the final coat on this beauty last night," he beamed, hoping Jennifer would be suitably impressed. She studied the lovely stairway and set up her camera on a tripod to take further pictures.

"Maybe you need me in the shots for scale or something?" he asked. "After all, I did all the work on this beauty," he boasted.

"Of course," she said. "It's a lovely piece of work, and you've really done a nice job, Jake. I think you deserve to get in a few pictures."

After lunch, Jennifer took out her notebook. "Okay, you guys, the editor wants the story finished and on the street during the week of March eleventh, and I've been tasked with negotiating an agreeable date for a final visit when I can get some 'finished state' photographs." She added, "At the minimum, we need pictures of the completed entryway, the living room, the dining room, and ideally, two or three bedrooms."

"You mean completely finished with curtains on the bedroom windows, drapes in the living room, artwork in the hall, and rugs on the floor... and no rubbish anywhere?" Bill said, adding facetiously, "how about Monday, April first?"

"Look," George quickly cut in, "things are coming along fairly well. I originally estimated completion on March thirteenth, and as of today, we have only slipped by three days giving you almost three weeks to get ready for your first booking. How would March eighth work for you, Jennifer?"

"Oooooh, that's really squeezing it. Do you suppose you two could deal with the sixth instead? There's a lot more to getting these images ready for publication than just snapping pictures. You have no idea how many hours I've spent airbrushing out junk no one saw the last time we were shooting."

George thought for a moment, hoping a compromise would work. "How about in between? Can we all agree to the seventh?"

It would be tight, but they all agreed, so Jennifer advised she would be over on the first plane that morning.

* * *

March came in like the proverbial lion, bringing cold rain and high winds, which, in turn, gave Seth the new project of cutting and clearing an eighty-foot uprooted spruce tree suddenly blocking Bill's driveway. The job took the best part of Saturday morning, leaving him the afternoon to relax in front of the TV with a cold beer and a sandwich. Engrossed by a fast-paced hockey game, it took him a minute to react to the ringing phone.

"Well, how ya doing up there, young man?" the unidentified voice began. "I just wanted to tell you I have a ticket back to Portland on March sixteenth. The folks at Johnson's will have the boat outside and will be doing some work on her before I take her back to Sandaray. Any chance you can come and give me a hand for a few days?"

"Sure thing, JB," Seth said. "The work at Bill's is wrapping up, and everything should be done by then. How about I fly in sometime on Sunday the seventeenth and stay till you're ready to come back here? I need to do a few things in town anyway."

"Great, I'll be staying at the Islander Hotel. Come and find me when you arrive."

Seth returned to the living room, his mind no longer on the hockey game. Finally, he had an ironclad reason to be in town for a few days, and certainly, he would have a chance to find out what, if anything, Scott had learned from his contacts in Washington.

* * *

By the following Monday, work at DeVoe Lodge had come to a standstill as they were forced to wait for the main stairway varnish to dry. Seth took advantage of the lull to get some computer time. He typed a short note to Scott:

Hi Scott,

JB wants me to come to town on the 17th to help get the *Linda-T* ready. I'll be there for three or four days. Can we meet? Hope all is well with you.

Seth

Bill, George, and the others were having breakfast when Seth arrived on Tuesday morning. "Good morning, guys, hope all's well," Seth said, adding, "Bill, mind if I use your computer again? Just need to check something. It'll only take a minute."

With a mouth full of toast, Bill nodded in the direction of the computer.

The telltale time stamp on Scott's email indicated an almost immediate response to Seth's message from the previous day:

Hello Seth,

No telling what world-shaking news may develop between now and then, but most likely I will be in the office sometime on the 17th. Call when you get into town. I have some information.

Scott

Seth's time at the B&B now consisted of a multitude of small final fixes. However, as March 17th approached, he became more and more preoccupied, speculating about what Scott had found out.

* * *

Seth's routine took an unexpected turn the Tuesday before his departure for the mainland. Late in the afternoon, as he walked south on the trail behind Emma's Café, he noticed the lights were on inside. Additional evidence of Emma's return included her red Toyota pickup truck parked in front, and the café door propped open by a chair. He went in.

"Hello. Emma. Are you here? Are you home?"

A frazzled Emma eventually emerged from the back room. "Seth…oh, hi," she said, forcing a smile. "Excuse my grungy looks, but this has been a real doozie of a day."

"What do you mean? You look great! But maybe you could use some assistance. What can I do to help?"

"Well, yeah. Actually, some help would be wonderful. There are about two thousand boxes of stuff still in the truck, and they all need to go in the back room."

It took less than an hour to unload, pack the perishables, and organize the other boxes. Soon only a briefcase and two suitcases remained. As Seth began neatly piling empty boxes, Emma put the briefcase on her desk and started up the stairs with the two suitcases. "I'll be right back. Then maybe I can find us an almost cold beer. Sound good?"

"Sounds wonderful, but can I suggest something even better? How about we go back to my place for a proper cold beer and some hot food. Interested?"

"Seth, that would be the highlight of this crazy day. Give me a couple of minutes to turn the water pump and heater on and I'll give you a ride down the hill."

Ten minutes later, Emma sat at Seth's kitchen table with a cold beer in front of her as he began preparing a meal. "Hungry? Been long since lunch?"

"Ha," she said, "right now I could eat the leaf right out of this table!" Soon he had chicken, rice and vegetables carefully prepared, plated-up and presented with a second beer. As she ate, he watched her begin to unwind.

"This is beautiful, Seth. You're a total lifesaver." As she looked up at him, he suddenly realized how much he had missed her.

"So when do you plan to reopen?"

She replied it would be as soon as possible, but she still had to give the place a thorough cleaning.

Seeing the genuine weariness in her face, he ventured, "Now I would offer you an after-dinner cognac, but my guess is you would really rather drive back up the hill and crawl into bed."

"You're a mind reader, Seth Martin. I really, really need to hit the sack." She rose, quickly put on her coat, and moved toward the door. Turning, she added, "I can't thank you enough for all this." Another time, she would have accepted his offer in an instant, but not tonight.

* * *

March 17th arrived and just before ten o'clock, Bill Harris drove Seth to the airport. In no time at all, he found himself back in the alien environment of the mainland.

The Islander Hotel, a stately old building with a commanding view of the harbor, had been carefully updated over the years, but its smaller than expected rooms were not overly appealing to the modern traveler.

"How're you fixed for rooms?" Seth asked the small, officious-looking man behind the counter.

"Your name happen to be Seth Martin?" the clerk responded.

"Well yes...yes, it is."

"Then you're all set in number twenty-one. JB Thompson told me you'd be showing up. He's in twenty-two. Just sign this and let me see your credit card."

Seth signed, then looked up. "Sorry, but I don't have a credit card."

"What do you mean—you don't have a credit card? I thought all stern people had two or three of 'em nowadays, but I suppose it's okay since JB said he would vouch for you and make sure you paid. Here's your key."

"Thanks. Oh, do you have a restaurant here some place?"

"Yup. The best in town just around to the right. JB's already in there."

"Great, and thanks again."

Seth pocketed the key, picked up his small bag, and headed for the restaurant.

Dominated by the original, exquisitely hammered copper ceiling, electrified gas lamps, and beautifully maintained wood paneling, this restaurant clearly surpassed for elegance any of the reproductions found along the New England coast. JB waved from his table near the window.

Seth greeted him with a handshake and a broad smile. "Welcome home. You're lookin' well."

"Sit down, young fellow. Looks like the winter hasn't been too bad to you, either. How are you? How is the place?"

A shiver went through Seth at the thought of what this old man would do to him if he ever found out about him and Linda. "Oh, the place is just about the same. Weather has been cold and windy, but there hasn't been much snow. Your home is safe and sound, so no problems there, and your traps are all ready, except for the warps. I've been working almost full-time up at Bill's. That's about it. Oh yes, Emma just returned to open the café. But tell me about Texas and your winter in the tropics."

"It sure beat last winter out on the island. Very nice to visit with Sis. We haven't had much time together since Martha died in 2002, and she came up for two weeks. We had good, warm weather most of the time, even hot on some days. Her house is near the shore, and most days, I got in a couple of miles walking but didn't do a hell of a lot more. We spent Christmas with my nephew and his family, but we didn't go anywhere to celebrate

New Year's Eve. In fact, neither of us really cared to stay awake for midnight. We both enjoyed the visit, but now I'm very glad to be home and keen to get back to work."

They sat for the best part of an hour eating and chatting. Seth filled JB in on who had been on the island over the winter but focused mostly on all the work going on at Bill's. He carefully avoided mentioning Dan and Linda's departure.

"Do you need any help this afternoon? I can be over at Johnson's by three, but there are a couple of things I'd like to do first."

"As long as it ain't raining, we'll start painting her bottom first thing in the morning. They pressure washed her yesterday afternoon, and I'd just as soon give her a full day to completely dry. Let's plan to leave the hotel tomorrow morning at five; that gives us time to eat breakfast first."

Seth politely took his leave of JB, eager to find a public telephone so he could call Scott.

* * *

Even ten years earlier, there would have been at least one phone booth somewhere in the three blocks he could see before him. But no, not now, not today…having a cell phone had become as necessary as having clothes! Eventually, after two more blocks, a sign caught his eye, announcing the location of the offices and the press room of the *Courier*. Although a long shot for a Sunday, Seth went to the door and knocked. No one answered, but it appeared to be unlocked and surprisingly swung open.

Three desks and a number of filing cabinets were crammed into the front part of the old, converted store, a door and hallway leading most likely to the main part of the operation. An attractive, middle-aged woman sat at the desk facing the entrance. "Sorry, but we aren't open just now. No one's here until tomorrow morning," she said politely looking up from a computer terminal. "Please pull the door hard on your way out. It has a wonky latch."

Seth closed the door firmly but remained inside. "You certainly don't look like a 'no one's here' to me. May I ask if Scott Young might be another 'no one's here' just now?"

She removed her glasses, depositing them on top of her generous head of auburn hair, and looked directly at Seth. "Okay, you hit the jackpot. There are only two working stiffs here at the moment, me and good old Scott. Just a minute." She picked up the phone, punched a button, and spoke. "Scott, there's a Houdini out here looking for you. No, he didn't give his name, but he's about six two, young, handsome, dressed like, and sorta smells like a fisherman. Uh-huh.... Is your name Seth?"

Seth nodded.

"He'll be out in a minute."

"Thank you."

The woman resumed typing while Seth studied a picture of the main street, showing what looked like this very same building but with horses and wagons parked along a cobblestone way in front.

"Is this a picture of this building?"

"Yes, it is, taken around 1890 they figure," she replied, barely looking up. Social chitchat was definitely not part of her Sunday agenda.

Scott Young came out of the hallway, thanked the woman, turned to Seth, and extended his hand in greeting. "Hey! Good to see you, Seth. Let's go get coffee."

An energetic slam latched the door and signaled their departure. They headed up the street to the Pepper Mill café reasoning it would be near deserted at this time on a Sunday.

"How ya been anyway?" Scott asked.

"Okay, I suppose. Just curious to know what you've found out."

"Yes, well let's get inside and order, and I'll tell you what I know."

Soon they were seated with coffee and croissants in front of them.

"Let's see," Scott began. "Your concern is that a fellow, whom I understand Sir Reginald Wilson has just hired, may in fact be the March 2011 leaker of super-classified government intelligence information. If your suspicion is correct, the Wilson Companies may have hired a dangerous employee who could seriously undermine Sir Reginald's new operation. You remain concerned, even though the FBI, the CIA, and two congressional oversight committees thoroughly investigated and were unable to prove his or anyone's guilt. But you believe he is the bad guy. Is that about it in a nutshell?"

"Yes, about it, in a very small nutshell."

At this point, Scott explained he had dug up the old stories and read everything he could find on the subject before calling any former colleagues or cashing in any markers for updated information. What he found essentially corroborated what Seth had laid out. The nature of the leaked information clearly narrowed the field of possible culprits to about twenty. As the inquiry went on and possible suspects were eliminated, the focus turned to three people: one Raymond 'Smitty' Walker, a Martin Steele and the fellow in question, Edwin Henderson. All had worked in the same CIA office on the development of super-secure data transmission equipment. Some even went so far as to speculate these men worked on a system called Pyramid designed specifically to protect the PDB, the document which had been proven to be the origin of the leak. But these things were never established as facts.

When the news media and the public found out the two prime suspects had high-level security clearances, worked in very sensitive positions, had been carefully vetted, and were highly trusted, the public outcry was understandable. All three understood the equipment protecting the PDB, and it appeared both had opportunity. The two crucial questions were, of course, why, and who had motive?

In the end, Walker had briefly gone back to his old job and Henderson had been totally cleared and reinstated in his former very sensitive job. Steele, on the other hand, while also being totally cleared, did not. Instead, the agency effectively ostracized him, giving him only low-level menial work. During the investigation, a mountain of circumstantial evidence had continually come out about Steele, and he had become increasingly portrayed as the bad guy, with Henderson being the good guy turned whistle-blower. Despite the fact that no charges were filed, it became clear that high-ranking people wanted Steele to be politely forced out.

Taking a sip of coffee, Scott paused. "Now, Seth, there's something you need to know about how this business works. If I believe my information will lead to something big, I'm very reluctant to share it until I've properly nailed down the story. When I started asking around about Henderson, for example, the responses were generally questions about his current whereabouts and work. From several conversations, it appears many in my old office share your skepticism about the entire investigation but are just waiting on the sidelines for someone to uncover the facts so the story identifying the real leaker can come out."

"I can certainly understand, Scott," Seth responded, adding, "but were you able to gather anything at all new from your conversations about Henderson, any other tidbits, such as his motivation for leaving so close to retirement?"

"Not exactly. It seems most of what I heard, I had already read. But that doesn't mean the story isn't still alive. It's actually got me really interested." Scott went on say he would keep at it, and because he had already planned to be in Washington for the funeral of his former editor, Archibald "Archie" Fraser, he would use the extra two-day leave he'd been granted to meet and talk with some of his former colleagues. "I'm owed a big favor by one of them; she's an excellent reporter and a nice person. I think talking to her might break the ice on anything new doing the rounds."

"Sounds good. When's the funeral?"

"March twenty-second, with full military honors at Arlington National Cemetery."

"Impressive! It's not just the average GI who gets buried there nowadays. He must have fought in some war."

"Yes, Archie got drafted out of school during World War II, served in the navy during the South Pacific island-hopping campaign, and went on to study journalism, ending up as a war correspondent in Korea. After being wounded and cited for bravery, he came to work in DC and quickly made his way to the top. He proved to be an interesting, insightful, superb leader, and one outstanding writer. All of us in the trenches of the newsroom loved the man—the paper won't be the same without him. In any event, the trip will also give me a couple of days to poke around and ask questions."

* * *

Seth spent the following week painting, fixing, greasing, testing, and helping with all the repairs required to get the *Linda-T* ready for another season's fishing. Finally, on the day before Scott departed for Washington, a giant crane lowered the refurbished boat into the water. In less than an hour, with all the final pieces in place, two of Johnson's mechanics joined JB for a sea trial.

"Seth," JB shouted from the deck, "I don't know how long we'll be, so you just go back to the hotel, and I'll see you in the morning. Unless something goes very wrong, we'll head home at nine."

"No problem, JB. See you at breakfast."

Walking back to the Islander provided excellent thinking time. *History may record I have now opened a can of worms—only this time, I'm not going to close it until all the rotten worms are routed out.*

Chapter Fifteen

In front of the Old Post Chapel at Fort Myer, a group of people waited to enter for the funeral of "Archie" Fraser... soldier, war correspondent, writer, husband, father, manager, and editor-in-chief.

Inside the chapel, Scott took his seat and looked slowly around, soaking up the atmosphere of this historic building. He noticed many faces of former colleagues and friends. *What a wonderful group. What an extraordinary leader.*

The thoughts given during the service were meaningful and the rhetoric eloquent. And later, as the captain of the honor guard presented the precisely folded flag to Archie's son and daughter, Scott found it very difficult to hold back his emotions.

With the service complete, military escorts led the family away, and the crowd slowly dispersed to the nearby Hilton Hotel to eat, drink, and reminisce. Scott soon found himself catching up with friends on events of the past two years. He told them about his life in Maine, of fishermen, farmers, and a subculture very different from the big city. They told him about Washington politics and the dark web. But the conversation always came back to Archie, the boss with a nose for a story and a desire to find and write the truth.

Scott mingled with the crowd, looking for Martha Aston. Having no luck, he wandered over to the buffet. Just as he helped himself to a shrimp, he felt a gentle tap on his arm.

"Hello, stranger. Haven't seen you around here for eons. How are you?"

"Hello, Martha," Scott said. "I'm fine, and you're looking great. Nice to see you."

As they chatted, a tall handsome man came up and stood next to her.

"Oh, Scott, this is my husband, Jerry. Jerry, this is Scott Young. He used to write for the paper but left for the simple life in Maine someplace."

The two men shook hands.

"Are you in the newspaper business, too, Jerry?" Scott asked.

"Not really. Only by marriage, I guess," Jerry replied, "but I sorta am in the service business. I work in the Safeway warehouse nearby where I'm a butcher."

"Great. Bet that keeps you busy."

As they spoke, an elderly gentleman approached, dressed formally in a tailor-made black suit.

"Excuse me for interrupting, but may I have a quick word, Scott?"

Scott straitened up as though coming to attention. "Yes sir, Mr. Daniels. Good to see you again." Scott extended his hand as though addressing royalty, a status which Norman Daniels never flaunted but carried because of long years as senior writer and number one investigative reporter for the *Washington Post*.

"How can I help you, sir?"

"I know you're in Maine now, and this is neither the time nor the place for such things, but I would like to talk with you about a story before you go back home. Here's my card, and

I've put my cell phone number on the back. Please give me a call."

"Yes, sir. But I'm leaving early Sunday, so I'll phone you this evening if you don't mind."

"Of course, that's fine. I look forward to talking with you then."

Scott pocketed the card, and Daniels quietly disappeared into the crowd.

"Imagine," Martha said, "the big guy wants to see you. Ha! You must have left a story unfinished or something. Say, what do you two think about the three of us sitting over there out of reach of these delicious shrimp? If I stand here much longer, I'm going become one."

The two men chuckled, and they all headed for an empty table by the wall. Soon Jerry left to get drinks. As he did, Scott leaned close to Martha and told her he would really like a few minutes to talk privately, not right there, but some place where they would not be interrupted. As it turned out, Scott's hotel and Martha and Jerry's apartment were only four blocks apart, so they decided to meet in the hotel lobby at eleven the next morning. Jerry would be working until mid-afternoon, so she wouldn't need to explain her absence.

Later on, back at his hotel, Scott phoned Norman Daniels. His second meeting of the day was arranged for two o'clock, but this one would take place under the dramatic spires of the Air Force Memorial.

Saturday morning brought fair skies but continued cool temperatures. After breakfast, Scott decided to walk a bit, take in the new scenery, and get his thoughts together for his meeting with Martha. His mind went back to an evening in the April before his departure. He had been working late and had gone into the conference room to look for a folder. Switching on the light, he had been surprised to find Martha Aston and Lucy McIntyre, the executive secretary to Archie Fraser, intimately and wildly engaged on the heavily carpeted floor, their clothes strewn all around. Locating his folder on a chair by the door, he had grabbed it quickly, looked at the two, mumbled an "excuse me," shut off the light, and promptly left.

Now, as the incident came back to him, he wondered about Martha. Certainly, she had married a strong, handsome man, but to what purpose? To provide the look of normalcy, or to be her husband? Professionally, Scott thought very highly of Martha; indeed, he had denied seeing anything when the subject of her possible affair with Lucy had come up two days later. He knew he had saved her neck and her job. Now he hoped he could cash in some chips.

Scott entered the lobby about ten minutes early, removed his coat, sat conspicuously on a leather couch near the entrance, and began reading a newspaper.

In less than a minute, a well-dressed, slim female figure stood in front of him. "Hi there, Scott," she said quietly, quickly diverting his attention from a climate change story to the business at hand.

"Hello again, Martha. Thanks for coming. Shall we go through for something to drink?"

"Sure, I'd love to."

Soon they were enjoying coffee and glazed doughnuts next to a large window overlooking the busy Jefferson Davis Highway.

"I'll get right to the point, Martha. I'm looking for information. I know you're interested in facts, and you work in a place where tons of them constantly bounce around."

Scott then told of how the two-year-old PDB leak story had made its way to Maine and, since he now had the opportunity, he wanted to ask if she had any new information about the story.

"Oh, this is the case where the three CIA guys were investigated as possible leakers. Seems they tried very hard to hang one of them, a guy named Steele, but in the end could pin nothing on any of them."

"Exactly the story. The three men were Henderson, Walker, and Steele. What I'm really after is any new stuff you may have heard about Henderson. Things like why he left so precipitously and where he's gone."

"Well," Martha began, "a couple of interesting things have crossed my desk. But first, I should tell you this is hardly "old" news. In fact, there is genuine continuing interest in this story in our newsroom. Norm Daniels himself has taken the lead. He can't stomach the idea of treason and simply won't stop until this bad guy is caught and properly locked up. But even he hasn't come up with anything new for a while."

She stopped and stared out the window, cradling her cup in both hands. "Let's see…you probably don't know, but during and immediately following the investigations, all of us who watched the story thought some unknown "puppet master" was pulling the strings, manipulating public opinion, and building an unsubstantiated case against Steele. Within a month of the close of the last investigation, Walker left, as he had been identified as a covert, temporary transfer from the White House Secret Service. Then, a few months later, Henderson, with a generous retirement pension within his grasp, simply up and quit. And Steele, well, he just disappeared.

"Perhaps you don't know, Scott, but for years, Steele had been one of the most creative and innovative computer systems engineers at the CIA. His awards, the ones we know about anyway, were numerous, so his ostracization came as a big surprise and his disappearance an even bigger one."

Martha went on to give Scott one very interesting tidbit from the investigation. For a lengthy period of time, Henderson's wife, Norma, had been having a carefully covered-up affair. The investigators initially looked into it but later discarded the information calling it "unrelated to her husband's alleged treasonous activity."

"It appeared she only wanted to get her jollies by screwing the mailman or someone," Martha said. "But recently, more on the subject has been uncovered, and it's changed my opinion somewhat. In fact, it might change the whole story."

"What exactly did you find out?" Scott asked anxiously.

"It all started about two weeks ago when I met my friend Dolores Duval at the health club. Dolores has been a very successful private detective around here for over fifteen years. She's a really sharp lady, and we've been good friends for a long time. I'm sure she's never breached any client confidence, but there have been times when she's pointed me in just the right direction for a good story. We hadn't seen each other for months, but that day, we happened to meet in the health club steam bath.

"As we steamed, I related my curiosity about a possible 'puppet master' and the sudden departure of Edwin Henderson. I asked if she had run into any clues as to why he'd left or where he had gone. All she knew was he had applied for some position with one of the Wilson Companies in Belgium. But more interestingly, she talked about doing a job in late 2010, gathering evidence of an alleged adulterous relationship involving Henderson's wife, Norma. Of course, she didn't say, but Edwin Henderson had apparently hired her to gather divorce evidence—photos, video, and so on. This kind of thing is Dolores's stock and trade, and she's exceptionally good at it. In February 2011, she duly delivered her report with all the incriminating evidence to her client.

A point in time well before Henderson or anyone else made the news created by the PDB leak and its investigation."

Martha stopped as Scott digested all she had said. After what seemed an eternity, she continued, "Dolores recalled the man in the pictures as someone she had seen on TV, possibly on the news or else in the papers, most likely a government official of some sort. A man whose face seemed strangely familiar but which she just couldn't place. Unfortunately, these kinds of cases make up more than half her work, and she looks at many faces with every job. While not being able to pull out his name, she's absolutely certain he's a prominent man."

"It's definitely interesting to speculate about Henderson's wife being involved with some influential official," Scott responded. "I can remember reading about the FBI discovering the affair, how they'd looked into it fully and deemed it irrelevant to the leak. Just think, if the guy involved held a high enough position to influence the investigation, she could easily have been using the leverage of their affair to help her husband. But I suppose if that had been even remotely possible, they would've pursued it at the time. As I see it, the fact the FBI and others did what they did meant one of several things. Either Dolores had uncovered more significant evidence than the government investigators had, or the man had been identified but clearly had no connection to the leak, *or* the lover used his very influential position to ensure the affair never came up during the very public leak investigation."

"Please," Martha interrupted Scott, "remember what we're talking about here is very privileged information given to me in violation of my friend's ethics and contractual agreement. If you use it, please be very careful. Dolores is my friend."

"Certainly. I understand, Martha, but my guess is if the FBI were to put her under oath during a criminal investigation, she would be legally bound to testify." Scott paused for a moment, thinking. "Just imagine, if she does remember who this man is, it could make a so-called irrelevant event very significant, perhaps changing the whole case."

"Dolores has said she'll let me know if some news image, TV picture, or book cover photograph ever triggers her memory enough to positively identify the man. Of course, it might lead to someone totally uninvolved. Whatever you do, please keep my relationship with her to yourself."

"I certainly will. And thank you, Martha. This has been a really interesting conversation, and I appreciate you keeping your ear to the ground."

"I think I owe you, Scott, so this is the least I can do."

They said their farewells in the main lobby, and as they hugged, she whispered, "Good luck. I really hope you get to the bottom of all this."

He checked the time. In two hours, he would be meeting Norman Daniels.

* * *

After a quick lunch, Scott asked the concierge how far it was to the Air Force Memorial.

"It'll take just under an hour to get there on foot, if you don't get lost in the mass of roads between here and there. Lots of folks walk in the fine weather. Here, take this map; it'll help."

Scott thanked the man, took the map, and started north along the highway. Though he had lived in that area for over ten years, he had never seen the roads from a pedestrian's perspective.

As he walked, his mind began to fill with several possible scenarios. Could the identity of Norma Henderson's lover affect the leak story? If Dolores Duval's client turned out to be Ed Henderson seeking evidence for divorce, why hadn't he filed?

Perhaps her lover was a prominent and wealthy business figure who ultimately could pay big bucks to keep the story under wraps a la Martha's "mystery force" theory. This could explain Ed's leaving a government retirement behind when he departed. On the other hand, Norma's lover might have been a foreign agent who cleverly used her to acquire intelligence information indirectly from Ed.

As he approached the memorial, he smiled and shook his head at his own speculations. *Let's face it, most of the people out here are just regular people, not millionaires, prominent business leaders, or spies. Three investigations have looked into Norma's affair, and none considered it relevant to the leaking of government secrets. That has to mean something.*

* * *

Scott arrived at the Air Force Memorial well before the meeting time. He took the opportunity to look and read. *What they died for was freedom, indeed my freedom. And one of the things that attacks freedom in the most vicious way is treason.* Suddenly Seth's story grew in significance.

As he stood in front of the jet-black marble slab, the reflection of a figure approaching from behind caught his attention. He turned and greeted his former colleague, Norman Daniels, with a handshake.

"Good afternoon, Scott, and thank you for coming. Now tell me, how are you getting along up there in the cold country with all those 'down-Mainers'?"

"Getting along just fine, sir. It's an entirely different world up there, but I really like it. I only write for a weekly, but it keeps me busy, and I have a great boss. Along the coast where we are, the locals are mostly merchants, farmers, or fishermen, and I hardly ever run into a politician. Things there just don't move as fast as they do down here, by any measure. But tell me, how have you been down here in the big city?"

"Surviving okay," Daniels responded, chuckling, "and thanks for asking. I've been fine but very busy. There seems to be a never-ending array of important things to look into and write about." Daniels paused and, in a perfect segue, launched into his reasons for wanting to speak to Scott. "My guess is you didn't come all the way here just for Archie's funeral. I hear you've been asking questions around the office for almost a week now."

Scott frowned. "Bush telegraph, as effective as ever."

Daniels continued, "You've been asking questions about the 2011 PDB leak, haven't you? You've probably heard I've been keeping a fire burning under the story ever since the whole mess supposedly ended. Now I understand you well enough to know something piqued your interest way up there in Maine, so why don't we just cut to the chase and focus on the leak story? I sure would like to know if you've brought anything new with you from the far north."

"Perhaps I have. One thing is certain, my looking into this story has made me very interested in finding out what really happened. Treason is serious stuff and should never be left unpunished." Scott continued, "What I've learned starts with a sternman, a lobsterman's helper, who, like several others up there, left a career elsewhere. This guy had been a software engineer who worked right around here and had social connections to a number of insiders.

"He said, at the time of the leak investigation, several of his friends, some of whom worked at the CIA, thought there was something very strange about the way Henderson, Steele and Walker appeared to be treated differently. To these folks and much of the public, I imagine, it cast a shadow on the investigation and gave the impression of very high-level manipulation.

"Then, last summer, my friend just happened to be working at Sir Reginald Wilson's annual gathering on Orran Island. There, he overheard several references to a Mr. Edwin Henderson, formerly of the CIA, being considered for an important security job in one of the Wilson Companies. He had become good friends with Sir Reginald and his son and daughter-in-law, and he simply didn't want to see these friends involved in hiring a possible traitor. Though it now appears this is exactly what has happened.

"We met in town just a few days before I left to come here for Fraser's funeral, so I quickly read all I could find on the leak as well as on Henderson and the other two men. Then I made a few calls to friends down here. Four things were apparent. First, this leak came from inside the CIA. Second, the investigations appeared controlled or, at the very least, flawed. Third, the three prime suspects were unequally treated both during the investigations and later after being cleared. Fourth, the investigations were closed, leaving some thieving, treasonous bastard on the street and possibly still working inside the CIA."

"That's most interesting, Scott," Daniels responded. "It's heartening to know others in the media are still paying attention to this story. I'd heard he was heading up the security efforts for one of Sir Reginald's new subsidiaries in London, and I agree, he certainly wouldn't have been my choice for the job."

As they talked, the two men slowly strolled around under the towering spires. Scott then added he had heard of a possible affair involving Norma Henderson. Daniels said the affair had been known about by many, but each investigation had independently deemed it irrelevant, so they continued to look elsewhere for leads.

"At least we now know where Henderson is," Daniels added, "although I doubt he would give me an interview if I were to just show up in his London office. As for the other two, Walker left the agency within months and is now back home with the Secret Service in the White House. I've spoken to him about the case but learned nothing new, so, for the time being at least, I accept their story of high-level, interagency cooperation involving something altogether different. The other man, Steele, could be on the back side of the moon for all I've been able to find out, but I sure would like to talk to him."

They walked in silence for a while until Daniels stopped and in a most determined tone said, "I really hate traitors, and someone in this case has gone to extreme lengths to get his hands on classified government information. After all this time, my guess is the power behind it is either Russia or China, but either would need inside help. Do you suppose your friend who recognized Henderson's name has enough pull with Sir Reginald to get me an entrée to meet Henderson in London? I'd really like to talk with him."

"Don't think there's much chance of that, but there's a very real chance he might show up at the next gathering on Orran Island."

"I've heard the press presence there is usually limited."

"You're right. Limited to one. We're not really wanted, but they always allow one, and it's been me for the past two years. They like the glitzy publicity despite what they say. But there's always a need for waiters and kitchen help…if you get my drift. I'll talk to my contacts and see what we can work out."

"Thanks, Scott, whatever you can do would be much appreciated. By the way, did you come up here by car or on foot?"

"On foot. Why do you ask?"

"Good. Let's walk this way toward the parking lot. There's one more thing I'd like to go over with you, and my car is down there, so I can drop you off at your hotel." Daniels began to describe his latest theory about who had leaked the information and why. "Do you remember reading anything about the 'Pyramid' project in your research?" he asked.

"Well, kinda. I think it must be a thing, a machine or whatever, designed to transmit and receive extremely sensitive information...like the PDB."

"Correct. The CIA developed it specifically to transmit the PDB, in a uniquely secure way, to the president wherever he happened to be. It uses some sort of fancy double-barreled encryption system that destroys the entire transmission the instant anyone tries to intercept the data. On the receiving end, it can only be read by the president, as verified by a key, a password, and two biometrics.

"The process goes like this: A handful of very trusted, highly cleared officers of the agency gather each morning to attack a mountain of current intelligence information with the objective of distilling it down to its essence. Their job is to create a concise briefing, focused on the most timely, important, and critical issues. When they're done, someone takes the result and types it into the Pyramid machine. Someone else proofreads it, and they push the transmit button. At the receiving end, it is displayed on the president's Pyramid machine, but only if he continues to hold the machine after verifying who he is. Pyramid has undergone extensive tests by the National Security Agency."

"Incredible!" Scott said. "You must have trusted contacts everywhere to know all this." *Could Daniels be the leaker?* A shiver ran down Scott's spine.

Daniels continued, "A lot of what I know came from sources attending a top-secret gathering of the agency division where Pyramid had been developed. The assembly, headed by the director of central intelligence, honored the project and its inventor."

"Ya going to tell me Henderson invented the thing?" Scott asked.

"No, I'm going to tell you Martin B. Steele did."

"I can begin to see why you might like to find him then."

"Oh, yes, I would certainly like to talk to Steele, but please don't get the wrong impression, Scott. I don't think he's the leaker, despite the fact he's completely disappeared from view. People who knew him, particularly Walker, who worked with him for nearly a year, all said his dedication to the project, the agency, and our country was absolutely beyond reproach.

"Remember the exact wording of the leak proved it had come directly from the PDB, and Pyramid had been designed and built solely for the protection of that data. You could describe it as Steele's baby. He would never have put so many years of work into it, only to kill it by giving its secrets away, no way! From what I've learned of Martin Steele, he would never sell his country out, not for anything.

"I believe the culprit has to be either the Chinese or the Russians. Despite what everyone believed at the time, somehow, they broke into the Pyramid data stream and successfully leaked a piece of a message, just to prove they could…a real 'gotcha' for their side!

"Of course, because of the leak, they had no choice but to stop using the system immediately."

Soon they were standing beside a very shiny, new BMW sedan. "Here we are," offered Daniels as he unlocked the trunk and handed Scott a brown manila file. "Jump in and take a look through this while we drive. You said Crystal City, right?"

"Yes, sir. It's the Marriott near the airport."

Scott opened the folder. There were several photographs on top, including three neatly marked—one with the name "E. Henderson," another "M. Steele," and a third "R. Walker." They looked like the type of mug shots that would normally be produced for a license or a badge.

"So you have no clue as to where Mr. Steele is, but you would like to meet him, right?" Scott began.

"I've done everything I can to find him. Perhaps if I were in the CIA or the NSA, it would only take a few seconds, but I'm not. You have any ideas?"

"Well, yes, I do."

"I'm all ears."

"I think I've seen this man and can locate him again," Scott said, holding up Steele's photo. If I can arrange a meeting, and the identity of the leaker comes out of it, are you willing to let me break the story?"

"Wow! If you have indeed located Steele, it could be a major breakthrough." With obvious excitement in his voice, Daniels added, "Scott, you're talking as though you're still down here in the middle of things and not up in the sticks, getting excited about some guy who just won a statewide cooking contest! But hey, I understand. Breaking the real story of this leaker would certainly put Scott Young and the weekly *Courier* in the headlines all over the country. I'll make you a deal. If you arrange a meeting with this guy, and he turns out to be Steele, and his help turns out to uncover the real leaker, you can have the scoop, I just want the leaker."

Chapter Sixteen

To the welcome relief of the commercial fishermen on Sandaray, April's fair weather got the lobster season off to a good start. JB and Seth worked long days to get the legal limit of traps in the water as soon as physically possible. JB's work ethic made him both a careful and an involved task manager, as well as a very hard worker. But on the Wednesday of the second week of April, their initial efforts being complete, he announced to Seth they would wait until Friday to haul next, thus giving them both a day off on Thursday.

* * *

Seth woke without the usual alarm. He stretched, enjoying the luxury of a non-workday, and lay there, looking at the ceiling and thinking. His mind focused on Scott Young. *I wonder what he learned down there in Washington.* Giving little thought to anything else, he got up, dressed, and headed straight to Emma's Café.

The place was deserted. No Emma, no customers, not even Kenny. Not really surprising since it was still relatively early. After all, the working folks were long gone, and all the tourists were probably still asleep. He sat at the counter, and eventually, Emma emerged from the back. "Well, if it isn't Seth Martin. What a nice surprise! It must be a month since I last saw you.

Thought you must have won the lottery and run off to sunnier climes or something," she joked, setting a steaming cup of coffee in front of him.

"We've been straight out since JB got back, but all his traps are in the water now, and today's a day off. You know I haven't had a decent breakfast since you closed up last fall. Any chance of rustling something up?"

"Oooo, I'm sure I can fix you up with something. The usual?"

"Of course. Thanks, Emma."

Within minutes, Emma returned with a perfectly cooked breakfast of eggs, ham, and fried potatoes. When she headed over to refill his coffee cup, he asked, "Emma, is your computer working?"

"Damned if I know. So far, I haven't needed it, so I've avoided the hassle and not even turned it on."

"During the winter, Bill let me use his up at the lodge, so I set up an email account to get a connection to the outside world. I'd like to check it. Is it okay if I use yours?"

"Sure, come on back. You'll have to dust it off and plug it in." She cleared a space on the desk for the keyboard and ran a rag over the monitor. "The internet should still be active since I keep paying their damn bills. There ya go."

Seth sat at her desk and powered on the machine. After about twenty minutes of updating the operating system and the antivirus programs, he logged on to his new email account to find a message from Scott.

> Seth
> Back from the funeral. Have some information,
> please stop in when you're in town.
> Scott

Shit. The email had been sent a week ago. *I need to get into town!* He shut down Emma's machine and hurried to the front where he found her serving Kenny coffee and a ballast rock. "Emma," he said anxiously, "did any of the guys in here earlier talk about going into town today?"

"No," she replied. "Didn't hear much more than the regular stuff about too much work, not enough money, and too many troubles with unhappy women, but if you're looking to get into town, the mail plane went over about five minutes ago, and if you're quick, you can catch the pilot at the post office. If he has room, you've got a way in."

Seth paid Emma for the breakfast, thanked her for the use of her computer, bid Kenny good morning, and bolted out the door. He ran full tilt up the hill to the junction with the road going to the store, where he slowed down, knowing the pilot would have to drive past him.

It took only fifteen minutes for the ride to the airport, thirty more for the flight to the mainland, an additional twenty for the cab ride into town, and in just over an hour, he was standing at the reception desk of the *Weekly Courier.*

"Is Scott Young in?" he anxiously asked the lady at the desk.

"Oh, it's you again. No, I'm afraid not. The editor sent him down to Johnson's wharf to get a story on some guy who just brought in a hundred-and-fifty-five-pound halibut. Want to leave him a message?"

"Yes, please. Tell him Seth Martin is in town."

"Anything else?"

"Yes, how long ago did he leave?"

"Ten minutes, I'd guess."

"Thanks."

Seth sprinted the mostly downhill half mile to Johnson's. Gasping for breath, he rushed over to speak to the first person he saw.

"Know where the guy is who caught the big halibut?"

"Yup. Go right down to the water and turn left. There's a big crowd; even the TV people are there."

"Okay. Thanks."

A sizable crowd surrounded the large contraption used to lift boats out of the water and transport them around. From its superstructure, some ropes and a scale supported one very large halibut. The picture told the whole story, and the scale made it officially a 153.5-pound catch. A TV interview crew stood in front of the fish, speaking with the proud fisherman. As Seth approached, he saw Jennifer Stanley busily taking pictures of individuals in the crowd. She waved him over, and in a second, they were joined by Scott.

"Damn, I'm glad you finally made it, Seth. We *really* need to talk."

"What's up Scott, you selling halibut now?" Seth joked.

"Can you get to the Lighthouse Restaurant in an hour? I can meet you there."

As the TV crew politely moved everyone else back from the fisherman, his big fish, and their interviewer, Seth whispered to Scott, "How do I find the Lighthouse Restaurant?"

"Just south about a mile along Route 1. It's on the left."

"Great. See you there."

* * *

Set on a high promontory commanding a beautiful view of the harbor, the Lighthouse Restaurant attracted vacationers, tourists, and yacht owners but not the average working fisherman. There were several tables on a large deck, but they, along with all but two inside, were empty. Seth took a table near the window where he could enjoy the view while watching for Scott and ordered coffee for two. The coffee and Scott arrived at about the same time. "So tell me," Seth began, "how did you get on in the big city?"

"There's a lot to tell, my friend," Scott began. "It's been more than three years since I left, and so much has changed. But it's still the center of our government and still humming with all manner of electric excitement and intrigue.

"For one thing, the 2011 leak story you spoke about is still an active topic of conversation in media circles. In fact, the top writer and investigative reporter from my old paper has never stopped looking for clues and evidence. He and I met at the funeral. We talked privately later. He knows a lot about the case and has actually got a prime suspect."

Seth's pulse quickened. "Really? Probably Henderson, right?"

"No, it's none of the original prime suspects. He believes it is either the Chinese or the Russian government who broke into the PDB transmitted data stream. It must have been quite a difficult job, so they leaked a bit to show us they could do it in the knowledge that we would immediately shut it down."

Anger welled up in Seth, and his cheeks flushed. "*Not possible!*" he cried. "It just can't be. There's no way those bastards could break into that data stream!" Seth stopped abruptly, and for a while, the two men sat and looked at each other.

Scott broke the nervous silence. "Your instinctive reaction is okay, Seth…or should I say, Martin?"

Seth slumped back in his chair. Game over.

"You have to understand, my friend, it was damn near impossible for me to have gone down there, knowing what you'd said, then talk with Norman Daniels, who's been watching this case since the beginning, and come away without finding out who you really were."

Seth put his head in his hands and momentarily closed his eyes.

"By the way, Daniels wants to meet you as soon as possible. A covert meeting up this way somewhere would be my suggestion."

Raking his fingers through his hair, Seth looked up and considered how he should respond. *I should have been more prepared for this moment. But this is the road to the truth, and this is the road I'm committed to, one hundred percent.*

Fixing his eyes on Seth, Scott finally added, "There's one more thing, one very important thing I have to ask you. Can you look me straight in the eye and say Martin Steele wasn't the leaker?"

Seth fixed his eyes on Scott and answered emphatically, "Yes, I can, absolutely. I am not the fucking leaker!" Then in very hushed tones, he slowly began to explain. "Look, Scott, I conceived the system, I built it, it's my creation. There's no way I would ever do anything to compromise it. It would be like killing my own child!"

Seth thought for a long moment, mulling over the real meaning of his words. "And Scott, there's something even more important you must understand. There's no force, nor reward that would ever induce me to betray my country. That's simply the way I am and the way I've always been, long before I took any oath to that effect. And no, it was definitely not the Russians, the Chinese, or the Iranians who were trying to rub our collective noses in something they had uncovered. With all respect to Mr. Daniels, that's simply stupid. If they really had found a way into the system, they certainly wouldn't try to get us to stop using it. They'd kick our asses with the stuff they could get from it on a regular basis.

"Many years from now, someone may be able to break their way in, but for the foreseeable future at least, getting anything out of that data stream is way beyond all of them," Seth paused, "and well beyond our country's best efforts as well. This leak must have come before the data ever entered the system. It's a fucking solid system…it works! No one with only thirty or forty samples has even a prayer of breaking it. Maybe some genius with three or four billion samples could, but even then, I seriously doubt it. Neither do I believe it could have leaked from the receiving end."

"Thank you, Martin. I believe you."

In a whisper, Seth replied, "Let's just keep 'Martin' out of this conversation, okay?"

"Of course."

As the restaurant filled up, Scott flagged a waitress for more coffee. He then explained he thought a meeting with Norman Daniels should be arranged, as soon as possible, in some conveniently located place where they would not be noticed. He suggested the hotel at Boston's Logan Airport. Big hotel, lots of independent travelers, people coming and going at all hours, the ideal place. The date would have to be set later. Seth agreed the location would be fine, but he would need as much lead time as possible since there were always unknown variables getting off Sandaray. "Can you come along as well, Scott?" Seth asked.

"Depends totally on my boss, Seth, but I think I can work it. I would certainly like to be there."

Changing the subject slightly, Seth asked, "Did you find out anything about Norma Henderson's affair? Do you think it's a part of the puzzle, or is it really, as the FBI put it, not relevant to this case?"

"It could be relevant if she happened to have been screwing some super high-level guy, someone high enough to influence the investigation. There is some talk he may be a person of public prominence, but officially no one knows who he is… or no one is saying. Most folks still have their money on the 'mailman' scenario."

As lunch time approached and the crowd increased, Scott and Seth rose to depart. When they passed the queue of waiting guests, Scott remarked in an obvious way, "I'll let you know when I hear from the *Boston Globe* about the *Jasper* interview, Seth."

Within two hours, armed with a few provisions, Seth had been transported back to the island by the Air Taxi service.

* * *

At five o'clock the following morning, the *Linda-T* slipped out of the harbor for the first haul of the season. During the past year, Seth had learned his job well, and now he and JB worked together seamlessly, each anticipating the other's moves, making the operation much more efficient and easier for both. By the last full week of April, life and work had settled back into a comfortable and profitable routine, although much of Seth's thinking remained focused on events from the past and their possible influence on his future.

Now weekends had become the time to get other stuff done or to just rest up. So, one Saturday, the day began with a late breakfast at Emma's. As he entered, several tourists were sitting at the tables, some discussing the day's plans, others studying one of Bill Harris's island maps.

From the corner by the window came Kenny's familiar voice. "Good morning, young fella, how ya doing?"

Seth took a stool two seats away and sat down, leaving ample room for Kenny's newspapers. "Doing great, Kenny. How about yourself?"

The question launched Kenny into a long tirade centered around a "frig'n raccoon'" that had somehow gotten into his basement and helped itself to a chunk of just about every one of his remaining stored potatoes. "The little SOB won't last long," Kenny concluded. "I now have three rabbit traps strategically placed around the potato bin. I'll get him soon, no more potatoes for him! How about you, Seth, you guys getting any lobsters?"

"A few," Seth answered, using the noncommittal island jargon that meant they were doing quite well.

In a moment, Mandy arrived, coffee pot in hand. She greeted Seth, took his order, gave Kenny his check, and disappeared through to the back.

As Seth finished his breakfast, Emma arrived with a cheery "Hello." She came over, filled his coffee cup, and then, in somewhat hushed tones, said, "Remember the day I arrived back from the mainland? You surprised me and really saved the day by helping and feeding me a fine dinner. Well, I'd like to return the favor by inviting you over here for dinner tonight. Are you busy?"

"No," Seth replied, surprised by the invitation. "I'd love to. What time?"

"How about six?"

"I'll be here." Seth paid Emma, thanked her again for the invitation, and headed up the hill to the store.

"Hear you've been out to haul every day since JB got back. Getting any lobsters?" BP asked in his usual nosey manner.

"A few," Seth replied as he carefully perused the shelf where BP had a small selection of wine. In less than five minutes, Seth had gathered all the things on his list and spread them on the counter.

"Oh, hold on a moment, Mr. Seth Martin…here ya go. Ya got another letter." BP handed over the envelope. "Just look at the stamp? Bet it's another one from the Wilsons over in England."

BP started adding up the bill, his mind clearly filled with curiosity and focused on the letter. "Wonder how they're doin' over there? Good 'ol Dan never did a decent day's work in his life, ya know. I don't know why Linda stuck with him all these years." When he had totaled the bill, he looked up, but Seth gave nothing away. "Ain't ya going to open it?" No answer. He handed the bag to Seth. "Well, that'll be thirty-seven eighty-five then."

Seth sighed, paid him, and headed for the door. He thought as he turned, *the guy can't help it. And after all, how else would people out here get the news.* "You have a good day BP."

He waited until he had returned to the fish house to read the letter.

> *Dear Seth,*
> *By the time this gets to you, Dad will probably have you working round the clock, getting things ready. I hope all is going well with both of you.*
> *Dan has been quite busy, and I must say his father seems positively impressed. Quite frankly, so am I. This is the first time I know of when Dan's work has been of any real importance. But he is keeping up with it and getting things off to a good start, so the business is coming together very well. Doing meaningful work is having a good effect on him!*
> *I'm planning to fly back for a short trip at some point. I feel bad being so far away from Dad.*
> *I really hope you're still there. I miss you, Seth.*
> *Love,*
> *Linda*

Seth folded the note neatly and then put the groceries away, his mind focusing on Linda. He made a silent pledge not to repeat his last encounter with her, but as he did, the emotion of the evening came back in powerful, exciting detail as he vividly remembered the overwhelming desire that had consumed them both. No pledge, indeed, no force he could think of, could have kept him from her, nor her from him. Shivers ran down his spine. Resolve or no resolve, pledge or no pledge he had to be damn careful.

* * *

Seth set out up the hill to Emma's in good time, the carefully wrapped bottle of wine in hand. The sun shone brightly high in the clear sky, but a moderate wind produced an almost fall-like chill in the air. The café sign said "closed," but out of habit, Seth tried the door. Finding it locked, he proceeded around to the back. He knocked gently, then a bit harder, and soon, Emma's voice came from a window above.

"The door's unlocked, Seth. Come on up."

Upstairs over the café, the same amount of space provided a bedroom, a bathroom, and one large living, dining, and kitchen area. The room featured a picture window with a spectacular view of the harbor. Seth greeted Emma and presented her with the wine.

"Wow!" she said with a tone of genuine surprise. "Here's a corkscrew. You could open up that beauty, and we can sample a bit before dinner, okay?"

"Great idea."

They carried their glasses over to the sofa and toasted the future.

"Well, the new season is underway for everyone," Seth remarked. "I see Mandy is still with you despite Bill's best efforts. Is she giving you as much time as she did last year?"

"Yes, she is. Mandy's great. She's a good, hard worker, and everyone likes her. She says Bill has offered her the same work schedule this year and thrown in a little raise to boot."

"Great," Seth responded, adding that from a customer's point of view, Mandy had always been outstanding. He started to ask how Emma's winter had been when a timer went off by the stove. "Hold the question please," Emma said. "It's time to eat. Bring the rest of the wine."

On a beautifully set dining table, Emma presented a first-class meal. Their conversation stayed generally light, eventually moving on to Bill Harris and what Seth had been doing up at DeVoe Lodge. Emma's comments about her ex surprised him, as he thought there was no love lost between the two. When the freshly baked rhubarb pie arrived, however, all talk of Bill thankfully ceased and they finished the meal in companionable silence.

After dinner, they moved to the sofa to enjoy the stunning view as the light of day slowly faded into darkness.

Seth held up his glass and touched hers. "To Emma. Thank you for an absolutely wonderful meal, in an absolutely gorgeous setting, with an absolutely beautiful hostess!"

"Thank you, Seth. You've made this a lovely evening for me as well."

They sat in silence for a short while, neither quite sure where to go next.

Emma sipped her wine and in a short while gave in to what had been a nagging, long-term curiosity. She started slowly, "You know something, Seth, it's been over a year since you just showed up one day and rescued my poor computer from being dumped overboard in some very deep part of the ocean. Clearly you weren't just another runaway, druggie, or misfit who'd come here to make a few bucks or hide from the law. Nope, you were—are—different. But despite my and Kenny's best efforts, we've found out nothing about you, where you came from, or why you're here." Emma stopped and carefully studied Seth's face for a reaction.

He waited before responding. Relaxed from the effects of a lovely meal, delightful company, and delicious wine, he found it very tempting just to open up to her. "Obviously I have a past, Emma. If you want, I'll give you a highlight or two if you promise to keep it to yourself and not ask any questions."

"Oh, come on, Seth, how about just a few questions?"

"Well, maybe two."

"How about twenty-two? I'll keep everything about you all to myself."

"Promise?"

"Yes, I promise."

"Coming here was a first for me. I had never been farther north than Boston and never even heard of Sandaray Island. My life began in the mountains of North Carolina, my father a school-teacher, my mother an artist and homemaker. After high school, I went to college at Virginia Tech, got a job, and about seven years later, left it to find out what it would be like to be a sternman on a Maine lobster boat. So there you have it. See, my background isn't anything spectacular. It's the future that's more important."

"Okay. Aren't you leaving out a few small details about things like girlfriends, marriages, divorces, children, and whatever work you did before becoming compelled to drop it all and go to a place you'd never heard of to do a job you knew nothing about?"

"Well, let's see, that sounds like five of the two questions you were limited to. Okay, the answers go like this: several girlfriends, no marriages, no divorces, no children, and a regular run-of-the-mill office job."

Emma carefully divided the last of the wine between their two glasses, sat back, and gazed out at the harbor, now illuminated by the rising moon. "You know, it's a virtual impossibility to keep anything secret out here, and word has it when you were over at the Orran Island bash last summer, something you overheard from one of the guests got you really excited. Is that true? Are you in trouble with the law or something?"

Her unexpected question instantly changed the mood. He had come to like Emma, indeed, to like her a lot, and wanted neither to avoid her curiosity nor offend her with deceptive falsehoods. So he answered cautiously and economically, "I'm not in trouble with the law, Emma, but yes, it's true something did happen on Orran. I overheard something very worrying about someone from my past, someone who had become the focus of interest by others in a very powerful international group."

He paused for a moment, put his wine glass on the table, and turned to face her. "This is strictly confidential, Emma. But I'll give you some background. I used to work in computer security. It's a business that touches everyone and protects everything imaginable, from the privacy of your grocery order with D. R. Fox to the most closely held government secrets. When a security system broke down at the place where I worked, three of us were suspended, and there was a big investigation. They concluded I had nothing to do with, it but the harassment and pressure really got to me and drove me to the point of wanting to quit. So I did. Packed up my stuff and headed north, hoping to find a new job and, I suppose, a new life."

"What about the other people they suspected?"

"In the end, lack of hard evidence meant no one could be prosecuted, but a crime had definitely been committed. And I'm ninety-nine percent sure I know who did it. I suspect he's the person I overheard being discussed in connection with a security job at one of the Wilson Companies, and I'd like to warn Sir Reginald somehow."

"Maybe you could tell Linda or Dan when you see them next. Tell them what you know."

"It could be awkward, but it's a good idea. Thank you, Emma." He took a sip of wine.

"So you're a techie geek! No wonder you were able to heal my computer so quickly. Thanks again for that." She paused. "No one will hear any of this from me, Seth, but I do have just one final question. I know, I've used up my quota. But the rumors say the newspaper guy, Scott Young, spent months trying to prove you were some runaway doctor." The bonus questions tumbled out. "Why did he think that? Are you also a doctor? Who are you, Seth Martin? And is that even your real name?" As she spoke, Emma's hand softly found Seth's, adding sincerity to her question.

Seth gulped and then, knowing he wanted very much never to lie to this lady, answered vaguely but honestly, to no question in particular, "Well, no. Not exactly…and now you've definitely overrun your questions!"

Before Emma could say another word, he rose, feeling decidedly uncomfortable, and looked at his watch.

"Wow, I really should go. And it's getting very late for someone who starts her business every day before four in the morning"

An awkward atmosphere replaced the warmth of a convivial evening. "I'm sorry, Emma. I shouldn't have told you any of this. Please just forget it. It's complicated."

They walked together to the top of the stairs. Seth stopped and took her hand. "Emma, you don't need to get sucked into my past. It is what it is, in the past. Bad stuff happened, and I left."

She stared up, searching his face for further meaning, but nothing was forthcoming. He shook her hand and, in what seemed to her a confusing gesture added, "Thank you for a lovely evening, Emma."

The handshake dissolved into a mutual hug. But as Seth released his arms, Emma suddenly pulled him closer and lifted her face, inviting a kiss. His heart pounded, but in an instant, he diverted his lips from hers letting only their cheeks touch. Quickly withdrawing and holding her gently by the shoulders, he whispered, "You're such a good, kind person. I'm not the man you think I am, and I'm certainly not worthy of your affections. Good night, Emma."

As he started down the stairs, she quietly called after him, "Good night, Seth."

* * *

During the following week, a deep, persistent low-pressure area made each day's work longer and harder. But by the early hours of Friday, JB and Seth had successfully hauled all JB's traps and had only to load up the week's catch and sell it to Frank and Carrie.

By midday, the work week was over. Seth headed for a long shower, a set of clean clothes, and lunch at Emma's. As he walked up the hill, he found himself recalling Saturday evening's lovely meal and the unfortunate way it had ended. Emma had become a real friend, but he had definitely said too much. He wanted to be honest with her, but then, in this close-knit community, even the most discreet people could, and did, inadvertently let secrets slip out.

All the seats in the café were taken, and Mandy was rushing about trying to take everyone's orders as quickly as possible. Apparently, Emma had gone somewhere, perhaps up to the store for more food. *So much for the lunch idea,* Seth thought, but he did manage to grab a nanosecond of Mandy's time to ask if she thought Emma would mind if he used her computer again. "Go for it," she said, "I'm sure she won't mind."

He logged in and found a three-day-old message from his former colleague Cheryl Murphy.

M,

I hope the winter is finally over for you way up there in the wilds of the north. Down here we have gone directly from winter to summer, skipping spring altogether. Felt just like a hot, muggy August day today!

There is a rumor going through the halls down here now that you may be interested in. A newspaper guy named Daniels has filed a Freedom of Information request for listings of all nonsecure phone numbers called by several of the heavies upstairs during the period November 2010 thru March 2011. Daniels has a long and solid reputation as an investigative reporter and makes no secret of the fact he's looking into the March 2011 leak. Now that it appears the request is going to be granted, you may want to get in contact with this guy.

There is also significant news on the personal front. At certain times of the month recently, John has been eating lots of broccoli, and it now seems to have done the trick as I am officially pregnant! It has been a long time coming, and we are both very excited.

I hope you are working hard and staying well. We miss you, I miss you.

All the best,

C.

Seth sent a congratulatory reply to Cheryl, thanking her as well for the information regarding Daniels. Then, quickly turning his attention to Scott, he sent an email asking if there had been any word about "the possible interview by the *Boston Globe*."

On his way back to the fish house, he began going over events that, for more than a year now, he had simply blocked from his mind. He reasoned the time had come to go back over everything he could remember with someone like Daniels. Daniels sounded like a safe bet. Certainly, someone very well connected, who had apparently maintained an active interest in the story long after the case ceased being news. The fact remained: someone committed a major crime, and somewhere, there were enough facts to nail the culprit. Gathering, validating, and compiling these facts would have to be done carefully and in secrecy lest the insider, almost certainly protecting Ed Henderson, find out and torpedo this new data-gathering effort.

On the evening of Tuesday, May 21st, Seth decided to watch an episode of *Star Trek: The Next Generation* on TV. Just as Picard ordered Warf to "fire photon torpedoes!" the telephone rang. Bummer.

"This is Seth Martin."

"Scott Young. Your meeting is on for Friday evening. You can get a bus from here at nine fifteen going directly to the airport. I would like to go with you but so far haven't come up with any reasonable justification for the time away. Have a good trip and a profitable discussion."

"Thanks, Scott."

"Good night, Mar...er, Seth."

The next morning, as they made their way out of the harbor, Seth asked JB if he could have Friday off.

"Need to go to town?" JB asked.

"Yes."

"You going to be back by Monday?"

"Yes."

"Okay, have a good time."

Chapter Seventeen

The bus schedule showed almost five hours for the ride down the coast to Boston's Logan Airport, so Seth armed himself with a novel, the local newspaper, and two candy bars. Surprisingly, he found the seats relatively comfortable, with the movies and complimentary snacks most unexpected. Not quite the same as riding the metro bus around Washington. The hours passed quickly, and by dinner time, he had checked in to the hotel ready and anxious for the upcoming meeting.

In an effort to divert his thinking, Seth turned on the TV, flopped on the bed with the remote control, and began searching. Wow! A charge for everything, and paying seven bucks to see Sir Alec Guinness blow up *The Bridge on the River Kwai* just didn't seem worth it. He shut it off and went back to his book. Just as he started reading, the phone rang. "Hello, this is Seth Martin."

"Daniels here. Can we meet at seven thirty?"

"Where?"

"My room, seven-eighteen."

"I'll be there."

* * *

A tall, well-dressed, elderly man opened the door. "Please come in," he said. "I'm Norman Daniels. It's good to see you again, Martin."

"You have me at a real disadvantage, Mr. Daniels. I can't remember ever having met you."

"Not at all surprising," Daniels replied, closing the door and motioning to Seth to take a seat. "Now before this discussion begins, it's important we share identification. Let's start with this." Daniels quietly opened a small attaché case, removing a US passport. "Just so you have no doubt about who I am, please examine this." Seth took the booklet and turned to the identification page comparing the picture to the face in front of him. Then, using knowledge that only could have been taught, quickly examined the pages for signs of tampering. Finally, with the identification complete, he returned the passport.

"Now I know who you are, sir, but I have little to prove to you who I am. Once again, Mr. Daniels, you have me at a disadvantage."

"During the 2011 congressional investigation that focused on you and two others, I sat in the press gallery taking notes. By the time they were done, I truly felt as though I knew you. My guess is you took extraordinarily little notice of the media people filling the seats behind you, so your disadvantage is easily understood."

Seth then offered his hand. "I'm very pleased to meet you, Mr. Daniels."

"The feeling is definitely mutual, Mr. Steele. Now would you like a soda or something before we start?"

Momentarily startled on hearing his real name spoken, he managed to ask for sparkling water.

Soon the two were seated across a small table, Daniels with a voice recorder, pad, and pencil in hand, and Seth with his glass of water.

"When you start recording, I would appreciate it if you called me Seth Martin, okay?"

"Certainly, Seth. The machine is completely out of habit. As I grow older, my memory just isn't as sharp or as trustworthy as it used to be. This recording goes no farther than my desk."

"Thank you."

"There are two very strong driving forces that are keeping me on the trail of this particular leaker," Daniels began. "The first is my love of our country and the hate I hold for anyone who commits a crime aimed at damaging our government, indeed our way of life. The second is my allegiance to the ethics of journalism and its demand for thorough, unbiased, and honest reporting." Daniels spoke with clear passion. "Something else you must understand is that the two of us would not be sitting here today if I thought for a moment you were the leaker."

"I appreciate your confidence, Mr. Daniels. You're absolutely correct, there is no way I would do such a thing. I am not the leaker."

"As a starting point for our discussion, I would first like to go over the highlights of the crime as I think it occurred."

Daniels went on to outline his vision of how it had all happened. According to documents and the testimony released during the investigation, on March 8th, 2011, at about seven in the morning, in one of the very highly protected rooms of the CIA headquarters, five people gathered to review several prepared texts, along with the very latest news and field dispatches. They boiled each item down to the essence of its story, then selected the most critical ones. These items would become the points of the PDB.

The process took a bit over half an hour and, when complete, the selected texts were entered into a special computer which the group would view to make their final edits. On March 8th, the first item received particularly careful attention as it centered on the details of a joint military CIA plan to capture or kill the number one man on the "most wanted terrorists" list. Several lengthy pieces were condensed by the group into half a page of facts, and then they composed the leading sentence. The uniqueness of this sentence later became central to the investigation, as it showed the origin of the leaked information could only have been the same PDB.

Daniels went on to describe the rest of the process. Once all the items had been reviewed and were ready to be sent to the president, one of the group pushed a button, and the text disappeared, leaving only a signature box. Using a special stylus, someone signed as the "Originator." A second message then came on the screen saying, "Awaiting Release."

At this point, the original group of five had completed their task, but they had to wait until the designated VIP released the text for transmission to the president. For this step in the process, the releasing officer would come to the same machine and identify himself not only with a badge, but also with a hand scan, a retinal scan, and a password. With this completed, the PDB text again appeared. He would read it and, if there were no questions or changes, sign, approve and release the document for transmission. With all this completed, the group members would carefully deposit their notes and documents into a safe-like container marked "Classified Waste" and depart.

By then the document would only have been seen by six people, and no copy remained viewable. Now it could only be accessed by one person, the president. His uniquely constructed tablet, activated by several biometrics, would come to life only when the president himself held it in his hands. Once active, he could select several communication actions from the screen. Touching the block labeled "PDB" sent a message to the CIA, triggering the transmission.

"Of course, we in the media were not privy to any of the classified discussions concerning how the message made its way to its destination, but as the investigations proceeded, it seemed more and more apparent to me the leaked information had to have been extracted from the system sometime after the release of the PDB but before the president received it. In other words, someone had to have listened in on the stream of transmitted data.

"With regard to the six people, my opinion, as well as the opinion of all the other investigating groups, was that their credentials, work records, polygraph interview reports, and sworn testimonies cleared them of suspicion. And I can't believe the president himself would do such a thing. All this led me to the initial hypothesis involving the Chinese or the Russian governments. With the authorized people essentially eliminated from suspicion, the only way the message could have been acquired had to have been through a breech in the data stream as it traveled electronically from the machine to the president.

"Signals intelligence experts testified about capturing this particular data, saying it might be possible but not a job for an amateur. It would take some world-class technicians with heavy-duty computers to extract any message from the equipment. Finding the leaker, then, seemed a choice among the six people who wrote it and someone or some group, even some government, who had immense technical capabilities. I believe the six were innocent, and I completely trust the president. So my best guess is the Chinese or the Russians. They both have the technical capabilities...well, perhaps the Iranians do too. They all have extremely effective computer and cryptanalytic people."

Seth thought for a moment, wishing he could mention the unique protection only Pyramid could give the data it carried.

"Of course," Daniels continued, "if the Russians were really able to break into the most secure data we have and read messages as sensitive as the PDB, why wouldn't they just keep doing it while keeping their processes very closely guarded? It's hard to believe they would let us know and pass up a major new source unless, of course, they had acquired it through a collection fluke or set of impossible-to-recreate technical events. In this case, making their acquisition public at least assured them we would discontinue using it.

"For the moment, let's assume the system performed as advertised and provided total security. Let's also assume none of the six people involved in its writing, or the president, leaked the data. Doesn't leave us with much to go on, does it? This is the main reason I wanted to speak with you. You, Martin…er… Seth, are said to know the processes better than anyone. I've been told you developed the concept and created the entire Pyramid system. Do you have any idea how someone else could have gotten their hands on this message?"

Seth found himself intuitively cringing at the sensitivity of the discussion, even the use of its classified code word, but he needed to give Daniels an answer. Mentally reviewing the inner workings of the system, he began, "I agree with your logic so far, Mr. Daniels, but I would stake my life on the security of those messages once they were in the data stream. In the year and a half prior to it being put into use, we produced thousands of test messages and gave them to the best computer, crypto, and code experts our country has. No one could read even one. The path from the PDB writers to the president, however, isn't quite as simple as you describe it. You make it sound like the console used to edit and control this document is securely connected directly to the president's tablet, but that's not exactly the case."

At this point, Seth again found himself wrestling with his desire to help identify the leaker and his obligations not to reveal any national security information. "Look, I'm bound by law and ethics not to tell you anything about how the system works. I can't even legally say the name of the project, even though you seem to know it." Seth continued with sincere emphasis, "But I, just like you, despise the leak of government secrets and very much want to see the person who did this locked up, their methods exposed, and a fine system put back into service. So I must ask you to please leave my name out of any discussions where system details may be involved."

Seth confirmed Daniels's description as being essentially correct but technically incomplete. What Daniels didn't know, and what hadn't been mentioned in the investigation, was the fact that after its release, the PDB passed electronically into a highly secure communications switching area. Here it waited until the president requested its transmission, at which time it left the building to find him wherever on the planet he happened to be. Seth explained this area, called a communications room, had been dismissed by the investigators as an unimportant place where hundreds of wires and fiber-optic cables got connected to hundreds of other wires and fiber-optic cables. A room built like a bank vault with access uniquely controlled so no one could enter alone or without valid reason.

"Not many people ever go in there, or really care about the communications room. It's commonly thought of as just a big junction box. Most of what is in there allows technicians to reroute any telephone, computer, or video feed quickly and easily to a new location anywhere in the building, anytime someone decides to play musical chairs with the office space."

"Got the picture," Daniels responded, "'junction box' rings a bell. We have a similar setup down at the paper, which we fondly call the telephone closet. The only time anyone goes in there is when office space is being rearranged."

"Exactly, but at the CIA, there are much more sophisticated communication systems, indeed, some unique and highly classified, that could be accessed there. Some, like the one we're talking about, even contain processing equipment. The common belief, however, is the signals, images, and data passing through this room are just ones and zeros transiting wires which, in most cases, is correct. With *this* system, however, one final bit of processing goes on inside the communications vault. It's there the message is actually encoded and injected into the secure data stream."

"Are you saying someone might be able to electronically intercept the message in clear text between the 'composing' computer and this very secure data stream by which it would ultimately be transmitted?"

"No. To intercept it electronically at that point is a literal impossibility, as the connection between the two boxes is a wire only nineteen feet long, and it is shielded. So no data passing through it can radiate a signal that could be intercepted, and the transfer takes only a nanosecond or two. After the message has been released for transmission, there is no copy whatsoever in the composition computer. Instead, the message is stored in the security of the communications vault as it waits to be transmitted. Of course, there is a very remote possibility someone could access the message file while it's sitting there waiting, before the president pushes the button requesting its transmission."

"I never heard about this room or its function during the investigation," Daniels said. "Everyone just assumed all the magic went on in the machinery at the composition console and only wires or radio waves or whatever carried it between there and the president's tablet."

Seth continued, "The motivation for this arrangement is security. We wanted the waiting message, as well as recorded copies of all messages, to be stored in a highly secure vault, instead of the composition room where others, even highly cleared others, could possibly have access."

Daniels nodded his understanding and concurrence.

"Without getting more technical about it," Seth added, "you can see the only place where this message could have been stolen is inside the communications vault. But for this to occur, several independent, major failures had to have taken place, the dual-access requirement and the locked vault door to begin with. Even if entry were possible, the thief would need a special password and knowledge of the equipment to locate the message, not to mention the very short window of opportunity.

"All this came out in the classified sessions of the investigation, where an FBI investigator testified the log for the communications room showed no entry between March fourth, 2011, at four seventeen p.m. and March tenth, 2011, at twelve twenty-five p.m. The guard's log supported this, showing a locked condition at every regular hourly check during that period. In simple terms, while the message remained there, no one even came close to having access to it."

Seth paused. He knew he was walking a very fine line. With his heart beating nineteen to the dozen, he continued, "I believe in this system. It didn't fail," he said with absolute conviction, "and I believe the six people involved had nothing to do with the leak. In my opinion, someone somehow gained access to the communications room between the release of the message at seven forty-four a.m. and its transmission to the president at seven fifty-seven a.m. During this time, the intruder accessed the box and copied the file."

Seth watched Daniels closely as the impact of all this new information began to sink in.

"But if this communications vault access is so difficult, how could someone get in there alone, undocumented, and unnoticed?"

Seth sipped his drink and answered slowly, "Following the investigation, many thought the whole process had somehow been corrupted by an unseen, very high-level, influential person. High-level enough, in fact, to protect individuals, or even bias judgments. If that's the case, anyone in such a position could probably arrange for a door to be left unlocked or a guard to be gone—even on the seventh floor of CIA headquarters."

Seth briefly debated how far he should go, but now, it seemed, he had nothing to lose. *In for a penny, in for a pound* he thought. *All the best brains in Washington have investigated this leak, and whoever did it is still running around free as a bird. Someone needs to pay for what they did and for ruining my life in the bargain.*

He picked up the narrative, "The best computer people in the CIA and the FBI have been over all the machines involved, including the one in the communications room. They found nothing showing any access during the time when this message must have been stolen. However, I believe there just might be evidence they missed. It's a long shot, but if I'm correct, I think I could prove who did it."

"And how exactly would you do that?"

"The remote possibility exists that some of the validation circuits we used during testing may have remained in place. I'm not certain, but I could find out, and if they are there, they might contain a clue."

"And how do you propose to find out?"

"A friend of mine at NSA helped with the system testing and validation. I could ask him. If any of the special validation circuitry exists, and he agrees with my assumption, the real problem becomes getting access to the machine. Even if data identifying the thief is there, I don't think the agency would let me in to check! And if they did, their security office would certainly be heavily involved. Remember, if my theory is correct and someone really got into the vault undetected and unauthorized, the security office had to have been involved in some way. If there is additional data in there, it needs to be extracted carefully and in a way which preserves its authenticity and, to my way of thinking, without the knowledge of the security office. Most importantly, the fewer people who know, the better, until it's all put together."

Once more, a quiet settled over the conversation. Seth then asked, "Scott Young tells me you have had contact with the DCI on several occasions over the years. Do you suppose you could get a private word with him under the cover of an interview?"

"That's a pretty tall order!" a surprised Daniels responded, hesitating again for a moment. "You think the thief is your buddy Edwin Henderson, don't you?"

"Damn right, I do!"

"And with the help of CIA security."

"Yes."

* * *

The two men contemplated what had been discussed. Daniels thought he might be able to come up with a way to put a word in the director's ear. "A couple of weeks ago, my editor came up with an idea for a series of articles covering the cause and effect of changes in the CIA mission over the past twenty years. I've been given the assignment, and a request has already been submitted for me to interview the DCI." He paused. "Tell you what, I'll do what I can to get a private word with him."

"Great! Perfect, Mr. Daniels. And I will do what I can to confirm my suspicion about the equipment. I guess the DCI is the level we need to go to get approval for what I'm suggesting."

"I also subscribe to the theory of some high-level inside influence," Daniels continued, "both to get the thief to the material and to affect the outcome of the investigations. The security office certainly has the tools to get someone in unnoticed. Along the same line, I've put in an official request, under the Freedom of Information Act, for a listing of all incoming and outgoing nonsecure phone calls made by several of the heavies on the seventh floor—including security. If it's approved, the information may also help to identify someone on the inside."

Changing the subject, Daniels asked Seth what he knew about Edwin or Norma Henderson and if he had any clues as to why Henderson had just picked up and left so close to retirement.

"You know, we worked in the same office," Seth began, "and on the same project. He worked well, but in time the whole thing got beyond his ability. He began contributing less and less, until finally, the boss took him off the project and put him on another job. I continued to work on it with the brilliant help of Smitty Walker, and about two years later, it passed its final tests and went online. They gave me a big award which really pissed Ed off since Smitty got mentioned but Ed didn't. After Ed stopped working on the project, we saw very little of each other, apart from a chance passing in the corridor.

"Early on, we socialized a bit, but he and Norma had a volatile relationship. I knew Norma fairly well and can completely believe the story of her having an affair. She is one self-assured, very sexy woman. Ed isn't the most engaging of guys, and I doubt he paid Norma the attention she needed and deserved.

"A few months before the leak, he hired a private investigator who, I understand, provided absolute evidence of her affair.

No names were ever mentioned, and when the investigation put Ed in the spotlight, the FBI looked into it but dismissed it as being irrelevant to the case. It all kind of died. I believe she may well have been bedding some very influential person and used potential exposure of their affair as leverage to somehow protect Ed. He's in England now I understand."

Yes that's correct. You're pretty sure he's the leaker, aren't you?"

"I think it has to be him. I don't trust the man, and I'm happy at least he's no longer working in our old office. He may have done it just out of spite for me receiving the award. I don't believe he should be trusted with any sensitive information, and I don't think he should be trusted in his job for Sir Reginald Wilson's new operation either."

"You know it took a couple of months to locate Henderson in London, but until Scott Young came along, I hadn't a clue about what had happened to Martin Steele. Care to tell me what *he's* been doing since he left?"

Seth answered slowly, "I left as a mental basket case on the edge of killing myself. The project which I'd put my heart and soul into for several years had been scrapped. I'd been accused of malfeasance, and even when they decided I hadn't been involved, the harassment just went on and on."

Seth stopped as the horrors of those days flashed through his mind with painful clarity. "I got to the point where I just couldn't take any more. Then, when the rumors went around of a high-level move to pin a treason charge on me, something snapped. I quit my job, packed a bag I could easily carry, and left town. I just wandered around for three or four days. Can't even remember where I went. I checked into cheap motels and tried to figure out the best way to end it all.

"Then one day I saw this picture of Patrick McDermott on a TV screen in a shop window, and it got me thinking. He just disappeared while out fishing in 2005. I thought, why not? I'm pretty sure I could just 'disappear' if I really wanted to. So I headed north. Got talking to someone on a bus and ended up with a job on a fishing boat in Maine. Funny the fishing connection!" Seth paused, as Daniels simply shook his head.

"No one knew me. No one bothered me. No one asked any questions. No one judged me. No responsibilities. I just made it up as I went along. Changed my name. Lived from hand to mouth. But I was forever looking over my shoulder. I needed to get farther away, further isolated. So I took a ride out into the Atlantic and ended up on Sandaray Island. Got a job on another lobster boat. Found a place to stay and gradually regained my sanity. Eventually, I realized I had to address what had happened and set the record straight. And along the way, I met Scott Young. He seemed like a good guy so I asked him for help. There's a lot more to the story, of course, but here we are. Here I am."

The seed of an idea to get Seth into the communications vault continued to germinate in Daniels's mind. He thanked Seth for the information and pledged the secrecy of its source, as well as Martin Steele's location and identity.

Seth's mind now turned to his friend at the NSA.

* * *

Back in his room, Seth went straight to the telephone, and with the assistance of the front-desk clerk, got the phone number of a former colleague and friend near Baltimore.

A female voice answered, "Hello."

"Hello, my name is Martin Steele and I'm looking for Fletcher Richardson. Do I have the right number?"

"You do. Just a moment, please."

"Marty! How the heck are you? Haven't heard from you for ages."

"Yes, it's been a very long time. Are you, Lucy, and the children doing okay?"

"Sure, we're all fine. But this is a surprise. Something up?"

"Look, Fletch, I need to speak with you privately. Is there any chance you might be free sometime tomorrow?

"Sure, you hit it perfectly. I'm off for two more days. Where? When?"

Seth explained he could probably catch the shuttle flight to Baltimore's BWI airport, arriving the next morning at 8:54 a.m. Fletch agreed to be at the coffee shop near the American Airlines ticket counter at nine thirty.

With the meeting arranged, the combination of excitement and exhaustion brought Seth deep sleep in less than five minutes.

* * *

The packed but short flight from Boston departed and arrived on time. Seth hurried to the appointed meeting spot, reminding himself that Fletcher Richardson, with whom he had worked for more than a year, knew him only as Martin Steele. The two of them had developed and completed the many tests that validated the function and demonstrated the effectiveness of the Pyramid communication system.

Richardson, a top-of-the-line computer expert, could design and build anything in the IT world. In his job with the NSA, he evaluated the purpose and capability of 'acquired' hardware, particularly foreign cryptographic and communications systems. He had the reputation of being someone who could get into the very bowels and brains of a system and uncover its vulnerabilities. Working together, they studied the Pyramid schematics and data flow diagrams, and then, by using very sophisticated, sometimes handmade testing apparatus, exercised every individual function in the machine, proving its proper functioning. Their final testing involved sending thousands of messages through and delivering the encrypted data to other NSA experts to see if they could decipher it. The whole process had taken just over twelve months. During those months, an intense and genuine mutual respect had grown between them.

"It's good to see you again, Fletch. You're looking great."

"You, too, Marty. You look just the same as the last time we met, except for the tan and the beard!"

They took their coffee to the most isolated place they could find, and Seth got right to the point.

"Several times during our project together, we installed process-monitoring devices, so we could watch the progress of a message passing through the system or record data for investigation out of real time. They let us keep track of exactly how all the processes were working. These monitoring devices clearly had no effect at all on the machine's functions and when we had completed the testing, we removed them."

"Yes, I remember the project and the monitors we installed."

"You proved yourself a master diagnostician, as well as a most skilled electronics mechanic. If you recall, during the validation process, we made several significant changes to the software, the firmware, and even the hardware. The point I'm trying to make is that, during those months we worked together, it became clear if anything ever failed within the system, and my organization asked your organization to help repair it, you would certainly get the call. Those months of testing also showed you were a really careful and thorough worker.

"For the past year, I've thought about the system and about you. Now I need to ask you if any of your testing devices got left in the box when it finally went into service."

"Martin, you should know me better! I would never do such a thing."

"I'm dead serious here, Fletch. I know your talent and abilities, as well as your methods, and I have the greatest respect for them and for you. We both know the project would never have succeeded without the efforts of you and your organization. But I also know you and I were working for quite different agencies with different objectives. We also both know an unwritten, unsaid code makes each of us put the interests of our own organization above all others."

Fletcher looked a little uneasy as Seth continued. "The project left your lab and went online, but then, almost immediately, somehow failed. I'm sure you must have read about it. The bottom line is…I'm now a fisherman, and somewhere out there is the thieving bastard who torpedoed it all by sending some things, processed by the system, to the news media. This became a massive embarrassment to my old organization, particularly months later, after the FBI and Congress both failed to find the person responsible."

"Yes. We heard about the big investigation on the news from time to time. I also heard your name, but it all stopped more than a year ago. Seems to me they couldn't prove any particular person did it, so they just blamed it all on the technology, isn't that just the way? So, what happened to make you take up fishing?"

"I'd love to share the story with you, but it has to wait for another day. Look, I'm asking you about the monitors. I've had a long time to think about all of this, and I'm pretty damn sure the theft must have occurred while the message was awaiting transmission in the processing box. I'm absolutely convinced no one intercepted the data downstream.

"That leaves either the originators or the receiver, and evidence, plus testimony, rule them out, at least in most people's minds. The security folk at my former place of work, as well as the FBI, are absolutely convinced no one could have been near the box during the processing of the leaked message. I think they're wrong, but I need a way to prove it.

"Fletch, please tell me, are you absolutely sure you left nothing in there that would tell us what went on in the box, in a way only you could ever have access to it?" Fletcher held his cup in both hands, alternately sipping and staring out through the large windows of the concourse.

"What you're asking is, did I hide some secret recording device inside your equipment, which might now contain information relating to the data lost back in 2011?"

"Yes," Seth replied in a very serious tone, "and if you did, its significance goes way beyond any interagency one-upmanship. It could lead us to a treasonous insider who worked in my old organization."

Fletcher tore a page from a small notebook, wrote down two sets of characters, and handed it to Martin. "On the main board of the J module, there is a chip labeled 'J1279.' It looks just like the one you soldered in there way back at the start. But it's not the same chip. I replaced it right at the beginning of our testing with an identical-looking one, so you couldn't tell it had been altered. Log on and search for an executable file named 'Fh_lark.' Executing the file will bring up a password box. Enter the first set of characters and another password box will appear. This is the critical one, as you have only fifteen seconds to enter the second password correctly. What you'll then see is the activity log beginning about the time you brought the thing to our lab, right up to today."

"My God, I knew it! I knew someone as careful and thorough as you would have some silent thing just watching every second.

This could be a real lifesaver. Thank you, Fletch. Thank you. I know this is the key to finding the leaker."

"Guess I'm just getting old, Marty, because I had fully intended to remove the thing before you came to pick up the box. But when departure day arrived, it just slipped my mind. Later, I debated calling you to tell you about it but decided to keep it a secret. Since the chip had absolutely no effect on the box's operation, no one else could ever access or use it. And, as you imply, if it ever came back to NSA because of suspected tampering, it would spotlight the jabroni who did the tampering in a millisecond."

"I can't thank you enough, Fletch. Of course, all I have to do now is get access to the box."

"Good luck, my friend."

"When this all sorts itself out, I'll certainly be in touch."

They shook hands with genuine sincerity and parted.

Later in the evening, Seth returned to Maine, and at ten the following morning was all strapped in ready to fly back to Sandaray.

Chapter Eighteen

Alex had been a full-time pilot with the Air Service for almost eight years and had learned to expect the unexpected—usually unpredicted weather or last-minute changes to the route or passenger list. Today fit the model exactly. Just as he had started the engine to leave for Sandaray, his cell phone had rung with a message to return to the terminal building to collect an additional passenger. And a very attractive Burberry trolley bag. Uplifting the bag, Alex glanced back into the terminal building but the extra passenger had not yet finished checking in. He loaded the luggage and proceeded around to the pilot's door to update his passenger. "I'm sorry," he said, "we're just waiting for one more."

Being unconcerned and in no hurry, Seth turned back to watch the maintenance being done on a fancy private jet off to their right. Eventually, the passenger climbed in next to him and almost immediately, they were on their way. As they taxied, she removed her scarf and turned to face Seth.

"At last…I didn't think I'd make it! Kevin's guys are the best, they are really accommodating …" Seth's head spun round at the unmistakable sound of Linda's voice. "Well, if it isn't Mister Seth Martin! Indeed, this is double good fortune."

Completely taken aback, Seth managed to get his words out just as Alex throttled up to taxi onto the runway. "Linda! Wow! What are you doing here? When did you get in?"

Linda could only mouth her reply as Alex applied full power for takeoff.

Once they were comfortably airborne and the noise level had decreased, Linda turned to Seth. "Got into New York yesterday and flew up here this morning. Didn't think I'd get out to the island until tomorrow, but, hey, here I am. Got a text from the Air Service saying they had a seat open on a plane just ready to leave for Sandaray. They gave me five minutes. Luckily, I only had to walk two hundred feet from the commercial terminal, didn't even have to run. I don't have a whole lot of time here, and I want to surprise Dad. He doesn't even know I'm on this side of the Atlantic!"

"Well, you certainly surprised me. How are you doing? How do you like London?"

"It's very different from life out here, of course, but I'm slowly beginning to adjust." She added Sir Reginald had planned a three-day visit to New York to give Blackstock and Henderson a conglomerate overview. She had flown over in advance to have two weeks on the island and to catch up, particularly with her father. She would then travel back to New York to be there when Sir Reg and the others arrived, and after the orientation, she would join the group to travel back to London in Sir Reg's private jet.

Noise made conversation difficult in the back seat of the Cessna 206, and even with raised voices, they had to lean in close. Seth expected the conversation difficulties, but not Linda's hand gently resting on his thigh.

A moment of quiet followed their exchange of general news. She moved even closer, her lips almost touching his ear. "I can't get over what happened. You turned my life upside down, you know. Where do you think we go from here?"

The warmth of her hand, the faint aroma of her perfume,

and the very closeness of her body were all seriously interfering with his thinking.

"Do you think there is a 'we'?" he asked.

"Do you want there to be?"

"It's wrong, Linda. You have Dan. Your dad is my boss. Our particular 'we' just can't and shouldn't exist."

"But facts are facts, and I know what I feel," she added quickly. "I think you feel something for me as well…don't you?"

"I do, but the way things are, it's a losing situation for everyone involved." Seth took her hand in his and leaned back.

They sat, unsure what else to say, as the plane began its descent to Sandaray.

Alex parked in the usual spot and shut off the engine. But even before the propeller had stopped turning, Bill Harris's pickup truck appeared by the left wing. Alex jumped out and asked, "Ya got three passengers for me, Bill?"

"Well, yes and no, Alex. They weren't ready to leave when you flew over, so I thought I'd come by anyway, let you know, and see if anyone else needed a ride. I'll take Linda and Seth now and be back with the others, okay?"

"Sure, no worries."

While Bill and Alex conversed, Linda and Seth deplaned, gathered their luggage, and headed over toward the pickup hopeful of a lift at least part of the way. Bill explained he didn't have time to get Seth down to the harbor but he would be happy to take them both as far as Linda's. They thanked him and put their bags and themselves in the back of the truck. The two-mile ride seemed long, noisy, and dusty, but it clearly beat walking.

Standing on the path outside Linda's house, Seth picked up his bag and turned to face her. "I'd better start down the road, Linda. It's been lovely seeing you again."

"Surely you're not in such a big rush. Come on in, and I'll make us some coffee."

Seth thought a long moment, debating between what he should do and what he increasingly wanted to do. Linda fumbled with her purse, looking for the house key.

What the heck. A cup of coffee with a friend is okay.

Carrying both bags, he followed her up the path to the house.

Seth deposited the luggage by the door while Linda headed straight to the kitchen. As he walked along the hallway, he looked into the dining room, remembering the Thanksgiving dinner with its delightful food but unforgettable acid rhetoric. Approaching the kitchen, he paused momentarily in the doorway to observe this beautiful and bewitching woman. He watched as she set out mugs. An electric coffee pot began percolating vigorously. He quietly came up behind her and put his hands around her waist. She stopped, acknowledging, accepting, and delighting in his touch. His hands soon moved farther around her, gently rubbing her midriff, his inner urges growing rapidly. In a moment, his hands were gently caressing her breasts. He kissed the back of her neck, and felt her shudder under his touch.

Sliding the coffee tray well away, she turned to take his face in her hands. Their lips met, warm, moist, wanting. She took his hand and led him toward the living room. Frantically discarding a minimum of clothing, she pulled him onto the couch. He entered her quickly, and they moved together with desperate, wild, all-consuming passion. Very soon ecstasy exploded mutually and completely. They lay, holding on to each other.

What now? Seth wondered. *Why did this feel so absolutely perfect, so right? Why is she wasting her life thousands of miles away with a man who cares more for himself than he does for her?*

He gently kissed the top of her head, and she turned to look up at him. A broad smile spread across her face, "Interested in coffee now?"

* * *

At the airport, Bill's passengers were finally boarding, and the plane was almost ready to go. Suddenly another truck roared up the dusty road. JB jumped out carrying two small boxes. "Hey, Alex, wait up! Do you have room these? Someone from Johnson's will pick 'em up and give you two others to bring out next time you're over. I got the steering all taken apart this morning and guess what, they've given me the wrong damn parts."

"No problem, JB," Alex said as he stowed the boxes.

In less than a minute, the plane was airborne again and heading back to the mainland.

* * *

For a moment, Bill and JB stood and watched the plane climb and turn north. They both began to walk to their trucks.

"You must be real happy Linda's back," Bill said.

"Linda's here?" JB replied in a questioning tone. "That's news to me!"

"Yes, I gave them a ride to the house a little less than an hour ago."

"Well, that's the modern generation for you. No phone call. They just show up. Must be the way of the big city, I guess." Shaking his head, JB returned to his truck, somewhat bemused.

Linda and Seth sat very close sipping their coffee. Linda began mumbling about some fancy gym she had joined in London, but Seth interrupted her somewhat brusquely. "Linda, look it's all really interesting but can I just stop you for a second.

I need to tell you something. Something really important—*really* important."

Taken aback at his sudden change in mood, Linda paused. "Oh, okay. Shoot."

"This is serious, and I need you to do something."

She put down her coffee and gave him her full attention.

"I need you to warn Sir Reginald about his new security chief over there."

"What, Ed Henderson?"

"Yes. He's a disloyal, unethical, and possibly very dangerous person who shouldn't be in such a position of responsibility. Tell Dan he needs to watch the guy closely."

At first, Linda expressed disbelief but admitted she had seen a slightly unpleasant and weird side to the man, even though they had only met socially.

"Dan works with him every day and seems to think he's God's gift to the security of the Wilson Companies."

"Oh yes, he's very believable, but mark my words, Linda, he's a rotten apple, and unless I miss my guess, he'll be in jail, where he belongs, sometime soon."

"Seth, that's pretty strong stuff. Are you absolutely sure?"

"Totally. He has a history. I can't tell you everything just yet. It's complicated. Just warn Sir Reg and Dan, okay?"

"Sure, I'll say something if I get the chance, but I don't imagine it'll go down well."

As their conversation turned to lighter subjects, Linda began tracing patterns with her finger on his chest. She expanded the area of exploration downward and discovered once more, and to her delight, his very aroused condition. As they became increasingly absorbed in each other, neither heard the sound of a vehicle pulling up to the front of the house nor of the front door opening.

"Hello, Linda? Dan? Are you here?" JB looked first in the kitchen and then the living room. His initial disbelief instantly turned to horror and disgust as he moved toward them. "What the hell is going on here?" he bellowed making straight for Seth. "You son of a bitch! Get away from her. Let go of her. You son of a bitch!"

In a flash, JB lunged toward him, grabbing Seth's arm and jerking him to his feet with one powerful pull. In virtually the same motion, JB freed his right hand and backhanded Seth with the power of a sledgehammer. The blow spun Seth violently away, loosening his arm from JB's grip. JB came toward him again. This time, Linda jumped to her feet and without a thought, flung herself between the two men, arms flailing, trying to separate them.

"Stop it, stop it, *stop it*, for God's sake!"

JB stumbled and landed awkwardly on a small table next to the couch, crushing it to the floor beneath him. He turned his head to see Seth grab his clothes and bag and bolt for the door. JB pulled himself up but knowing he had no chance of getting his hands on Seth again, screamed at the top of his voice, "Now get your ass out of this house, get your shit out of my fish house, and get off this island before the sun sets, or you're a dead man, Seth Martin! *Get out of here now!*"

In a flash, Seth bolted out the front door and ran full tilt across the lawn. At the tree line, he stopped to wipe away the blood trickling from the corner of his mouth. Keeping an eye on the house, he got himself dressed.

He saw JB come to the door, still shouting. "Keep going, you son of a bitch, and don't ever come back here. Don't you ever touch my Linda again!"

* * *

Closing the door and returning to his daughter, JB seethed, "As for you, Linda, get yourself dressed. I'm ashamed of you. You should be ashamed of yourself. You're a married woman. You've taken vows! I can't believe you did this. What would your mother have thought?"

Linda moved toward him, but he continued, "I don't want you anywhere near me. In fact, I don't want any more to do with you! You hear me? Nothing! Ever!"

"You hurt him, Dad," Linda whispered, "I saw blood."

"If he hadn't slipped out of my grip, I would have beaten the bastard to a pulp, and by now, he would be just where he belongs…dead, not running across your lawn!" JB stomped out of the house, slamming the door behind him.

As he drove down the road, tears filled his eyes and a terrible pain welled up in his chest. *How am I ever going to survive this? How can I live without Linda?* he thought, sobbing.

Seth watched from a hiding place in the woods, happy he had not chosen to start down the road until JB had passed.

* * *

Back at the fish house, he washed out his mouth, examining the cut his teeth had made in his tongue. At least, it had stopped bleeding, though it would be a while before it stopped hurting. He quickly packed all his belongings into the old duffel bag and the one suitcase he now had, left the door key on the kitchen table, and beat a hasty path over to the ferry terminal. There would be no ferry until Tuesday, but just in case someone might be going in, he walked along the wharf, looking around.

No luck. Not a single fishing boat had docked, and the only boat moving around in the harbor was the *Fair Morn*. He turned back toward the terminal and noticed a man, woman, and two children coming around the corner of the building and starting out to the wharf. Despite the excruciating pain in his jaw and mouth and acutely aware his appearance must be pretty off-putting, he ventured over to talk to them in case it might lead to a ride to the mainland. "Hi, I'm Seth. You folks going in by any chance?"

The man answered, "We are. My cousin's Ronnie Moody. He's going to take us into town. You want a ride?"

"I do. You think I could tag along?"

"I'm sure he won't mind an extra passenger. Come on. Actually…are you okay, buddy? Looks like you've been in a spot of bother."

"Oh, just a bit of a scrape, but I'm fine. A lift would be perfect." *Boy am I a lucky man, in more ways than one.*

In twenty minutes, they were all loaded aboard the *Fair Morn*, bound for Rockland.

Seth thanked Ronnie for letting him come along and immediately went aft to be out of the family's way and to be alone with his thoughts. Feeling sick to his stomach, he stood in the stern, looking back, reliving the last few hours. *You complete asshole. Just look what you've gone and done now!*

Seth had come to know JB well during the past year and thanked his lucky stars his boss had not had a gun. If he had, Seth would certainly be a dead man. He watched as Sandaray began to shrink in the distance. *What a fuckin' mess! Poor Linda. I've wrecked things between her and her dad. Don't imagine Dan will be very bothered, though. Actually, come to think of it, if anyone deserves to be chased by someone with a gun, it's him! They say he's had a hundred women for every man she's been with.* Conceding no one ever described life as being fair, Seth tried to put thoughts of Linda aside and focus instead on what to do next.

As he stepped onto the floating dock at Johnson's Marina, he turned to the skipper.

"Thanks, Ronnie. You're a life saver."

"Any time, my friend. See ya back on the island."

Seth could only wonder if that would ever happen again.

With no idea of what to do or where to go, he eventually found a cab and asked the driver to take him downtown to the only place he could think of, the *Courier* office. He hoped someone would be there despite it being late Sunday afternoon. No such luck.

Suddenly craving a cold beer, he wandered up toward the Pepper Mill café.

"Bud Light please," he said to the guy behind the counter, and remembering they had a pay phone, added, "Could I get some change as well, whatever it takes to make a local call?" Seth put a five-dollar bill on the counter, and in a moment, the drink and several coins replaced it.

"It'll cost you fifty cents."

"Thanks."

At the pay phone, Seth dialed Scott Young's cell phone number.

"Hello, Scott here."

"Hi, Scott. This is Seth Martin. I'm in town and need a big favor. Can we meet?"

"Son-of-a-gun, I thought you planned to be back on Sandaray by now. I actually need to speak with you as well, so yes, let's meet. Where are you now?"

"I'm at the Pepper Mill. Give me some directions, and I'll walk over."

"Okay. It's pretty simple, but it'll take you fifteen or twenty minutes. Just head up Main Street until you get to the light, turn right, come up the hill as far as the school, and it's the building directly opposite. I'm on the third floor. You'll see my name on the door buzzer."

It took Seth just over ten minutes to get there.

Sitting in his small, uncluttered, minimalist apartment overlooking the bay, Scott asked about the meeting with Daniels. Seth relayed the conversation almost word for word, concluding with his belief that the leaked message had been stolen during the thirteen minutes while it waited between release and transmission.

"Right now, Scott, I believe I know where, when, and how someone stole it. The FBI, by the way, has offered proof showing no human had access to the vault when the file must have been taken, but I'm convinced an unauthorized, unrecorded, unwitnessed access occurred, and if I can get to the machine, I think I can prove it."

"I suppose since the PDB is involved, the machinery is locked up like the crown jewels."

"The crown jewels are easier to get to by far than this stuff. Daniels says he has a plan that would get me in. He gives it a fifty-fifty chance of success. We should hear something by next week."

"It sounds like your trip got the ball rolling a bit. I hope it all works and you can get proof on the table of who this treasonous bastard is. But you could have waited on the island till Daniels sent word. What brings you into town on a Sunday evening? Don't you need to be out hauling with JB tomorrow morning?"

"In a word, no."

Seth explained his rapid departure in the most general of terms. "JB has been upset these last few weeks because of me disappearing on short notice. Well, something happened this morning ending my employment with him, so I caught a ride with Ronnie, and now I'm here just to see you, and then head south to Washington."

"Care to share more? Everyone I've talked to said you two were a dynamite team out there, working well together, enjoying each other's company, and bringing in lots of lobsters."

"Suffice to say, JB did what he had to do. He had no choice."

"Well, that's too bad. But you're not going to start down the road tonight, are you?"

"No. I don't think I can face any more traveling right now. I'll find somewhere to stay and be on my way in the morning."

"Hell, stay here, Seth. I keep the extra bedroom made up just for times like this. Come on, I'll show you."

"I'd really like a shower if you don't mind," Seth said as they walked to the spare bedroom.

"Sure. Just make yourself at home. You should have everything you need in there. And take your time. I'll try and figure out what to do for dinner."

Seth felt a surge of relief. At least he had a roof over his head for the night. Hopefully, in the morning, things would look a bit brighter.

Scott suggested they go for dinner at a restaurant just a ten-minute walk away. "The walk will be good for us and we can have a couple of drinks and still get home legally."

Scott had been surprised to see Seth show up like this. It seemed completely inconsistent with his impression of the man. He thought of Seth as a conscientious worker, careful, considered, and organized in his thinking. He wondered what had actually happened back over on the island.

They ordered food, but when it arrived, Seth only picked at his. He seemed much more interested in drowning his sorrows.

At exactly midnight, Scott manhandled a totally hooched up Seth back to the apartment and deposited him, fully clothed, on the spare bed. *I don't fully understand everything he's told me. A lot has to be missing, but something pretty bad has definitely happened.*

The next morning, the two men parted, Scott for a news conference in Augusta and Seth for the local pharmacy and some painkillers. He only had a couple of hours to wait until the bus departed, taking him south to Boston.

* * *

On Sandaray, a morose JB sat at his kitchen table, thinking. He remembered vividly a day long ago when rage and violent thoughts had almost destroyed his marriage, and a shotgun in his wife's hands came near to ending his life. He picked up the phone and dialed Linda's number.

She answered, barely audible, "Hello."

"I know you don't have any food in the house, so get dressed. I'll pick you up in ten minutes."

Like most islanders, JB would usually have opened the door and walked right in, but this time, he hesitated on Linda's doorstep as the memory of the previous afternoon flashed through his head. He reached for the doorknob and then pulled his hand away. Maybe this was a mistake. Maybe they both needed more time. But Linda suddenly appeared in front of him. Coat in hand, she pulled the door to, and they walked in silence to his truck.

Soon they were in his kitchen, and for a long moment, father and daughter simply looked at each other. Then he took her in his strong arms and hugged her as only a father could hug a beloved child. Tears came to his eyes.

Chapter Nineteen

The journey from rural Maine, via Boston, to suburban Washington, DC, on public transportation, consumed just over a day and a half.

By Tuesday afternoon, Seth, his duffel bag, and his small case were settled into a hotel outside the famous multilane circle of concrete that surrounded the nation's capital city, the Washington Beltway. The hotel catered to businesspeople who needed a no-frills room for several nights at a relatively modest price. It suited his needs perfectly.

Seth unpacked his things and dialed Norman Daniels. After five rings, a message came on: "You've reached the telephone of Norman Daniels. I'm sorry to have missed your call. Please leave a message." A beep followed. Seth identified himself and gave the name and phone number of the hotel. That was all the information Daniels would need.

As the afternoon dragged on, the impact of the traumatic event 48 hours earlier combined with a long, not so comfortable bus ride, brought overwhelming tiredness. Seth knew he needed to sleep but all he could do was think about Linda. He picked up the phone and dialed her number. No answer. *God, I hope she's okay. I hope JB hasn't done anything irrational.* He laid down, but with his wide-awake brain focused totally on Linda and last Sunday, he got up, dialed her phone again, paced around the room, dialed once more. Where is she? What's going on back in Maine? Has JB gone after her, maybe injured her? He knew the latter was very unlikely but, at this moment, he felt almost anything was possible. He was living his worst nightmare.

Finally, he decided to take a walk. The warm spring air felt good but the pain produced by his thoughts remained a constant.

Later, back in the hotel room, he phoned her again ... and again. By ten thirty PM, after trying at least twenty times, exhaustion overcame him and he slipped into a deep sleep.

At ten minutes past midnight, the phone he was still cradling gave an explosive ring. He jumped up, accidentally casting it onto the floor. Quickly, with his heart pounding, he located the handset and shouted into it, "Linda, Linda, is that you?" But it wasn't Linda.

* * *

During the previous two weeks, Daniels had immersed himself in everything he could find relating to CIA policies and actions over the past twenty years. In addition to reading a mountain of documents, he set up a meeting with the previous director of operations.

His preparation for the interview with Director Malcolm "Mac" Mitchell had been thorough and had included how he might broach the subject of the leak and Martin Steele...assuming they got a private moment or two. He would use the opportunity to quietly tell Mitchell about new information which had come to light about the events of March 8th. Hopefully, this would lead to an expanded conversation and ultimately the okay to allow Steele access to the Pyramid box.

Then, realizing the improbability of a private word, he decided to formulate a backup plan. The idea came quite quickly. He would take with him a copy of his latest book, appropriately autographed for the DCI. Inside, he would place a sealed envelope marked

"Eyes Only—Mac Mitchell." The note would be as succinct as possible explaining how he had spoken with Martin Steele and become convinced the evidence identifying the leaker might still exist within the Pyramid system. Acquiring such evidence would, of course, take DCI authorization. Finally, he would suggest a private, perhaps covert, meeting with Steele to explain it further.

When the day of the interview came, Daniels arrived at the security building outside the CIA headquarters compound at the appointed time. He passed through the usual visitor inspection routine, metal detector and briefcase inspection. No cell phone, check; no tape recorder, check; no camera, check. Once completed, a young security officer came to escort him to the meeting. They drove through a wooded area into what looked very much like a modern industrial campus where parking lots, buildings, and roads were separated by small, well-groomed lawns with immaculately trimmed shrubs.

A circular drive led to a large, seven-story building with a grand ceremonial entrance. But they continued on until they reached a ramp leading down into a VIP basement parking area. From there, an express elevator transported them to the top floor, and after a short walk, they were in the DCI's anteroom.

The surprisingly small room had only two desks, several chairs for visitors, and two filing cabinets. A lady sitting at the only occupied desk rose to greet them. "Mr. Daniels, welcome. I'm Anna Evans, the director's secretary. He knows you're here, but he's running a couple of minutes late. He won't be long. Please have a seat."

Daniels sat, thinking again about the questions he would use to frame the interview while, at the same time, wondering if his young security escort would be joining them. Soon the door opened, and three men emerged. Without missing a word or a thought in her telephone conversation, the very efficient

Anna Evans nodded to the young security officer, directing him to escort Daniels into the DCI's office. The security man did as instructed and then followed, taking a seat in the corner of the room. Anna entered quickly behind them, collected several files from the DCI's desk, and departed, closing the door behind her.

Mitchell rose and extended his hand. "Nice to see you again, Norman. Please sit down."

The DCI stood an impressive six feet, two inches tall. He sported closely cropped, dark hair graying at the temples and had the most piercing blue eyes Daniels had ever seen. *Natural or tinted lenses?* he mused as they shook hands. Around the walls, impressive photographs and memorabilia told the story of his thirty-one years of service to the agency. They marked him as one of the very few who had ever risen through its ranks to the top position.

With very little preamble, the interview began. The questions were concise, the answers succinct, only twice requiring the response, "I can't talk about that." To both Mitchell and Daniels, the twenty-five minutes passed in a blink.

"You're a good interviewer, Norman, and a hell of a good writer. It's been a pleasure talking with you."

"And with you, too. This has been most helpful."

Placing his copious notes in his briefcase, Daniels added, "Oh, I almost forgot. I've brought you a copy of my latest book. It's my first attempt at fiction. A mystery, but not at all like the kind of mystery you live with here every day. I hope you enjoy it." Passing over "*The Girl from Nowhere*", he added, "Thank you again. I really appreciate your making time for this interview today."

As Daniels and the security officer left, Anna rushed in with a file. "They're gathering in the briefing room, sir. You have five minutes to read this!"

In the anteroom, Daniels handed his notes to the security man to review for possible classified information. Noticing

223

Daniels marking time, Anna went over and asked if he would mind autographing her copy of his new book. They went to her desk, where he signed. "Have you read it yet, Ms. Evans?"

"Just the first three chapters, but it has me hooked. I'm really curious to know who this girl is."

"Well, you'll find out in due course. I hope you enjoy it."

As they were talking, Mitchell came out of his office en route to the conference room. "Thank you again for the book, Norman. I'll be contacting you with my critique!"

The young security officer read through Daniels's notes quickly but carefully. Soon, with the review complete, the two were back in the elevator heading out.

"Forgive me, but we haven't been introduced. I'm Norman Daniels."

"Finlay Morrison," the young man responded. "I'm very pleased to meet you, Mr. Daniels. My girlfriend also has your new novel. I hope she finishes it soon, so I can borrow it. She says it's terrific."

"Thank you, Finlay. I hope you enjoy it, too." Soon the elevator delivered them back to the basement, and in moments, they were driving back toward the security building just outside the campus.

"It's been a while since I visited your headquarters here, but tell me, who introduced this strange policy of reading everyone's notes?"

"Well, it's only been the procedure for the last year and a half, and of course, it only applies to those without a security clearance. The director has always been a real stickler about security, but a couple of years ago, a classified document, one very possibly originating here, got leaked to the press. When the investigation concluded, and no one could be identified as the leaker, he put in about a dozen new policies.

"Today, for example, you might have been sketching the room we were in or the funny-looking model satellite on his desk. It may sound crazy, but on the other hand, the leaked document didn't just grow little feet and walk out all by itself. We look through everyone's briefcases and bags now, even his."

In less than ten minutes, Daniels again found himself negotiating the heavy traffic of the Washington Beltway as he returned to his office.

With no call by six o'clock, Daniels began to wonder whether or not Mitchell had seen the note. *Well, there's always tomorrow, and at least Steele's now in town. Maybe I'll just have to be patient.* But at nine fifty precisely, just as he had decided to turn in for the night, his cell phone rang.

"Norman Daniels speaking."

"I read your note, Norman. Of course, I'm interested. Is M here in the local area?"

"Yes, he is."

"Good. Can you both get to the parking lot at Great Falls Park at twelve thirty tomorrow?"

"Indeed, we can."

"I'll be in a maroon minivan, license plate KFI-9851. We can talk then."

"Excellent. See you there. Good night, Mr. Mitchell."

Daniels called Martin to tell him about the afternoon's meeting and the one now set for the following day. "Your arrival has been very timely Steele. I'll pick you up at quarter to twelve."

"Great," Martin responded, "I'll be ready."

∗ ∗ ∗

The next day brought beautiful weather with a temperature of about seventy-five degrees, no wind, and only a few scattered cumulus clouds overhead. A perfect day to go to the park.

Daniels had planned their trip precisely, and they drove into the parking lot at exactly twelve thirty.

"Over there," Martin said, pointing. "KFI-9851, just by those trees."

Daniels parked, and in less than a minute, the three men were seated comfortably in the back of the minivan. The director spoke first.

"Just so you know, none of what we say is being recorded, but I'm sure you also know we're being watched very closely. There is no need for introductions. I remember Mr. Steele quite well, but this is your meeting, Norman. What's your proposal?"

"The subject is the leak of classified information which occurred on March eighth, 2011. Ever since it happened, I've been interested in the case and have continued looking for additional facts because the who, how, and why of the leak still remain a mystery.

"Now, after talking with Mr. Steele, I believe there may be previously undiscovered technical evidence pointing to what happened and who did it. As you know, Martin developed and created the system to which we're referring. After the leak, you very sensibly took the system out of service and had all the equipment looked over multiple times. However, no evidence of tampering or unauthorized entry ever came to light.

"Steele and two other engineers were investigated over and over, yet even today, no one can say how the message got out. Martin now believes a record exists in a Pyramid processing box that could show additional system activity for the day of the theft. If this data is still there, which Martin believes it is, it could point to the person involved, provided no one has tampered with the hardware, of course."

Mitchell almost exploded, "Oh come on! If such records exist, as you suggest, I can't believe our finest computer security people, the finest crypto people, and the finest FBI guys couldn't find any trace of it during the inquiry. Believe me, they went over and over the whole damn system with a fine-tooth comb. What makes you so sure such a record exists now, two years later?" He paused for a short moment then, pointing an accusing finger at Martin added, "By the way, how come *you* didn't know anything about this during the investigations a year and a half ago?"

Martin replied, "There is a simple reason, let me explain. During the system testing, we moved all the hardware over to the National Security Agency because they have the nation's best capability to break codes and evaluate crypto equipment. We wanted to validate all its processes and see if they could successfully extract a message from the data stream. During testing, one of the NSA guys put data-catching hardware devices into the system to monitor the progress of the encryption and the transmission.

"One of these devices recorded who logged on to the system and some of what they did, so if troubles later developed, they could go back and figure out what happened. When the tests were completed, all the catching devices were supposedly removed and the system returned to where it is today. I never gave it another thought. However, a week ago, an NSA engineer confirmed to me that one of the little catchers is still inside! It's accessible only from the console in the communications vault, and doesn't even appear to exist unless a person knows exactly how to find it.

"Once addressed, a time-sensitive multi-password scheme, known only to the guy who helped in testing the system, kicks in. I've spoken to him, and I now know how to find it and get to its data." Martin paused to let this sink in, then continued, "During the year following the closure of the investigations, I spent a lot of time going over all the facts and virtually rebuilding the system in my head. The data stream concept works, it never failed in testing, and I believe it never failed in actual use. There is just no possible way the message could have been intercepted en route.

"This leaves only two other possibilities: Either one of the six writers or the president leaked it, or someone stole it from the communications vault during the thirteen-minute period when it was awaiting transmission. I believe it to be the latter, but until last week, I had no way to prove it. Now I believe the evidence remains stored in the communications box itself. And I know how to get it out. If I'm correct, we should be able to prove unequivocally someone had access to the console on the morning of March eighth, 2011, no matter what the written security logs show."

Mitchell remained on the defensive. "As I'm sure you are aware, our security people, the FBI, the whole damned lot of them found no evidence of anyone entering the communications vault at any point during that day. Also, what you might not know is that our computer security people spent weeks searching through both the composition console and the communication box, looking for what you now say you can extract. In all their searching, they found nothing."

Martin slumped with disappointment. "You mean they took the machine apart?"

Mitchell quickly responded, "No. They searched using nondestructive methods only. I didn't allow them to disturb its capability, hoping the system itself might eventually supply some answers. I'd ordered it to be taken off-line and left in an operational condition until the culprit had been identified. So no. No dissecting of hardware. At least not yet. The same security guys also spent a lot of time studying the receiving tablet, again with no results."

"If it remained operational but off-line, I'm quite sure I can extract a log file of events," Martin said, "but if they've played around with the hardware, there's just no telling."

"Your argument to get at the box in the communications room is quite compelling, but if you think I can just snap my fingers and allow you in there, you have another thing coming. First off, you have no security clearance. No one knows where you've been or what you've been doing for more than a year now. On top of that, during the investigation, a large amount of admittedly circumstantial evidence pointed to you as the possible thief."

Martin tensed up as he remembered the total humiliation of the investigation and the feeling of being railroaded.

"Second, there are those who will say letting you into the vault would be like letting the fox right into the hen house, perhaps even giving you an opportunity to plant false information linking Walker or Henderson to the theft."

Martin's face flushed in anger. Instinctively he rose, his head hitting the roof of the minivan with a resounding boom. "I'm not a mole or a traitor, Mr. Mitchell. I put a lot of my life into perfecting the Pyramid system. There's no way I would sell it, or our country, down the drain and I guarantee you my name is not in the log for the eighth of March."

Daniels grabbed Martin's arm tightly, restraining him. "Easy, Martin. You have to try to see this situation from his point of view. Remember, you just disappeared for more than a year." A tense silence ensued.

Eventually Mitchell continued, "Steele, I wouldn't be here today if I had any real doubt about your loyalty. So let me tell you how it is...I think you might be on to something. You think the theft happened in the communications vault and that it occurred at a time when all the evidence showed no one could have been in there. This means we had an undetected entry. An entry by someone who knew enough about the system to capture a copy of the PDB and then get out without being noticed by security or anyone else. If that's the case, we not only have a thief to find but also some inside helpers, most likely a person or persons in security."

At this point, Daniels broke in, "I agree, but this gets us onto another thing that has continued to come up and might be very relevant."

Daniels went on to explain how the FBI had always dismissed Norma Henderson's affair as irrelevant in this case. But new information seemed to indicate the man involved may have been a high-level government official. Perhaps, someone at a level high enough up to influence the investigation of her husband, Edwin.

"Norman, are you suggesting Henderson's wife might have blackmailed someone in security to protect her husband?"

"Yes, I am. It's very possible your security office is compromised. It's their people, after all, who guard the vault and monitor its multiple alarm systems, and it's their people who can turn off those alarm systems or ignore them. Remember, Henderson had been an object of the original investigation, and, although no longer part of the Pyramid project at the time, he knew a lot about it and probably still had an access code when the leak happened."

Mitchell squirmed in his chair, "And it's someone from the same security office who would have to sign off on Martin getting into the vault now." He folded his arms, studied the faces of the other two, and thought for a long while. Then he leaned forward and looked directly at Martin. "What you've said is the leak happened because an agency person, helped by other agency people, probably from security, stole a PDB and gave a section of it to the press…and then deliberately tried to frame you?"

"Yes. I think so, sir."

"This is a tough situation, to say the least, but if I make arrangements giving you access to the vault unbeknownst to security, do you really think you can get your hands-on hard evidence of who the thief is and when they did it?"

"Yes, sir. I do."

"And if I arrange for you to get in and you get caught, I lose my job and we both could end up in jail. Hmm…you okay with that? And all the while, those same inside bastards have a big laugh and continue to undermine our agency and our country? There's a lot at stake here, Mr. Steele, and almost as bad is the case where you get in, don't get caught, and come out with real, solid evidence but are then accused of manufacturing it."

Daniels interjected, "Martin could have a knowledgeable person carefully looking over his shoulder to make sure he wasn't stacking the deck in any way."

"That's certainly a possibility, but they would need to be razor sharp, fully computer-literate."

"They could do all the entries while I watched," Martin added helpfully, "ensuring I never touched the machine."

The director nodded, considering the possibility. "If you do go in there, we don't want anything to happen that would give even the slightest impression the evidence had been tampered with."

Martin responded, "There are plenty of computer engineers and hardware and software experts based in the Directorate of Science and Technology. None of them played any part in either the production of the system or the investigation of the leak. I'll bet most of them don't even know the system exists. Most of them don't even work in the headquarters building. We could get one of them to do most of the entries. They could be wired and carry a camera to record the entire operation."

The DCI sat back, put his hands behind his head, and considered the implications of it all. "You two are no doubt aware many of the folks you're referring to are under cover of some sort. I don't want this to compromise them or anything they're doing either."

"Look," Daniels said, "yesterday, despite all the strict procedures you have in place, I made it all the way up to your office in such a way I'd bet no more than five people ever saw me. Imagine for a minute you grease the skids for a car with two unrecognizable passengers, three if you want another witness, to just pass through the gate and park underneath near the express elevator. These guys could quickly zip up to the top floor, where the vault door would be unguarded and the alarm deactivated. Two minutes to open the vault, ten minutes to gather data, another minute to relock the vault and leave. Same car drives out the entrance, job done, all in less than thirty minutes and no cover compromised."

Mitchell turned to Steele. "What do you think your chances are?"

"If the data hasn't been destroyed by some Houdini messing with the equipment, I'll bring the whole file back. Look, Mr. Mitchell, this project occupied my whole world for years. I would bet my life on the electronic security it provides. I'm ninety-nine percent certain the culprit is someone who knew the system and got into the vault at just the right time."

Again, Director Mitchell paused. "Thank you for the information, Steele. My inclination is to deny your request. But I'll think on it and get word back to you. Don't call my office on this subject. Anna knows I've spent this hour with my wife and two children, having a picnic lunch at Great Falls Park. I'll join them now. Please stay here for five minutes and then quietly leave."

Daniels and Steele shook the director's hand in turn. Mitchell departed quickly and headed for the main park building.

Chapter Twenty

The following Monday morning, Daniels's phone rang, breaking his concentration on a story for the forthcoming Wednesday edition. "Daniels," he bellowed in frustration.

"Good news, Norman, my secretary, Anna, found your missing cufflink. She says she's going out for lunch today at the Italian place by the bank in McLean. I'll ask her to take it along. Can you meet her there?"

"Great, I'll stop in…will twelve thirty work?"

"Perfect, she'll see you there."

Valentine's Bistro served excellent food and, being convenient to both the agency and many businesses, attracted large lunchtime crowds. Indeed, as Daniels entered, several people were waiting to be seated. He searched the crowded room and spotted Anna, seated with a man in a booth along the back wall. He bypassed the queue and went over.

"Anna, good to see you again," he said extending his hand.

"Hello, Mr. Daniels. I'm glad you could join us for lunch. This is my husband, Peter."

"Pleased to meet you," he responded, shaking hands with Peter as he slipped into the seat opposite Anna.

An excellent meal followed, with the conversation centering on Peter's work as a general construction contractor and Norman's latest book. When the check came, both men reached for their wallets and Anna for her purse. "Let me get this," Peter said.

"Well, let me contribute," Daniels replied removing a bill from his wallet. Across the table, Anna removed an envelope from her purse and, covering most of it with her hand, pushed it toward him. Daniels placed the bill on the table in much the same way and quickly retrieved the envelope, palming it on the way to his pocket.

"Okay," Anna said as she handed the money to Peter, "but it has really been our pleasure."

"Mine, as well."

The three left the restaurant, pausing outside the door for casual words of farewell.

* * *

Martin lay propped up on the bed, totally engrossed in his book when the phone rang. "Martin Steele," he answered.

"Can you meet me in front of the diner at five o'clock?"

"Yes, of course, Mr. Daniels. Have you an update? Is there a decision?"

"Yes. I'll pick you up and give you a briefing."

At exactly the appointed time, a black BMW drove up in front of the diner. Martin got in, and they headed west out of the suburbs into the countryside.

"Before I forget, you shouldn't answer the phone with your name—at least for a while. Remember, there is no such thing as a private line." Daniels then explained the DCI had approved the project. Of course, he would deny meeting with them in the park, saying he had gone there only to have lunch with his family. He also added that, if the subject of an unauthorized access to the communications vault ever came up, he would prosecute the offenders to the fullest extent of the law.

He handed Martin two carefully handwritten cards. As Martin read, Daniels turned off the main highway, and in a matter of minutes, they were traveling down streets between what seemed to be an unending group of windowless concrete buildings. They were all about the same size, none with more than a building number showing. Each had an entrance with a small parking lot nearby. Daniels stopped, leaving the car idling. He nodded over to his left, "See the sign over the entrance? It's 111200. Remember the number and the building. You need to be here at four thirty tomorrow morning. It all begins then."

They were in the middle of the largest collection of data centers in the Western Hemisphere, the very heart of the internet, all hardened block houses full of computers.

"I'll take you back to the hotel now. Read these notes…they're pretty comprehensive, but if the situation requires, improvise carefully. Do your best and remember, if something goes wrong, you're on your own. If you're caught, you could even be thrown to the wolves." Daniels paused as Martin glanced at the cards. "If you want out, now is the time to say so, Martin."

"I'm absolutely in, Mr. Daniels."

They drove in silence back to the hotel. "Good luck, Martin," Daniels said sincerely. They shook hands, and Daniels departed.

* * *

The instructions on the cards were crystal clear. In just under nine hours, he had to be in the parking lot of the data center they had just left. Problem one was transportation. He considered his options: rent a car, take a taxi, hitchhike, or borrow a bike. *Yuk.* After a minute of deliberation, he went to the front desk. "Hi," he said somewhat shyly. "I have a problem. Perhaps you can help me."

"Try me."

"Well, my car's broken down, and I need to get out to Ashburn tomorrow morning at four thirty. Are there any taxi companies operating at that hour that could get me out there?"

"Yup. Should be able to fix you right up. Where exactly do you need to go?"

"111200 Edison Drive."

"Okay, just give me a minute." The clerk picked up the phone and, in a moment, had made Martin a reservation to be picked up at four. Martin thanked him profusely and decided, rather than heading back to his room, he ought to eat.

Despite a lack of appetite, he recognized he needed to be as sharp as possible in the morning, so he ate the healthiest food he could find in the now familiar diner.

Back in his room, he went over all the things on the cards one more time. He laid out clean clothes for the morning, tried to concentrate on the TV, and read half a page of his book. Nothing diverted his interest or sped up the passage of time, and when he finally drifted off to sleep, he woke less than four hours later, a full thirty minutes before the alarm.

At three fifty-five, he made his way to the front desk of the hotel. There he found the night clerk and an apparent hotel guest engrossed in a late-night B-rated movie. Both were commenting on the action when a commercial break interrupted them. The clerk looked up at Martin. "You the guy who needs a taxi to Ashburn?"

"Yes, I am."

Turning to his companion, he joked, "Guess it's time to tear yourself away from the western, Eddie!"

"Sure thing." The man smirked, taking his jacket from the back of the chair. "If you're ready, buddy, so am I. What's the address again?"

"111200 Edison Drive."

"Oh yeah, guess it would be Raging Wire or Fairmont, maybe. One of them two always seems to need someone in the middle of the night."

On their way out to the data center, Martin thought how surreal this whole thing felt, like something right out of a movie. He wished they had let him take more of the tradecraft courses all the operations people took, back when he worked at the agency. *This kind of a thing would be all in a day's work for them…but not for me*, he thought nervously.

At four twenty precisely, the taxi pulled up to the door of 111200 Edison Drive. Martin paid, tipped the driver, and got out. The cab disappeared around the corner of the huge building, leaving him alone in the silence of the pre-rush-hour morning. Aware of the numerous surveillance cameras keeping watchful eyes on him, Martin casually crossed the street to the parking lot, carefully studying the two cars parked near the opposite end. Even though neither looked occupied, he stood out of the lights, under a tree, and waited. A cool breeze rustling through the leaves made the only sound. Not a soul could be seen.

He waited and waited for what seemed like an eternity. He kept checking his watch. Eventually, at four twenty-eight, the sound of an approaching vehicle caught his attention, and in a moment, a black Chevrolet Suburban pulled up in front of him. *Here we go*, he thought as he walked to the driver's side of the car. The window opened. "Mr. Steele?"

"Yes. Sidney Johnson?"

"Show me."

Martin gave the driver a signed photo taken when he left the agency. Sidney carefully compared it with one he had and the face in front of him, then returned it.

"Your turn," Martin said.

The driver handed over his agency badge and government ID. "J379KD. Just right."

"Get in the back."

Within five minutes, they were in a nearby residential area, parked in front of a well-kept row of townhouses. A small man in his mid-forties emerged from the trees next to the end unit and quickly went through the same identification drill with the driver. The man climbed in next to him.

"Martin Steele."

"Phil Palmer."

"Got the thumb drives?" Martin asked.

"Of course!" Phil snapped. "Got the vault door combination?"

Silence. Then Martin turned to his cohort, extending his hand. "Sorry. First time I've ever done anything like this." They shook hands. "I know you're a computer expert, but that's all. Can you say anything more about what you do?"

"Oh sure. I work with systems using software and firmware to make hardware do stuff. I'd have to kill you if I said anything more. How about you?"

"Just an average lobster fisherman from Maine who used to do just what you do and who today hopes to retrieve critical information from one very special system."

"And you would have to kill me if you said anything about what such a system does?"

Chuckling, he answered, "Of course!"

For a while, they rode in silence, then out of curiosity, Martin asked, "In the meeting, someone suggested you should wear a wire and bring a concealed camera. Did you?"

"I am wired and I have a camera."

"My instructions say I'm to do the work."

"Yes, but you'll need to talk your way through what you're doing as much as possible. I'll be recording everything, including this conversation. When we're done, I'll keep all the recordings and the thumb drives."

"Great."

At the main gate, an armed guard came up to the driver, who duly presented a paper and his badge. Almost immediately, the massive vehicle barrier disappeared into the road, and they were on their way in. In less than a minute, Sidney stopped the Suburban at the barricaded entrance to the VIP parking lot where his badge and the letter again worked their magic. Inside, he explained he had a key to put the elevator in "out of service" mode.

They would all go up to the top floor together where he would shut the doors, immobilize the elevator, and wait, ready for a quick departure in case of any last-minute adjustment in the guard changeover schedule. "I figure you'll be a max of twenty-five minutes, so I'll wait inside. When you're back, signal with three sharp knocks, and I'll open the door. Chances are good no one will even try to use any of the elevators until well after seven, but I'll keep ours there and out of service till you return."

They reached the top floor at five fifty-four. The elevator door opened, and Sidney scanned the corridor for security people. They did not expect to see anyone, as the guards had already done their hourly checks.

In less than a minute, Martin and Phil were in front of the communications vault. Martin knew he had only minutes to get in there and get the job done, but he paused for a short moment as the enormity and importance of what they were doing hit him.

With clammy hands, his heart pounding like a jackhammer, Martin began to turn the combination lock. After the final digit had been set, he glanced at Phil and started turning the large wheel-like handle. The pins disengaged. They both listened intently: no alarm, no hurried footsteps. The thick, heavy door swung open easily.

Inside, the myriad of racks, panels, switches, and neatly marked cables were just as he remembered. Against the back wall stood a work bench for splicing wire or fiber-optic cables. Next to the bench stood a rack housing the Pyramid equipment, labeled SYSTEM K. "There's the system," Martin said, pointing. He pulled out the sliding keyboard and began the login procedure carefully explaining every step.

Phil recorded each move and verbal comment. From a command prompt, Martin invoked a program to search for Fletch's hidden file "Fh_lark." In a flash, it appeared. He sat back for a moment. "This is it, Phil." When he executed the file, a password prompt came up. Martin typed in the characters and then pressed enter. A second password prompt appeared, with a number in the upper right, counting down from 15. Martin typed another set of characters. As the descending numbers got down to 8, he hit ENTER. The screen went blank. Martin's heart stopped beating. Suddenly, the log appeared. *Must be a really big file*, he reasoned. He rapidly scrolled to the beginning of 2011 and then to March 8th, 2011.

"It's here! See the activity logged on March 8th, 2011? This is what we're after! These entries are the reason for this whole operation. Give me those thumb drives, please. I hope we can copy the entire log onto one."

Phil did as requested. In a moment, Martin, seeing one drive had the capacity to store the entire file, quickly made a second copy.

"Be sure they know these are the same," Martin added as he handed Phil both drives. Then, while continuing to describe each of his actions, he logged out, closed the console, returned the keyboard to its place, and looked up at Phil.

"Everything recorded?"

"Every word, every keystroke."

"Okay. Let's get out of here."

The two men turned away from the equipment and moved swiftly for the door. Phil arrived first and eased it open, peering gingerly out into the corridor. He stepped out. Martin shut off the lights and followed, his hands shaking as he closed and locked the massive vault door.

We've got it. We're almost done. Stay calm, stay cool. His watch showed the time: 6:18 a.m., three minutes behind schedule and about thirty-five feet from the elevator.

Phil led the way, his agency badge in clear, unobstructed view hanging on a neck strap. Behind, Martin kept his jacket buttoned in an attempt to look as though he had closed it over his badge by mistake. They were both acutely aware this short walk represented the time of greatest risk. They were vulnerable since contact with any person would almost certainly lead to disaster. With each step, the adrenaline pumped harder. They continued down the hallway, the only sound being their own footsteps.

Between them and the elevator were the closed doors to four separate offices.

Martin began imagining all sorts of scenarios. *What if someone, just finishing up an all-nighter, popped out of one of those doors? Or an early-bird came down the corridor eager to catch up from a quick departure yesterday? What if the fire alarm went off?* He suddenly became aware of his rapid and shallow breathing. Only twenty feet to go now. He had to keep his cool. *Don't rush, don't run. Pretend this is your normal workplace, and you're just very late leaving. Take regular steps, breathe normally, left foot, right foot. Easy, only fifteen feet to go now.*

Suddenly, the snap of a latch on a door behind them signaled someone entering the corridor. *Remember, people in this corridor are the norm, that's what corridors are for. Just keep walking, pay no attention. Left foot, right foot.* Heavy steps were heading in their direction. *Shit! I've finally got the absolute proof of my innocence in hand and some guy just trying to go home is going to sound the alarm.*

Every instinct told him to run, but he had to keep walking. *Act normal, not too fast. Left foot, right foot.* Only a few more steps and they would be at the elevator. Suddenly, the corridor became deathly silent. Neither dared turn. *Maybe it's a guard signaling the watch office for help. Hold your nerve.* They were almost there now. Two steps, one. Now they were in front of the elevator door. Phil's knuckles made three sharp knocks.

In a room somewhere behind them a telephone rang.

Silence.

Then someone started talking loudly. This was not looking good. The elevator door remained firmly closed.

Phil knocked again.

Nothing. *What the hell was keeping Sidney?*

More footsteps.

Just before they turned to take a quick look, the elevator door slid open, and they stepped inside. "Quick get the damned door shut," Phil whispered, "I think we're in trouble."

The door closed. Sidney pressed *P* and they were on their way down. The annunciator light displayed their excruciatingly slow progress: 7… 6… 5. It felt like they would never get there. Neither dared breathe.

Finally, the elevator stopped, and the door opened to a silent, almost deserted parking garage. No alarms. No guards. This felt much better. They stepped out and hurried some thirty feet to the car. Martin and Phil got in the back, Sidney jumped in the driver's seat and in seconds had the Suburban running.

"Let's get the hell out of here," Phil muttered.

* * *

No one spoke for the first ten minutes of the ride, until Martin finally leaned forward.

"What happened back there at the top, buddy? You scared the shit out of us?"

"Funny thing about me and them elevators," Sidney responded, "this is the second time I've had to hold one out of service while someone who wanted not to be seen either delivered or picked up something on the top floor. And both times the bloody key stuck. I hope you weren't too worried!"

Martin glanced at Phil.

"Sure is an interesting business we're all in, ain't it?" Sidney added.

No one spoke.

Soon they were traveling west on the Leesburg Pike, a large multilane highway quickly filling with commuter traffic going in both directions. In a few miles they would turn off toward their destinations near Ashburn. In the car, the atmosphere lightened as both Martin and Phil gradually began to relax. The operation had been a total success. They had the evidence in hand. They had done it!

With obvious sincerity, Martin turned to face Phil and said, "Thank you for all you've done to make this—"

But he never completed the sentence. A deafening explosion suddenly showered all three with broken glass as, from out of nowhere, a huge concrete truck slammed into the right front side of the Suburban. The impact spun the car around, forcing it through the adjacent traffic lane and onto the median. It skidded across the grass, hitting a drainage ditch, rolling completely over, and coming to rest upright in the left lane of eastbound traffic. Two other vehicles immediately joined the mayhem, one crashing into the Suburban and the other sideswiping it before spinning out of control and coming to a stop just off the roadway.

Drivers approaching slowed, rubbernecking as they made their way past. In seconds, a green Ford pickup truck, which had been four cars behind the Suburban, made a screeching left turn onto the median stopping near the mangled car. Two men jumped out. They wrestled with the crunched-in doors on the right side but to no avail. One then went around to try the left rear door and, with brute force applied to a lug wrench, managed to pry it open.

"Looks pretty bad," he shouted to his companion. "They're all unconscious. Get over here and help me get this guy out of the way. The other one is our man." The two worked quickly, carefully sliding Martin onto the ground.

"That's good. I think I can get all the stuff without dragging him out."

"Be sure to check his pockets carefully, Jim."

In seconds, his search uncovered everything they were after. They hastily returned to the pickup and quickly rejoined the ever-increasing stream of westbound rush-hour traffic.

Minutes later, sirens announced the arrival of fire, rescue, and police vehicles, followed shortly afterward by a fleet of ambulances. The teams worked quickly and efficiently, treating Martin and Phil first before dispatching them to the hospital. Although it took nearly thirty minutes, using special cutting tools, to free Sidney, the side and front air bags saved him from all but a minor bang on the head. Soon he, along with the somewhat dazed truck driver, was also on his way to hospital. The uninjured drivers of the two other vehicles declined medical attention and used their cell phones to arrange towing and transportation.

Chapter Twenty-One

Norman Daniels had slept fitfully during the covert file retrieval operation. Eventually, when frustration and restlessness gained the upper hand, he dressed and drove to Martin's hotel arriving well ahead of schedule, just after seven in the morning. Even though he knew Martin couldn't possibly be back there for at least another half hour, he felt much better waiting in the parking lot, rather than in his bed.

As he waited, he felt his eye lids become heavy, and in no time at all, waves of tiredness overwhelmed him.

The sound of a car horn woke him with a start. Glancing around and then at his watch, which showed 9:05 a.m., he suddenly realized he must have missed Martin. He bolted out of the car and rushed into the hotel lobby. "Can you please ring Mr. Martin Steele's room?"

"Sure thing. Just a second, please."

After a long wait, the clerk reluctantly hung up the phone, "Maybe we caught him in the shower. He's definitely not answering." A chill crept over Daniels as he turned to leave.

"Thanks for trying. I'll catch him later."

Daniels drove to the diner, wondering if Martin had perhaps gone out for breakfast, but when, after a careful check, he found no sign of him there either, he decided to head back to his office and wait.

Stopping off at the newsroom, he asked one of the staff for the current police reports from northern Virginia. He thought these might indicate if there had been some sort of trouble. He scanned the contents. One entry caught his attention:

"0830 5 June 2013. Major traffic accident near Sterling on Route 7 at about 0655. Four vehicles involved. Four people injured, one seriously. All taken to Reston Hospital. Eyewitness reports indicate a cement truck traveling at high speed initially impacted one vehicle, which eventually collided with two others. EMTs on site in under ten minutes."

Could this be Martin and his colleagues?

He phoned the hospital and said he had heard about a bad accident on Leesburg Pike.

"I understand the injured from the accident were brought to your hospital."

"Yes sir. That's right."

"Can you tell me if a Mr. Martin Steele is among them?"

"I'm sorry, sir, but I'm not permitted to give names."

"Can you say anything about them? How many people were involved? Were there any fatalities?"

"I'm sorry, sir."

Frustrated, concerned, and curious, Daniels phoned the DCI's office.

"Director's office," came the voice of Anna Evans, calm as ever.

"Hello, Anna, this is Norman Daniels. I just called to thank you for the lovely luncheon yesterday and to ask you if you received a package this morning."

"Lunch was indeed most enjoyable Mr. Daniels. And yes, everything arrived by courier this morning, but I understand your friend has stopped off in Reston for a while."

Nonplussed, Daniels simply replied, "Reston...ah... oh, I see. Thank you, Anna. Have a good day."

"You as well, Mr. Daniels."

Daniels stood beside the office window staring out. He tried to get his head around the shocking events of the previous few hours. It appeared Martin's car had been in an accident resulting in him being hospitalized. His companion must have been released and able to deliver the data as planned to Anna Evans. Somewhat relieved, he resolved to go to the hospital later in the day. But for now, he had a pile of issues needing urgent attention.

* * *

At the hospital that evening, Daniels officially identified the man they were treating as Martin Steele. The head nurse, relieved to have his identity, gave a comprehensive update on his condition.

"His left leg and hip have been badly ripped up. He is scheduled for surgery tomorrow morning. He has some minor cuts and bruises, but our main concern is head trauma. The only reason the ER didn't send him up to the ICU on a ventilator was his good oxygen level and CT scan. But we've still not been able to communicate with him."

"Can I sit with him for a while?"

"Sure, but only for a few minutes. Try talking to him."

Daniels attempted conversation, but Martin remained unresponsive. Finally, when nothing he did seemed to get through, or even elicit a response, he went back to the nurses' station.

"Nurse, can I ask about the others who were traveling with Martin. How are they doing?"

"The driver has been kept in for observation but will probably be released within the hour. The other passenger, a Mr. Palmer, has undergone surgery for severe lacerations to his right arm. He'll almost certainly be released later this evening."

Confused, Daniels wondered how the thumb drives had made it safely to Mitchell's office if Palmer was in the hospital. Still, it seemed the mission had been accomplished… somehow.

Daniels then asked about the prognosis for Martin.

"It's really too early to say."

* * *

Twenty-four hours later, having undergone an intense four-hour operation to repair his hip and leg, Martin had still not regained consciousness. The official condition report listed him as, "serious but stable."

An additional thirty-nine hours later, a nurse making her rounds routinely asked, "Martin? Can you hear me, Martin?"

This time, his eyes partially opened and, as he became more aware of his surroundings, he tried to speak. "Lin…ah…Linda?"

"Well, hello you!" the nurse answered, adding, "It's Martin, isn't it?"

"No…uh…no…Seth…er…Mar…tin…no…no…Where am I? What happened?"

"You're in the hospital in Reston because you were in a car accident. A truck collided with you and your friends' car. Can you remember anything?"

He tried to recall what had happened. "Car…uh…it…a… uuh…a pickup truck? Uh…JB driving the truck?"

The nurse switched on his bedside light.

"Can you see me, Martin?"

He moved his head and looked carefully. "Ye…yes…yes I can. You're not… Linda…are you?"

"No, I'm your nurse, Betty Stone. Just rest now, Martin, and I'll be back to check on you shortly. We sure are glad you're back with us!"

Chapter Twenty-Two

The day after the accident, as the surgeons, doctors, and nurses fought to save Martin's leg, DCI Mitchell called Mr. Sailor into his office.

"Morning, Dave. What's the latest from the hospital on Steele and the others involved in the crash?"

"Well, Sidney Johnson, the driver, had the fewest injuries. They released him a few hours after getting to the hospital. They kept Phillip Palmer in for surgery to repair lacerations to his arm and then let him go home. Both are doing as well as can be expected. Steele, however, has been banged up quite badly and will be in hospital for a while. Apparently, as the car rolled over on its left side, a steel post penetrated the rear door or window and skewered him, doing significant damage to his leg and hip. He also sustained a bad head trauma and now has amnesia. Hopefully just temporary. His condition is serious, and the prognosis is not great. He's scheduled for major surgery this morning. If the surgeon is as good as they say she is, he won't lose his leg. His amnesia is still an unknown, but at least the initial evaluation indicates there's no brain damage."

"Dammed unfortunate set of events, Dave."

"At least he's in good hands over there."

DCI Mitchell rose from behind his desk. "I have to say it, Dave, I'm anxious to find out what's on the thumb drive. Do you think they got something? What do you think about getting Palmer in here to take a look at it?"

"Good idea. He's certainly qualified to decipher whatever might be on there and explain it to us. All we need to do is give him a Pyramid system briefing."

"Okay. You folks contact him, get him up to speed on Pyramid, and give him what he needs. He's to work here. Don't let anything leave this building. We'll meet on Saturday to see what he finds."

* * *

By the following afternoon, Phil had been given a briefing on the Pyramid system and a desk in the same workspace Martin had used to build the original equipment. Although slowed by his immobilized right arm, Phil studied the system information and schematics carefully. Then he looked through the copied file, finding and reading the entries for March 8th, 2011. It all seemed quite clear. By evening he felt ready for the high-level briefing.

On Saturday morning, about fifteen minutes before the appointed time, Phil went to the conference room, where all seemed in order. A laptop computer had been set up, so he went to it, but before he could check to see if it had a port for the thumb drive, the door opened.

DCI Mitchell led the group into the room and, once they were all inside, quickly set about making the introductions. "Good morning. I know you don't all know each other, so, for the record, to my left is Dr. Fredrick Bassett, the FBI investigator who headed the Bureau's 2011 PDB leak investigation. To his left is the indispensable Mrs. Anna Evans, my secretary for over twelve years, and at the end next to her is Mr. Phillip Palmer, computer expert from a division of our DDS and T. To my right is Mr. David Sailor, acting Director of Security. Mr. Ian Cunningham, the Director of Security, who worked with Dr. Bassett during the original investigation, can't be here today as he's involved in the Presidential Summit in Ankara. Mr. Martin Steele is also unable to attend as he's still recovering from his injuries in the hospital. Finally, again for the record, I must remind you the classification of this discussion is Top Secret, Pyramid."

After a short pause, the DCI continued, "Early this past Wednesday, Mr. Phillip Palmer, accompanied by Mr. Martin Steele, covertly entered our seventh-floor communications vault and made a copy of a hidden file stored in the Pyramid equipment. For validation of their actions, they made an audio and video recording of every step in the operation. Because of the covert nature of their entry, they departed in the same manner. The sensitivity of the classified recording equipment and the potential value of their collected data caused us to assign a tail to follow Palmer until the equipment and data were all back in this office.

"The plan had been for Palmer to be dropped off at home, then return during regular work hours to deliver the files and equipment here. Regrettably, however, the brakes failed on a large, loaded cement truck, causing it to crash into the car carrying Palmer and Steele. The tail, two men from our operations directorate, were on the scene in less than a minute, secured the equipment, and immediately returned here."

Then the DCI held up a thumb drive and asked that it be passed to Phil. "Now, Mr. Palmer, please show us what this file looks like and tell us what it has to say."

Phil began. "Thank you, sir. First, I want to say it's a real shame Martin…uh, Mr. Steele can't be here to give this presentation. I wish him a speedy recovery. However, I'm pleased to be here on his behalf. I think you'll be very interested in what we've learned.

"Just one thing before I start. Now that I understand the Pyramid concept, I have to say this is an exceptionally fine system. It seems a terrible waste to keep it offline. Martin Steele did a fine job designing it." Phil paused and glanced around the room. Although the faces were impassive, he could feel the anticipation.

"The information I'm about to share with you clearly shows who copied the now famous, stolen PDB back in March 2011. I'll explain what happened." Phil brought the laptop to life. "On the morning of the theft, the composing team had completed the original PDB at about seven thirty a.m. At seven forty-four, the Director of Operations officially released it for transmission. The message then left the composing station for temporary storage in a module located in the communications vault.

"On the screen now, you can see a segment of the log showing the major events occurring in the processing module on the morning of March eighth. Remember, this equipment is in the communications vault. Each line of the log starts with a set of numbers. First is the system time. It reads year, month, day, hour, minute, second, and millisecond. This is then followed by the gross event description. Here, the first line shows the computer console being activated by a person using the valid badge JK478 and a personal password. This action gave 478 internal access to the machine. Note the date and time—March eighth, 2011, seven thirty-five. You can read the rest yourselves. The fifth line down shows JK478 copied the message, bound for the president, in its clear text, unencrypted form, onto a removable thumb drive, serial number SSUFOD63 at seven forty-six. It's as simple as that. About eleven minutes later, the president requested and received the message with no system errors occurring."

2011-03-08 07:35:22:528 Console Activated by JK478
2011-03-08 07:36:46:948 New device detected USB DISK s/n SSUFOD63 System

2011-03-08 07:44:10:332 Message PD13845779 released by TPL1432

2011-03-08 07:44:11:411 Message PD13845779 stored awaiting call System

2011-03-08 07:46:21:307 Message PD13845779 copied to F:\ USB DISK s/n SSUFOD63 Console.

2011-03-08 07:50:45:829 Console Deactivated by JK478

2011-03-08 07:57:00:229 Message PD13845779 called by PT014489

2011-03-08 07:57:01:249 Message PD13845779E created by system

2011-03-08 07:57:02:119 Message PD13845779E transmitted to PT014489

2011-03-08 07:57:06:639 Message PD13845779E received by PT014489 errors = 0

2011-03-08 07:57:08:127 Message PD13845779A message archived by System

2011-03-08 07:57:09:621 Message PD13845779A archived errors = 0

The group studied the screen. Mr. Sailor spoke first. "Mister, or Miss, JK478 appears to be the thief. However, our security records show no entry into the vault whatsoever between March fourth and tenth. Could this log be recording actions made from an outside location—the composition console, for example?"

Phil responded, "I've studied the schematics and wiring diagrams and can say, absolutely, it's a literal impossibility for that to be the case…or for this data to have been accessed from anywhere other than the console inside the communications vault. JK478 had to have been in there for this log entry to exist. Whoever it was must have gotten in the same way we got in on Wednesday morning—by knowing the guards wouldn't be looking and the alarm system wouldn't be active. The room is basically a bank vault, and it has only one entrance."

An uncomfortable silence filled the room.

Bassett eventually spoke. "It seems as though Director Mitchell has an additional problem on his hands. But I have a fundamental question regarding this log information: How do we know Mr. Steele, or you, just didn't go in there on Wednesday morning and write all this in the computer, then copy it and bring it here?"

"Martin did all the work, and I observed his every move, recording both video and audio. He explained everything he did before doing it. I photographed every move he made and recorded every word he said. These recordings have all been delivered to Director Mitchell."

"Mr. Palmer," Sailor said, "from what I have read about this incident, several computer experts from both the agency and the FBI went over all this equipment. So how is it they didn't come up with this file?"

"The answer is simple: They couldn't find it. Indeed, if I had been called in to help, I wouldn't have found it either. Moreover, if anyone had run across it by accident, they couldn't have accessed it without two passwords. This file is stored on a chip installed as part of the NSA system validation. Fortunately, it had not been removed with the rest of the NSA validation hardware."

"This log clearly tells me two things," Mitchell observed. "First, the thief, who is still running around, is a CIA person with both a valid badge and enough influence to gain unescorted entry to the communications vault. Second, contrary to what some believe to be the case, the leaked message was not intercepted by the Russians or anyone else."

"Yes, sir, absolutely. As you know, the primary Pyramid system logs show no anomalies in the data or the data stream. That message went to the president without any sort of error. It is quite clear this is the only possible way the message could have been copied."

"Dr. Bassett," the director continued, "what do you need to get an arrest warrant for this person, and how quickly do you think it can be done?"

"I'd need depositions from Palmer or Steele, as well as a certified copy of the log together with the real-time recordings of its acquisition. And, of course, an identification of JK478. Not just the person's name, but also the facial recognition images made during his or her entry to the building on the morning of the eighth."

"If it's okay with you, I'd like to send Mr. Palmer downtown to your office for the deposition, Dr. Bassett. Please let Anna know when you want him to be there, and she'll deliver him. We'll have to wait for Martin Steele's, but rest assured, we'll get him to you as soon as we can. Mr. Sailor, you'll have to verify the identity of the person wearing badge JK478. Anna, please take one copy of the log file and arrange secure delivery of all the rest of the equipment and data to Dr. Bassett. I want this to get moving as fast as possible. Are there any questions?"

There were none.

* * *

Director Mitchell returned to his office mentally redoubling his resolve to get to the bottom of what now looked to be an awfully bad situation. "Anna, get Sailor in here as soon as possible. I need to talk to him."

"Yes, sir."

The acting Director of Security arrived almost immediately. "Come in, Dave. Have a seat. What sticks in my head most from this morning's meeting is your question. The more I think on it, the more it bothers me. We had a profoundly serious problem two years ago, and it may still be with us today. Circumstances have provided us with a unique opportunity. It now seems almost certain the leaker is one of our employees. It also appears someone in our security office helped them. Cunningham won't be back for a few more days. You're in charge, and I want you to look into how the hell someone could get into the vault and out again without being detected. I hate to say this, but trust no one, and report only to me. Understood?"

"Absolutely."

"What really galls me as well is the way the location frequently dictates the punishment. When a security event of this magnitude happens here, we have investigations, and eventually the truth is found. Perhaps someone is embarrassed in the press, loses his or her job, or goes to jail. But when things of this magnitude happen in the field, where many of our folks work…people die."

"I understand, Mac. I'll get right on it."

* * *

The following morning, in the downtown apartment of Private Investigator Dolores Duval, Walter Duval placed a mug of coffee on the stand beside his sleeping wife. He leaned in close and whispered, "It's eight thirty, darling, time to get up."

She stirred slightly, moaned, then slowly opened her eyes.

He moved closer and kissed her lovingly. "Good morning, Dolores. It's eight thirty and you have a ten o'clock appointment."

"Oh, Petroski can wait," she responded, wrapping her arms around his neck. Their lips met once more, but only briefly as he pulled away.

"I'll bring your fruit and toast in a moment, and meantime, here's your coffee. Remember, Petroski is a valuable client, you can't afford to lose him."

Dolores straightened the bedclothes, and sitting back on two large pillows, picked up the TV remote and the coffee mug. The morning show was on, with several talking heads speaking about the latest local Washington, DC, news. When the program resumed after a commercial break, the story focused on a press conference that had been hastily called by the Secretary General of the United Nations in New York. The picture showed seven people lined up, each behind a microphone, in front of a room full of reporters and cameramen.

"We're expecting the arrival of the Secretary General momentarily," the announcer said.

Dolores sat straight up in bed. "There he is! That's him!" she exclaimed as Walter entered the room with her breakfast. "It's him, I'm positive!"

"It's who?"

"Put that stuff down, Walter, and look at the TV. Tell me who the third man from the right is—the guy next to the lady in the dark purple outfit." As she spoke, the camera panned away to the far left, where the Secretary General was getting ready to speak. "Pay close attention, Walter, he might introduce all these people. I'll be right back. I must go pee."

Walter stood at the foot of the bed, watching and listening as the Secretary General explained that this multinational group would be leaving that evening, twelve hours in advance of the original schedule, giving them two full days on site before the start of the Ankara summit. It was all part of the dynamic nature of this level of diplomacy, he explained, as he opened the question-and-answer session.

Dolores returned and stood with Walter in front of the screen. "Did you get his name?"

"No, not yet. Only question went to the guy second from the left, an economist called Professor Hermann Von Echter."

Dolores crawled back into bed, still glued to the TV.

"Next question."

"Eric Johnston. Aljazeera. My question is for Mr. Cunningham. Mr. Cunningham, everyone knows you work for the CIA. So what exactly is your role in this Middle East conference?"

The camera moved to the third person from the right.

"So that's who he is! Mr. Sneaky Cunningham of the CIA… well, well…" She could barely contain her excitement as she listened to his response.

"First of all, I'm on leave from my employer, and I'm only working for the United Nations during these meetings. I've been invited to join because of my twenty-five years of experience in high-level security matters. Think about it: This is the first time in over six decades a comprehensive solution for the Middle East has been so close. The last thing any of us want is for some security breach to ruin it for all the millions involved."

"Okay. I'm done. You can watch whatever you want now. I've got what I need!"

"You've got the remote, darling. Besides, I need to leave for work."

And with that, Walter moved close, kissed his wife goodbye, and headed out to join the morning rush hour.

Without touching her breakfast, Dolores picked up her cell phone and called Martha Aston. "Hi, Martha. Haven't seen you for months. How about meeting for an early lunch today?"

"Great idea. Where?"

"I've got an appointment at ten, downtown on F Street, but will be done by eleven thirty. How about meeting at the Old Ebbitt Grill around then?"

"That's just a short walk from here. I'll meet you outside."

"Super, see you later."

Dolores dressed, put several files in a small briefcase, and departed for the city center.

* * *

It was a fine day but hot and steamy as Martha Aston waited by the three large arches marking the main entrance to the Old Ebbitt Grill.

Right on time, her friend Dolores Duval rounded the corner.

"Hey, Dolores. Good to see you. Let's get inside, out of this heat."

Initially, their conversation was typical of two friends who hadn't seen each other for several weeks. "How's Walter?" "How's Jerry?" "How's work?" They ordered lunch, and as they ate, Martha studied her friend. "So, what's up, Dolores? This was all a bit cloak-and-dagger!"

Dolores opened her briefcase and took out an envelope. "You remember what you asked me for back in March? Well, here it is at last." She passed the envelope to Martha. "My guess is that you'll give it to Norman, but please let Scott know as well." She leaned close across the table and in a whisper, added, "Most importantly, no one has to know where you got this, understand?"

Martha opened the envelope and read the note. "Holy shit, Dee!" she exclaimed, quickly shoving the note back into the envelope.

"I thought that might be your reaction!"

* * *

In his office, Norman Daniels was writing the last of several emails. For him, it had been an unusually busy morning, but finally he was able to take a break for lunch. As he rushed out, he nearly ran over Martha, who was in the act of knocking. "Martha! I was just leaving."

"And I was just coming to see you."

"Is it something quick?"

"Will only take two seconds."

Norman ushered her in and returned to his desk. Without a word, she took the envelope out of her purse and handed it to him.

He read it and thought for a minute. "This is very timely news," he said, quickly adding, "Who else knows?"

"As far as I know, only the source."

"Dolores Duval?"

"Funny, I can't remember."

"Damn. This certainly changes things. Thanks, Martha. Please keep it to yourself, okay?"

"In fairness to Scott Young, we should let him know, don't you think?"

"Certainly. I'll see to it."

Martha left, closing the door behind her.

Forgetting lunch for the moment, Norman immediately phoned Director Mitchell's office. When Anna Evans answered, he identified himself and asked if she could tell Mitchell he had an urgent note for him. Anna called back almost straightaway, saying a courier was on his way.

Norman secured his desk, picked up his cell phone, and walked to the main entrance, the resealed envelope carefully tucked in his pocket.

Within minutes, a car drove up and stopped directly in front of the door. A smartly dressed gentleman jumped out, identified himself, took possession of the envelope, and headed straight back to headquarters.

Norman proceeded down the street to his favorite lunch place, thinking about the note Martha had just brought him. *I'll bet Ed didn't want to use the proof of his wife's adultery to secure a divorce; he wanted it to provide protection for his plan to steal classified information and pin the blame on Martin Steele. The timing of Cunningham's overseas trip is fortuitous, as Mitchell now has the perfect opportunity to investigate. Cunningham probably won't be back to work for at least four or five days.*

On returning to his office, Norman received some more exciting news, this time relating to another one of his many projects. Several months earlier, the editor had assigned him a feature article on the world's fastest-growing conglomerate, the Wilson Companies, founded and led by Sir Reginald Wilson. Having formally requested an interview with Sir Reginald, he was both delighted and alarmed to find it had been approved. It was scheduled for two days' time at ten thirty in New York City.

Norman dropped everything else, quickly made plane and hotel reservations, and began reviewing his notes and files. *I wonder whether their security officer from London might be there, too...*

* * *

The following day, Norman Daniels returned to the hospital to visit Martin. He spoke with the nurse before going in. "Good evening, Nurse Stone. How has our friend Martin been doing these past two days?"

"In short, very well. He had a major operation on his leg and hip on Thursday, and we're pleased with how things went. He's been incredibly lucky. He may end up with a bit of a limp, but that certainly beats losing his whole leg. His memory has also been creeping back slowly. He seems to remember you now. He's in the same room as before. I'm sure he's awake and would like to see you."

"Thank you. I won't stay long."

"If you can hang on for twenty minutes or so, his surgeon should be here. Her name is Dr. Karen Burr. Great surgeon, lovely person."

Daniels went in, greeted Martin, and very quickly noticed an improvement in his memory. Although unable to recall many details, he did remember their very first meeting in Boston.

"Do you know Linda?" Martin asked.

"Well, I know three Lindas I can think of. Why?"

"Fragmented conversations with her, whoever she is, keep coming back to me. I think she's going to be in New York very soon, but I have no idea why, or even why I care."

"Could she be someone you met on Sandaray Island up in Maine?"

After a long pause, Martin's face flushed as a whole set of memories came spilling back. In a split second, he saw Linda clear as day. They were together in her house. Then suddenly JB appeared. "Oh, my God! Linda! I hope she's all right."

"All right?" Daniels asked, trying to keep Martin focused. "What do you mean, 'all right'?"

"I had to leave... Oh, Linda's going to New York. I tried to phone her...need to talk to her...Ed will be there as well. You must tell them about Ed."

"Who must I tell, Martin?"

"Ah...I think..." Martin thought hard, but before he could construct an answer, the door opened and a tall figure in medical attire entered.

"Hello, Martin," she said. "How are you feeling today?"

"I think I'm feeling better, Doctor. Uh...yes, definitely better."

The surgeon carefully checked his bandages, drain, and the local anesthetic delivery tubing. She studied his vital signs display, smiled at Martin, and then turned to Daniels.

"His leg and hip are going to be okay. He should be up and about in two or three days and out of here in a week or so. Full healing will take a while, however, and he may have some permanent impairment. The post that impaled him could very easily have killed him. He's one very lucky man."

"Thank you, Doctor."

Once they were alone again, Daniels tried to return to their previous conversation. "Martin. Who is Linda? Should I contact her?"

Martin motioned Daniels closer. "Look, so much is coming back to me now. I read the log! It's Henderson. I read the entries and recognized his badge number. And he's going to be in New York for three days. Linda told me. Please tell the big guy, you know, the man we met in the van."

"I'll do my best. But tell me, who is Linda?"

"She's Sir Reginald Wilson's daughter-in-law," he answered quietly. "I met her in Maine, and I worked for her father. I'll ring her as soon as I'm out of here. Just forget I mentioned it."

Daniels nodded without fully comprehending.

"The important thing is to get the fact that Henderson will be in New York to the powers that be. I'm sure they must have read the log by now. This is their big chance to get him."

* * *

Daniels went home, encouraged by Martin's diminishing amnesia and his revelation about the contents of the log. Coupled with Dolores's identification of Ian Cunningham as Norma Henderson's lover, he now had some major new pieces to add to the picture he had been trying to put together for two years. He picked up the telephone and left a message with Anna Evans about Martin's condition and improving memory, adding cryptically, "And by the way, EH is due in NY imminently for a three-day visit." Next, he dialed Scott Young to brief him on the latest developments. That night, like all journalists on the brink of a big scoop, sleep did not come easily, but he was relaxed knowing the timing of his trip could not have been better.

Chapter Twenty-Three

At CIA headquarters, Anna Evans buzzed Director Mitchell. "Dr. Bassett on the secure line."

"Thanks, Anna." Mitchell picked up the green phone on his desk. "Mitchell."

"Mac, I've just found out a federal arrest warrant has been issued for Edwin Henderson. Our information is he arrived in New York yesterday evening for a three-day meeting starting tomorrow. I'll contact the New York Field Office to locate and arrest him as soon as possible."

"Thanks for the information and the fast work, Fred."

"Any leads on the helper yet?"

"I'll be in touch as soon as we have something concrete."

"Thanks, Mac. Much appreciated."

* * *

Thursday morning brought beautiful weather to New York City, so Daniels chose to walk the few blocks from his hotel to the offices of the Wilson Companies, east of Times Square. By ten fifteen, he had made his way to the reception area on the twenty-ninth floor.

He found the door slightly ajar so knocked gently and entered. An attractive middle-aged lady looked up from her desk.

"How can I help you?"

"Good morning. I'm Norman Daniels. I have an appointment with Sir Reginald Wilson."

"Oh, Mr. Daniels, we've been expecting you. I'm Marylin Holtz, Sir Reginald's secretary. He's running a bit late, I'm afraid, but he'll be with you shortly. Can I get you a cup of coffee while you wait?"

"I never turn down a good cup of coffee. Just black please." Daniels studied the large photos of Wilson Engineering's operations while he waited.

"Here you are, Mr. Daniels," Marylin said, handing him a steaming mug of coffee. "If you want to see more detailed pictures, there's a good display in the conference room. There are people setting up for lunch in there, but you'll not be a bother."

Daniels thanked her for the coffee and strolled into the adjacent conference room. The photographs told the story of one branch of Wilson Engineering—Wilson Laboratories. They showed everything from spectacular views of the earth from space to images of the inside of an atom. This company had been Sir Reginald's idea only four years before, and now it employed thousands and made millions. *This guy has a real knack for being in the right place at the right time, knowing it, and taking advantage of it.* As he moved around the large conference table, now covered with a linen tablecloth, an old phrase came to mind: Nothing succeeds like success.

A few minutes later, Marylin appeared at the door. "They're all set, Mr. Daniels. Please come this way."

Sir Reginald Wilson sat behind a large oak desk at right angles to a long oak table stretching the length of the room. He rose and greeted Norman, extending his hand, "I'm pleased to meet you, Mr. Daniels. Please let me introduce two gentlemen who are the kingpins of our new operation in London. Our Office Chief, Mr. Robert Blackstock, and our chief of security, Mr. Edwin Henderson."

As they shook hands, Daniels took in the details of Edwin Henderson—clean-shaven, slicked-back brown hair, and gray unfathomable eyes. Wearing a blue, pin-striped, three-piece suit with coordinated tie and handkerchief, he presented as a man with impeccable dress sense and surprisingly good taste in cologne.

As always, Daniels had done his homework carefully, so his questions went right to the heart of each subject. Sir Reginald's responses, regarding his companies' capabilities, were historically accurate, technically up-to-date, and enthusiastic. He clearly had a positive, far-reaching vision for both his organization and the world.

Blackstock, an engineer and longtime Wilson employee, gave candid, precise, and optimistic answers, pointing out several times, however, that the London operation still needed time to get on its feet.

Henderson spoke of his extensive CIA background, explaining how the unique requirements for security in the London office were being addressed. At times, his answers extended into mini security lectures, but generally, the man could not be faulted.

Despite his burning curiosity about Henderson's reasons for leaving the CIA, and the relevance of his wife's affair, Daniels restrained himself, keeping his questions focused on the upcoming article.

The intensity of the session absorbed all four men to such a degree that they ran well overtime. Eventually, Sir Reginald stood, effectively bringing the meeting to a close. "Thank you, Mr. Daniels, but enjoyable as this has been, we are, as you pointed out earlier, on a very tight schedule. Please feel free to write to any of us if you need further clarification. For now, though, it's almost noon, and luncheon will be served in five minutes. I hope you'll join us, Mr. Daniels."

Leaving the office, they exchanged business cards and shook hands once again. Sir Reginald and Blackstone headed toward the restrooms, while Daniels and Henderson walked into the conference room, Henderson commenting on the excellent photographs and the way they showed the diversity of the Wilson empire.

"This is a huge operation, Mr. Daniels, a fact your interview certainly underscored. But what really amazes me is how Sir Reginald keeps on top of it all."

Daniels did not reply, but he thought, *What amazes me even more is the fact that I am engaging in casual conversation with a possible traitor and threat to global security!*

Daniels and Henderson took their seats along with the other guests.

Sir Reginald rose and tapped his wine glass. "Welcome, and no, this is not going to be a luncheon filled with speeches, but for the benefit of those of you who haven't yet met them, I'd like to introduce our visitors. First, here to my left is Mr. Norman Daniels. Mr. Daniels is an author, syndicated columnist, and longtime investigative reporter from Washington, DC. He is preparing a series of articles on our worldwide operations. And on my right is Linda Wilson. Her husband—my son, Dan—is currently holding the fort down over there in London. Linda has been on vacation for a few days, visiting her home in Maine, and is here to get a better feel of what the company is all about. So now, please enjoy the meal and the rest of the conference activities."

As the wait staff poured the wine, Daniels leaned toward Sir Reginald. "I neglected to ask you during the interview if you were interested in fiction."

"Yes, I suppose I am. Why? Are you planning on writing something a bit more creative?"

"Well, yes. I've actually just finished my first novel. If you'd like a copy, I have one at the hotel and would be happy to bring it for you right after lunch."

"Thank you, I'd like that. I'll be at my desk all afternoon. Feel free to drop by."

Meanwhile, Marylin Holtz sat at her desk eating a sandwich, minding the door and answering the phones. It had been an unusually quiet morning but, with the luncheon soon ending, she knew it would only be a matter of minutes before all the busyness would resume.

She was slightly surprised when two well-dressed men, whom she did not recognize, entered the office.

"Good afternoon, gentlemen. How can I help you?"

"I'm Ronan J. MacPhee and this is Wallace Innes. We're here to speak with Mr. Edwin Henderson."

Marylin replied, "Mr. Henderson is with the luncheon group in the conference room just now and is scheduled to give a talk at one o'clock. If you wait here," she said, motioning to several empty chairs, "perhaps you can catch him on his way out and make arrangements for later."

"Thank you, we will."

Right on schedule, the conference room door opened, and people began to emerge. MacPhee and Innes went to the door and waited, watching as the group passed. Henderson emerged second to last. MacPhee addressed him, "Mr. Henderson?"

"Why yes. Who's asking?"

"Can we have just a moment to speak with you...in private?"

"Sure. I only have a minute, though, so how about we go right in here? Everyone else will be gone in a second, so we can close the door if you like."

Once all the guests had left the conference room, Henderson quietly closed the main door.

MacPhee spoke now in a very formal tone as he showed Henderson his credentials, "I'm Special Agent Ronan J. MacPhee of the FBI and this is Special Agent Wallace Innes. Are you Mr. Edwin Richard Henderson?"

"Yes, you know I am. What's this all about?"

"Edwin Richard Henderson, I'm arresting you on the federal charge of releasing classified information. You have the right to—"

Henderson interrupted him with a laugh and a grin. "So this is it? The guys in Brussels told me this would happen. Every time a new staffer gets invited to New York for the first time, there *will* be a significant practical joke of some kind. The only trouble is, right now, I'm expected to give a presentation, so can we just put this off for an hour or so?"

"I'm afraid this is no practical joke, Mr. Henderson," Innes replied. "We're here to carry out an arrest warrant issued by Judge Harold Baker of the Eastern District of Virginia and signed yesterday." He took the warrant out of his pocket and laid it on the table. "It'll be better for everyone concerned if you just come with us peacefully."

The grin quickly disappeared from Henderson's face, and he started backing away. "Uh, there has to be some mistake. I'm just here for three days from England. You must have the wrong person." He retreated farther down the long table.

"Mr. Henderson," Innes continued as MacPhee moved toward him from the opposite side of the table, "our orders are to bring you to Washington immediately. It'll certainly be easier for all of us if you just come along without any argument. You can examine the warrant if you like." Henderson just stared in disbelief.

"Look, guys, I live and work in England. I'm only here for three days. Umm…if you just say you couldn't find me, I assure you I'll be out of the country and on my way back to London before midnight."

"But *we* have found you," Innes continued, "and we have a lawful order to escort you back to Washington."

"Okay, *okay*, I'll go with you. Just let me read the warrant first."

MacPhee handed him the warrant. He read it carefully and, as he did so, he moved to put a few more feet between them. When he got to the last page, he threw the document at MacPhee, simultaneously aiming a kick to his groin. But both MacPhee and Innes were experienced and lightning fast. In a split second, Henderson found himself restrained on the floor with the cold steel of Innes's weapon pressed firmly against his neck.

They handcuffed him and left the room, stopping briefly at Marylin's desk. MacPhee handed her a business card. "We have taken Mr. Henderson into custody in compliance with a federal arrest warrant. Please call Special Agent Elizabeth Truxal at our New York Field Office for further details. Here is her card."

They departed, leaving Marylin studying the card and momentarily speechless. The ringing phone refocused her attention, "Front office," she answered.

"Hey, Marylin, this is Russ. I'm in conference room eight forty-four, and there's an anxious bunch of folks down here, waiting to hear from Mr. Henderson. How about giving him a swift kick in the butt and telling him to get down here pronto?"

"Oh, Russell, I'm afraid he won't be able to make it. Something's just come up. Please can you fill in for him?"

"Well, okay, I'll do my best, Marylin, but what's happening?"

"Russell, just go care for the group. I'll explain later."

"Okay...uh, later over dinner, maybe?"

"Do a good, professional job, Mr. Boyd. Bye." She hung up and, despite the recent bizarre chain of events, smiled smugly. *Mmm...dinner. I thought he'd never ask!*

Taking the card, Marylin quickly headed over to Sir Reginald's office, knocked once, and entered before waiting for the usual response.

"What's up, Marylin?" he asked, looking up from his desk.

"The FBI has been here, and they've arrested Mr. Henderson."

"What? Seriously? What on earth for?"

"They say it's a federal warrant. If we have questions, we're to call their New York Field Office. I have a name and a number."

"Have they left?"

"Yes, sir. They didn't waste any time handcuffing him and hustling him out."

"Let's see. Our head of security here is Mr. Boyd, correct?"

"Yes. He's now giving the orientation lecture in place of Henderson."

"Right. Get someone else from security to take over the lecture and get him up here right away."

"Yes, sir."

"And while you're locating people, you'd better find out where Henderson's wife is. I'll need to tell her what's happening. I presume she doesn't know yet."

"They've only been gone a couple of minutes. No one knows anything about this except us...for the moment."

Ten minutes later, Boyd burst through the door and stood in front of Marylin's desk. "At your service, Ms. Holtz," he said, grinning at her.

"Not now, Russ. The old man wants you in his office. Mr. Henderson has been arrested by the FBI."

"The FBI! Bloody hell," he muttered, rushing toward Sir Reginald's office.

Boyd knocked and entered in one swift move.

"Mr. Boyd, our chief of security in London, Edwin Henderson, has been arrested by the FBI." He handed Boyd the special agent's card and asked him to get in touch as soon as possible to find out the details.

"Yes, sir. Do you need anything else?"

"No, not for now. This has all just happened. They've only been gone about fifteen minutes."

"I'll get right on it," he said, leaving quickly. He stopped briefly at Marylin's desk, just long enough to say, in a very serious tone, he would be in his office.

Boyd stared momentarily at the business card, sighed deeply, and considered the questions he needed to ask. A minute later, he picked up the phone and dialed.

"SSA Truxal. How may I help you?"

"Yes. Hello. My name is Russell Boyd. I'm chief of security for the New York office of Wilson Companies. I'm told you have information regarding Mr. Edwin Henderson, one of our employees, whom, I understand, you have arrested."

"I can tell you this, Mr. Boyd: Mr. Henderson has been arrested pursuant to a warrant issued by a Federal District Court. At this moment, he is being transported by car to the Washington, DC, area."

"Can you tell me anything about the charges?"

"The charge alleges Mr. Henderson illegally removed classified material from his place of employment in March 2011. If you need more information, you'll have to contact the federal prosecutor in Alexandria, Virginia."

Boyd did as Truxal suggested but, after several calls, realized no one would tell him much more, since Henderson had been arrested for a crime occurring well before his arrival at the Wilson Companies. Satisfied he had done all he could, Boyd reported back to Sir Reginald. As he entered the office, he found a distraught Norma Henderson being comforted by the head of the company.

Gently easing himself from Norma's grasp, Sir Reginald turned to Boyd. "Mrs. Henderson, this is our New York chief of security, Mr. Boyd. He has the latest on your husband's situation."

Boyd briefed them both on all he knew, concluding by offering Norma his card and assuring her she could call their office anytime for updates.

Wiping her eyes, she politely thanked the two men. With no further comment, she picked up her purse and headed for the door.

"Please wait a moment Mrs. Henderson. Your husband is an important person in this company, and we'll do all we can to get this sorted out as quickly as possible. We're here to help."

She stopped short of the door. Boyd continued, "I presume you'll want to go down to be near him. May I help by arranging a car to your hotel or transportation to Washington, perhaps?"

From the tone of her voice, he could tell her thoughts were already miles down the road toward Washington. "Well, a ride to the hotel would save time—yes, thank you. You're very kind to offer."

Taking Norma by the arm, Boyd led her out. "We can arrange everything in my office; it's just this way."

* * *

Ten minutes later, Norman Daniels reappeared clutching his book. He approached Marylin's desk and asked if he could briefly see Sir Reginald. Somewhat to Daniels's surprise, Marylin responded politely, "I'm so sorry, Mr. Daniels, but Sir Reginald has been caught up by an unexpected emergency."

"Oh, what a shame, but I suppose such things are to be expected in an organization as large as this. I've brought him a copy of my book. Could you please see he gets it?"

"Of course."

Daniels took out his pen and laid the book on the desk to sign. There seemed to be a flurry of activity as people came and went from the boss's office. He closed the book and pushed it across to Marylin. As he turned to leave, Sir Reginald's door opened, and three words escaped, setting his pulse racing: "Henderson...federal crimes." Scarcely able to contain his excitement, Daniels quickly left the building. *So this is it. It's really happening. Just as we hoped.*

Back at the hotel, Daniels gathered his things, trying to distill the jumble of facts now prominent in his mind. He had set out with a singular objective, to find out what made Sir Reginald Wilson tick, and had returned with both a candid insight into the man and a potentially explosive story.

Suppressing his reporter's instinct to grab the headline first, he picked up his cell phone.

"Scott. Daniels here again. You can start writing your story now..."

*   *   *

As the car carrying Henderson proceeded southwest, on the three-and-a-half-hour trip to Washington, David Sailor waited patiently outside the DCI's office to discuss the results of his investigation into the 2011 unauthorized vault entry.

Several people came out, followed by a somewhat irritated Mac Mitchell. Mitchell turned directly to Sailor. "Dave, have you had any lunch yet?"

"No, sir."

"How would a ham and cheese sandwich from downstairs sound to you?"

"Great."

"Anna, can you arrange two ham and cheese sandwiches for us, please?"

"Coming right up."

They headed into Mitchell's office and closed the door.

Sailor explained that, as a result of his intensive investigation, he had put a security watch officer named Lawrence Hart on administrative leave with pay, pending a full review. "I discovered this guy had come on duty in the Security Watch Office on March eighth, 2011 at six thirty a.m. At about six fifty, he disarmed the alarm system on the communications vault and then, about eight fifteen, reactivated it. In both instances, he made none of the required log entries or took any note of the door-open signals received. Additionally, he admitted rewriting the hourly vault door check sheet to indicate "locked and checked" at seven and at eight o'clock. As a result of this, all official records showed the vault had been secured on March fourth, 2011 at three minutes past five and not opened again until March tenth at twelve twenty-three p.m."

"And what did Mr. Hart have to say about why he broke all those rules?" Mitchell asked.

Mr. Hart is a veteran of fifteen years and initially tried to justify it as one of those unusual things that 'just seem to happen in this building sometimes.' But when I pointed out its possible connection to an act of treason, his tune changed quickly to one of 'only following orders from above.'"

"So this must have involved another security person as well," Mitchell said in a serious tone, looking directly at Sailor.

"I pushed Hart, and he finally confessed it was not one of our people..."

"Okay, okay...just stop there a moment Dave. This is all starting to make sense now..." Mitchell paused. "Ed Henderson's wife was having an affair with Ian Cunningham."

"Holy shit Mac!"

"This situation has become a massive double-banger—a really bad one too."

For a long while, both men were silent until the buzzer on Mitchell's desk sounded.

"Sandwiches?"

"Yes, please. Bring them in, Anna."

Anna sensed the tension immediately. Quickly and quietly, she placed the sandwiches and iced tea on the desk and departed.

Eventually, Sailor stated the obvious. "The formal charges are the domain of the FBI. Regardless of what he thought at the time, Hart has aided and abetted a crime, and it appears as though Cunningham is in the same boat. What we need to do now is turn Hart over to Bassett and get this investigation reopened."

"You're right, of course. I'll speak with Bassett and keep you up-to-date."

Sailor picked up his sandwich and the glass and made his way out the door, stopping at Anna's desk. "Anna, how much do I owe you for this?"

Anna looked up and replied, "Not a thing, Mr. Sailor. The boss runs a tab in the cafeteria, so it's already on him." Just then, the buzzer on Anna's desk sounded. "Sir."

"See if you can get Dr. Bassett on the secure phone, please."

"Right away."

The red light blinked, indicating the call had been put through. Mitchell lifted the receiver. "Fred."

"What can I do for you, Mac?" Bassett asked.

"We now know who fixed things so Henderson could get into the communications vault on March eighth. He is one of ours, of course. His name is Hart, and we have him on administrative leave for the moment, but we'd like to get him, and this whole thing, into your hands as soon as possible."

"I can see the need for speed here. Has he been cooperative?"

"Indeed, he has. But Fred, this is going to explode when you talk to him. It's going to lead to a very big fish, which I want thoroughly fried, so feel free to go easy on Hart if it'll help."

"Give me a minute, Mac. Hold on, please."

Over the phone, Mitchell could hear muffled voices, then Bassett came back on the line, saying he could arrange the initial questioning of Hart for two o'clock on Saturday, June 15th.

Mitchell agreed.

* * *

Despite his busy schedule, Bassett continued to review the first leak investigation's reports, trying not to speculate on what he might soon learn. With the solid proof of how the document had been stolen, things had moved to another level. Now his task would be to prove to a jury just how Henderson, and others, were guilty of federal crimes, including conspiracy and perhaps treason.

* * *

Lawrence Hart opened up like a book. During the questioning, he described in fine detail how Cunningham had convinced him to "look the other way" with regard to the vault entry. But Hart could provide nothing related to Cunningham's motivation. Bassett suggested the CIA keep him on administrative leave until such time as charges, if any, were formally presented.

Chapter Twenty-Four

Two days after the Middle East summit concluded, the advisory group sent by the UN returned to New York. On their arrival at JFK airport, the secretary general welcomed them back and, speaking of their work in glowing terms, described their efforts as "highly successful."

Originally, Ian Cunningham had planned to spend the night in New York, but an early arrival into JFK and onward flight availability allowed him to get home the same evening.

During a late supper with his wife, Ruth, he enthused about his trip and its historic achievements. The visit had really boosted his political status, and he was riding high on the wave of success.

"So what's been happening here, Ruth? Have I missed anything interesting?"

The wave broke unexpectedly, and catastrophically.

"Oh, you'll never believe this, but some former agency employee got himself arrested! By all accounts it's a pretty serious charge—mishandling classified material, conspiracy, and possibly treason. Apparently, he'd worked at the headquarters for almost twenty years."

Ian felt his pulse quicken. "Did you catch his name?"

"Henderson, I believe. Yes, Edwin Henderson."

Cunningham felt sick to his stomach.

"You okay, hon?" asked Ruth.

"Sure...it's just...a shock...a surprise." Trying to maintain his composure, his worst fears now finally realized, he said the only thing he could think of, "Are you sure his name was Henderson?"

"Yes, and by the look on your face, you obviously know this guy pretty well."

"Err, I do...did. He used to be one of our top guys in communications security."

Cunningham rose, somewhat unsteadily, and made his way over to the desk. With more than a little trepidation, he turned on the computer to see what the latest news bulletins were reporting.

There were several stories, all connecting the arrest with the 2011 PDB leak. The magnitude of the news coverage left no doubt more stories would soon be emerging. Indeed, by eight the following morning, when his wife came down for breakfast, the story dominated the TV offerings. Cunningham knew it would only be a matter of time before the FBI would discover his involvement and come knocking at his door.

At nine fifteen, he picked up his briefcase to leave. Stopping momentarily at the door, he turned, hesitated, then walked back over to Ruth. He took her in his arms and kissed her tenderly.

As he headed out the door he glanced back to wave as he had done every workday for the last twenty-five years.

On his way into the office, he phoned the DCI.

"Director's office," Anna answered.

"Good morning, Anna, this is Ian Cunningham. Is the boss in?"

"Welcome back, Mr. Cunningham. Yes, he is, just a minute please."

Mitchell came on the line. "Hello Ian, welcome back to the States. Sounds as though you folks did a bang-up job. Enjoy the trip?"

"Yes. It turned out to be a pretty grueling schedule, but, thankfully, very successful. How's everything with you?"

"Up to my ears in alligators as usual Ian. When does your flight get into Washington? I'll send someone to meet you."

"Thanks, Mac, but there's no need. I changed my flight and got home last night. I'll be in the office in an hour or so."

"Oh, okay...okay. I'll see you shortly."

Cunningham detected a difference in Mitchell's tone and knew immediately something had changed.

He pulled the car off the road and stopped. Gripping the wheel, he began to hyperventilate. He loosened his tie and opened the window. *I'm in real trouble here. Mitchell knows. How the hell does he know? I need to think this out before I do anything.* He turned his car around and headed west into Virginia's horse country.

In just a short while, the Blue Ridge Mountains came into view. A perfect day and, under normal circumstances, he would have reveled in the beauty of the area. He slowed near the bottom of a hill and pulled off into a gateway, under the shade of a giant white oak tree. He shut off the engine, took out a small notebook, and began writing.

* * *

Just after midday, Ruth Cunningham's phone rang.

"Hello, Mrs. Cunningham, this is Anna from Director Mitchell's office. Is Mr. Cunningham still there?"

"No Anna, he left several hours ago. I would guess about nine thirty or so."

"Oh, I see. He called earlier, and we were expecting him sometime this morning. He hasn't shown up, though. If you see him or he calls you, please tell him the director had to leave for downtown and won't be available until after three. They can catch up then."

"No problem, Anna. I'll be sure to tell him."

* * *

After years of marriage to a man in the security business, Ruth had become accustomed to the police visiting their home. So it came as no surprise when a police car pulled up in the driveway and two people, one uniformed and one in plainclothes, came to the door.

"Mrs. Cunningham, I'm Detective Simon Richardson of the Loudoun County Police, and this is Officer Melissa Powell. May we come in, please?"

"Of course, but my husband's not here at the moment." Ruth sensed nervousness on the part of her visitors as she ushered them into the living room. "Maybe I can help?"

"Please sit down, Mrs. Cunningham. It's you we actually need to speak to."

"Oh, has something happened? Ian hasn't shown up at work yet. Has there been an accident? Where is he?" The questions tumbled out as the normally self-composed Ruth Cunningham began to realize something had very definitely happened to her husband.

"I'm very sorry to have to inform you but...there's been an incident, and Mr. Cunningham has died."

Ruth's hand shot to her mouth, "No, it can't be. He was just here...he only left a couple of hours ago. No. There must be some mistake."

"I'm afraid not. It's been confirmed ..."

"What's been confirmed? What are you saying? What's happened? Has there been a traffic accident? Sometimes Ian just pays too much attention to his thoughts and not enough to the road." Wide, dark eyes stared in disbelief at the officers.

"The evidence points to an apparent suicide," Richardson answered.

She responded with a sharp intake of breath, "Oh my God! Ian would never...he would never do such a thing. Maybe you've got the wrong man."

Struggling to make sense of it all, and nervously running her fingers through her auburn hair, Ruth frantically tried to come up with alternative, more feasible scenarios.

"You do know he works at the CIA, don't you? He just got back last night from the big peace summit in Ankara. Maybe he's gone under cover? Maybe this is part of a plan? Maybe someone pretended to be him, and now they're dead?" She knew she was rambling. "Have you spoken to his office?"

"Yes, we talked to a Mr. David Sailor, your husband's deputy. He'll be here shortly."

She gasped. *So it's the truth.* "Tell me, how...ah...how did it happen?"

"A single gunshot."

"Oh, my God!"

"There's just one other thing. He left a small notebook, and it has a message apparently meant for you." Richardson handed her the notebook, which she took but didn't open. Instead, she just clutched it to her breast. Whatever it contained; she could not bring herself to look just now.

Another car pulled into the driveway. Two people came to the door and knocked. Officer Powell let David Sailor and Anna Evans into the house.

During the next few hours, speculation about the cause of Cunningham's death spread through the news media relentlessly, due to his prominent part in the just-concluded Middle East summit. Whatever the reason, it must have been profoundly serious, as the local police soon called in the FBI to assist in the investigation.

Within two days, with the help of still-classified, state-of-the-art forensics, documented proof of Cunningham's suicide became publicly available. This quickly changed the focus of the news stories from potential assassination to speculation around why such a prominent, successful man should take his own life. The media blamed the extreme stress of his job, particularly recently, for pushing him over the edge.

* * *

For Sir Reginald Wilson, the news of Cunningham's death was timely, as it conveniently diverted media attention away from the arrest of Edwin Henderson. The ramifications for his organization however, were significant. On top of needing to appoint an interim director of security in London, Sir Reginald found himself in a very unfamiliar position. In his entire working life, he had never made such a bad judgment of character. He could still not believe he had been hoodwinked so convincingly. The next time he received a heads-up about an employee, and particularly when it came from members of his own family, he would not be so dismissive.

* * *

Days later, on the seventh floor of CIA headquarters, Mitchell and Sailor discussed Dr. Bassett's request for any other evidence that might add to either the Henderson or the Hart prosecutions.

Sailor offered his opinion: "We have been through every-thing of Ian's, but the only thing we've found of significance to the case is an envelope from Henderson containing several very graphic pictures proving Ian's adulterous affair with Norma Henderson. To me, it's clear Henderson found himself in a fortuitous position once he knew the identity of his wife's lover. I believe this knowledge changed his plan from divorce to blackmail.

"Personally, however, I think Cunningham has paid the price for his indiscretion, and the world really doesn't need to know any of this. It's your call, Mac, but if it were up to me, I'd put the whole envelope in the shredder."

"You and I know such a thing is both illegal and unethical," Mitchell replied, "but I think it would be much better all around if this particular information never got out. I'll talk to Bassett and see if we can protect it somehow. In the big picture, it only provides a motive for Ian to pressure Hart. If it ever does get out, it'll almost certainly be the only thing anyone remembers about one exceptionally fine government servant—and that would be a damn shame."

Just over a week later, in a meeting on an entirely differ-ent subject, DCI Mitchell passed the envelope of incriminat-ing evidence to Dr. Bassett. They had previously spoken on the phone, with Bassett essentially agreeing to its minimal value in this case. He said he would lock it up but made it clear that if the court ever asked him about it, he would not lie.

In the weeks which followed, Henderson—having been granted bail—his wife, and their longtime attorney, began preparing for the upcoming trial.

Chapter Twenty-Five

After being released from the hospital, Martin spent a little over four weeks in the Dulles Health and Rehab Center in nearby Herndon. Getting back to full health had become his top priority and gave him a new purpose, at least for the time being.

He had been extremely fortunate to survive the accident, and, as the rigorous physical therapy routine continued, his mobility improved daily. He looked forward to, and greatly appreciated, the visits from Norman Daniels and Cheryl and John Murphy, which provided a welcome diversion. He enjoyed hearing news from the outside world and, more importantly, the inside tidbits they brought regarding the reopened leak inquiry.

Although he desperately wanted to talk to Linda, he had no success reaching her. And, as the memory of a many unanswered calls began to return, it gradually dawned on him that she obviously wanted nothing more to do with him.

Martin also thought a lot about his future and, at Cheryl and John's suggestion, decided to submit an application for reemployment with the CIA.

In a remarkably short time, and to his great surprise, he received a positive response. On the upside, this meant a regular paycheck. On the downside, he would be working in the computer maintenance department, albeit temporarily, pending the completion of a final security check. The agency also proposed a part-time schedule at least until he completed outpatient physical therapy.

* * *

August 21st had been set as the date for Henderson's trial, but on August 7th, during a pretrial hearing, Henderson's lawyer asked for the log of events, extracted by Steele, to be validated by independent experts. The substance of his reasoning centered on the fact that all the people involved in obtaining this information were CIA insiders. Indeed, he pointed out, the person who actually retrieved the file had himself been one of the prime suspects during the original investigation. The judge considered the request and ruled the Pyramid event log be validated by third-party certification, attesting to its authenticity. Only then would it be considered admissible evidence. Within an hour, the ruling had been delivered to the federal prosecutor's office, where it quickly turned into a request to CIA security for approval of independent access to the Pyramid system. By the next day, the request lay on DCI Mitchell's desk.

Mitchell read the request carefully; then he got up and walked to the window, considering the possibilities. Complying with the judge's order would mean the end of Pyramid as a viable security tool. He had to assume any invasive, independent access to the system would compromise technology undoubtedly years ahead of its time. However, to refuse access might be perceived as a large-scale cover-up. In the worst-case scenario, complying with the order could put the technology into the hands of the nation's enemies. At best it would certainly allow justice to be done, sending at least one, and possibly two, guilty people to prison. At the same time providing a stunning example of what would happen to anyone considering such an action in the future.

He reread the request a third time and thought for a long moment. *This is a big one; better sleep on it and decide tomorrow.* He then called Anna and asked her to set up a fifteen-minute meeting with Sailor for early the next day.

* * *

The following morning at seven fifteen, Sailor knocked on Mitchell's office door. "Good morning, Mac. What's happening?"

"And good morning to you too, Dave. Thanks for coming over. Look, I've thought a lot about the judge's requirement for an independent validation of the Pyramid log, and I want your take on it before making a final decision."

"Well," Sailor began, "if you agree to it, Henderson and probably Hart will end up in the slammer. If you don't agree, Henderson will go free and Hart will likely only get a slap on the wrist. But, as we both know, it's not quite so simple. Compliance would involve outsiders probing into a security system way beyond any of today's technology. If it were up to me, I would deny the request. Not punishing Henderson would be regrettable but not nearly as regrettable as someone using the Pyramid technology against us."

"I see we think along the same lines, Dave," Mitchell replied, handing the paper to Sailor. "Our formal reply shouldn't need my signature, but if it does, just send it by. You know my position."

* * *

Three days later, the secure phone rang on Mitchell's desk.

"Mitchell."

"Mac, it's Bassett. I've just been advised the federal prosecutor has dropped all charges against Henderson."

"Well, guess there's no real surprise there."

287

"You know the bastard is guilty, Mac. Looks to me like you've lost your marbles. Think about it, tomorrow one treasonous SOB will walk out of there absolutely free!"

"This has been a difficult decision to make, Fred. It's complicated, but, at the end of the day, we all have just too much to lose. I'm confident we went the best way." *And if you knew what I know about our current world status, I'm sure you'd have made the same decision.*

* * *

The next day, a grinning Ed Henderson and his wife, Norma, walked hand-in-hand out of the federal courthouse in Alexandria, Virginia. A short way down the street, the finality and magnitude of what had happened struck him. He stopped, turned to his wife and, with the look of relief that could only be understood by one just spared the guillotine, took her by the shoulders and said, "It's done! It's all over, Norma. Let's get back to London as quickly as possible."

"Yesterday, they said you'd be a free man by the end of today, so I booked us on the last flight tonight. We're all set."

By midnight, they were on their way to Heathrow. During the flight, a very relaxed and confident Ed slept like a baby, while Norma reviewed the past, frequently centering her thoughts on Ian Cunningham, a fundamentally good man and a very caring lover. She closed her eyes as the tears fell silently. *This is going to take some getting over.*

* * *

Two months and two days after his arrest in New York, Ed Henderson returned to his office in London, only to discover his badge and password no longer gave him entry. Instead, the receptionist handed him a restricted visitor badge and directed him to Mr. Blackstock's office. There an irate Ed waited for twenty minutes to be ushered in.

Robert Blackstock rushed to complete a note in the margin of a document. He looked squarely at Henderson.

"Come in, Ed. Have a seat."

"Thanks, Bob, how's everything been?"

"Very busy, lots going on as usual. But it's been a difficult time for us all, as you can imagine."

Ed waited.

Blackstock stretched, gathering his thoughts. He had made a thorough review of all available facts surrounding the arrest and had a good understanding of the company's position following a rather pointed conversation with Sir Reginald. Ed would be returned to his former position but closely watched.

"First of all, the office, the organization and Sir Reginald welcome you back." He stood and they shook hands. Then, with a brief chuckle, he reminded Henderson his badge problem had been the result of an automatic system Henderson himself had installed right at the start of his time there.

"We had to have someone cover your position while you were away so, fortunately, we were able to borrow Fionna Walsh from our Nuuk, Greenland, office. She's expecting us."

With that, the two men went to the security office, and Ed's return to work began.

* * *

During the following week, Ed became reimmersed in the complex world of corporate security. Norma worked to clean up the apartment as they both recovered from the release of stress and jet lag. Ed sensed Norma's pleasure at returning to London, though their relationship, if it could still be called one, continued to be quite distant.

He knew the stress of the previous two months had broadened the gap between them. Too much had happened, and now, being forced together constantly seemed only to exacerbate their differences. He had a genuine fondness for Norma, but the sexual attraction had long since disappeared. As far as he was concerned, they had no future together. He knew Norma felt the same, particularly after she had told him, in no uncertain terms, how his actions towards Martin had been despicable. Both had ample grounds for divorce.

By late Thursday afternoon, Ed had begun to get back into the swing of things. He had also made up his mind to help Norma in pursuing their divorce, and things were returning to a sort of normal state. Dinner was planned for seven and, as had been his habit in the past, he decided to take advantage of the fine weather to go for a walk and be alone with his thoughts.

In no time he had reached Hyde Park. Finding a vacant seat overlooking the Boathouse on the Serpentine, his thoughts turned to his nemesis, Martin Steele. Steele's efforts, which had unmasked and almost hanged him, stood as irritating and intolerable facts that only heightened his resolve to make the man really suffer. Martin Steele represented unfinished business which must be concluded.

Some of his ideas for exacting revenge had been incredibly involved, but that evening, watching the paddle boats glide serenely past, a unique scenario took shape in his mind. *This will work! I'll get the son of a bitch this time.*

As he walked home, he continued to think and plan. Knowing the mental solitude provided by walking would soon vanish, he stopped on the front step of his apartment building for a moment, relishing the ingenious simplicity of his new idea. He smiled, oblivious to the sound of traffic, the comings and goings of the other residents, and the dark shadow in a third-floor apartment window across the street.

All three shots hit him. One shattered his skull, splashing blood and brains on the wall behind him, and two pierced his chest, making gaping, gushing holes in his back. He collapsed, blood cascading down the steps. Bystanders scrambled for cover in doorways and behind parked cars, fearing the work of a terrorist. The emergency services appeared almost immediately. Edwin Henderson was pronounced dead at the scene.

Chapter Twenty-Six

March 8, 2016, somewhere outside Washington, DC

Martin had spent most of the day working on a design for a new cryptographic subsystem, but so far all his efforts had ended up in the burn basket. Part of the problem came from his inability to stop thinking about the events which had occurred on the very same day, five years earlier. He glanced at the clock. Five years, seven hours, and some minutes since Ed Henderson copied the PDB and leaked part of it to the press, triggering a chain of events that severely altered the course of his life. A quick calculation also reminded him that one year and eleven months ago, his former colleague had been mysteriously murdered.

Martin had been reassigned to his former communications security office, and for the past six months had been working to update and repurpose the Pyramid technology. Ironically, he now worked in the very room where he had been programming when news of the infamous leak had broken.

With temperatures in the high seventies, most of Martin's colleagues had locked up and gone home to enjoy the unexpectedly good weather. But Martin had nothing and no one to rush home to. His leg had really been bothering him, so he paced around the office for a while, wondering whether he'd reached his daily allocation of painkillers. Walking continued to be painful, and while short distance mobility remained generally fine around the office and his apartment, he still needed the reassurance of a cane when he went out and about.

He returned to his desk feeling a little more comfortable and looked up at the clock on the wall. Although it showed 4:30 p.m., in his mind it suddenly became 4:30 a.m., and the place was not Washington, DC, but Sandaray Island. He sat, closed his eyes and pictured sternman Seth Martin standing on the dock, as he had done so many mornings, ready and eager to do a day's work lobstering on the *Linda-T*. He could almost smell the sea air and feel the cool breeze.

"Go home, Martin. Get some exercise and enjoy the sunshine." The voice of his boss brought him back to reality. "Don't want you spending another night here. You'll get it sorted."

Opening his eyes, Martin responded in a detached tone, "Night, David. Have a nice evening." But the feeling of being there, on Sandaray, on JB's dock in the early morning lingered in his mind, refusing to go away.

Eventually, realizing he had become totally unproductive, he also packed up and left.

At home, the flashing light on his telephone announced a waiting message. "Hello, Martin. Scott Young here. Sorry it's been a while. Hope you're doing okay. Give me a call please."

Martin called Scott immediately.

"Scott, how are you doing? I'm sorry I've not been in touch for a while."

"I'm fine, thanks. I know we've got some catching up to do, but I need to tell you some news from Sandaray. It's not good, I'm afraid."

Martin's heart sank. He could not face any more dramas.

"I'm afraid JB Thompson is dead."

"Oh, no! How? When?"

"Two days ago. I just called Linda to offer my condolences. She's quite broken up, as you can imagine. It seems JB caught his sternman smoking a joint, fired him on the spot, and then went out to haul by himself. Ronnie Moody found him after noticing the *Linda-T* circling near a string of JB's traps. A med-evac helicopter rushed him to the mainland, but he died in the hospital emergency room."

"I can't believe it, Scott, he always seemed in such good health. I wonder if he had a heart attack." *I know he could get wound up. Almost cost me my life.* "What a massive loss to the island and the whole fishing community. Tragic. Don't suppose there are any funeral plans yet?"

"I understand his sister, Ethel Griffin, will be coming up from Texas, and Linda, of course, will fly over from London, so it will probably be at least two, maybe three weeks."

"Thanks, Scott. Could you email me when you know more?"

"I certainly will. But tell me, how is everything going for you down there in the big city?"

"Lots of interesting work I can't tell you about keeps me quite busy. You know how it is! How are you getting on?"

"Doing okay. Still covering the cooking shows, lobster boat races, and other such exciting local news. Oh, you remember the story I did about the renovation of DeVoe Lodge? Well, the American Institute of Architects is publishing a book that features a section on the renovation with a number of Jennifer Stanley's photographs and chunks of my articles. Getting published by those guys is a big feather in both our caps."

"Scott, that's great news. At least you're making the national scene in a positive way. Please congratulate Jennifer for me." Martin paused. "Look Scott, I'm still annoyed they sealed everything up, denying you the big Henderson scoop that Daniels promised you. Guess you must still be pissed."

294

"Well, to a degree, but hey, life goes on. I still can't quite get over the FBI arresting Henderson at exactly the same time Daniels was there interviewing Sir Reg. Boy did he have one major scoop handed to him on a plate. But you know, he phoned me about it first and wrote nothing. I appreciated that very much. There's no question he's a man of his word. Just imagine, maybe someday they'll take the wraps off all the facts, even let *you* speak freely about it, and then I'll get the scoop."

"I certainly hope so; you deserve it."

"Oh, I have a new project on the go too. Maybe I'll hit the big time with this one!"

"And what exactly might that be?"

"I've written a novel."

"No kidding?"

"It's semi-fiction and was accepted by the very first publisher I approached. In fact, they liked it so much, they sent me a big advance."

"Wow, Scott! Congratulations. When will it be out? What's it about? What's it called? Err…and what is semi-fiction?"

"Semi-fiction is what I call it. It's fact treated to a generous amount of artistic license. You may have run into some of it posing as news somewhere along the line. They tell me the book will be out the fifteenth of next month. It's called *Reason to Leave*."

"Interesting title. I'll keep my eye on the *New York Times* bestseller list!"

"Thanks, Martin, I hope you find it there. And if you get up this way for JB's funeral, please look me up. It would be nice to catch up over a drink or two."

"Will do, Scott. Take it easy."

Martin hung up. The news had dealt even more of a blow than finding out about Henderson's release. But at least he finally knew Linda was okay. He slumped into a chair as thoughts, memories, and images of Sandaray once again flashed through his head. It made his earlier daydream seem particularly uncanny.

He closed his eyes and there, just as real as before, he saw JB at the wheel of *Linda-T*. He spoke out loud, "JB, please forgive me. Please forgive Linda." JB turned and, with a voice as clear as if he were standing right next to him, said, "I forgave her right after it happened, Seth. And I eventually forgave you too." Then, as quickly as it had appeared, the image vanished.

He sat for some time in a part-dreaming, part-waking state and, when reality again returned, opened his eyes to find the room in total darkness.

Chapter Twenty-Seven

The day before JB's funeral, Martin took leave from work and made his way north to Maine and ultimately to a reserved room at DeVoe Lodge.

It felt strange being back on the island, particularly as he recalled the details of his departure. He wondered what people knew about the events that had occurred. Had JB ever told anyone? It seemed highly unlikely that Linda would have said anything. He had come back for a single purpose and was determined to focus only on this.

Martin was surprised to be greeted by a receptionist on arrival at the lodge. *Big changes here,* he considered. *Bill is obviously doing well.*

* * *

The following morning, Martin walked the short distance to the church. The service was not due to start for another twenty minutes, but every seat had already been taken. He spotted many familiar faces. Indeed, it looked as though every local had turned out to pay their final respects to one of Sandaray's best-loved residents. He saw Scott Young in the far corner and carefully made his way over to join him. They whispered greetings. Scott nodded at the cane.

"I'll tell you later Scott, but I'm fine." Which was more than he felt. *I sure hope I can stand through this whole thing.*

During the typical Protestant service, JB's sister Ethyl gave an emotional eulogy and, later, when JB had finally been laid to rest, everyone respectfully dispersed down the road from the cemetery, most heading toward the Wilsons' house to gather, reminisce, and remember.

Martin walked somberly beside Scott. It felt inappropriate to engage in social chitchat, so they reminisced about JB and what life on the island would be like without him. Then suddenly, he heard a voice from somewhere behind, calling his name, or rather his other name. He had failed to notice Dan and Linda, but he immediately recognized Linda's voice. He turned, and his heart skipped a beat.

"Seth? Seth, is that you?"

He stopped to let Linda and Dan catch up.

"You look so different...younger, no beard, and you have a cane. What happened to you? Are you...?" her words trailed off mid-sentence.

"Yes, it's me," he said quietly. "Linda, I'm so sorry about your dad. I couldn't believe it when I heard ..." He paused, unsure whether to say more. Scott filled the uncomfortable silence.

"I really respected your father, Linda. My sincere condolences," Scott said instinctively placing his hand on her arm.

"Thank you, Scott. It's good to see you again. I appreciate you coming today." Then, turning to Seth she asked, "Why the cane, Seth?"

He responded as succinctly as he could.

"A large cement truck lost its brakes. I was pretty lucky."

The four walked together for a few minutes in silence until Dan, trying to lift the mood, started discussing the great success of the London office with Scott, adding details of how he and Linda would soon be moving to New Zealand. He proudly informed them of his father's decision to charge him with starting up yet another new branch of Wilson Engineering.

Taking advantage of the situation, Martin moved closer to Linda. He needed to muster all his resolve not to place a comforting arm around her as she finally succumbed to her pent-up emotions. She stopped to take a handkerchief from her pocket. Speaking through her sobs, and wiping away the tears, she quietly mumbled, "Dad forgave me…and you…the same day you left. You need to know that. You should also know he really thought the world of you. We spent a lot of time together afterward, just talking about life, values, understanding, and forgiveness. It's the closest we'd ever been."

Although staggered by the premonition of JB's forgiveness, Martin also knew he had done a bad thing, so it seemed only fair to have spent so long living in purgatory. He didn't know what to say, so he let Linda continue.

"Being alone with Dad also helped me get my head around our marriage. It's not perfect by any means, but things seem to be getting a bit better, and we're both looking forward to New Zealand…a new start together, and who knows, perhaps even a family."

"I phoned you several times. I worried about you after what happened."

"I know. You probably imagined all sorts of dreadful things. I just couldn't bear to talk to you. I'm sorry."

"Don't be, I understand. Thanks for being honest with me. I'm genuinely happy for you both, and I wish you the very best of everything."

Martin and Linda stopped at the end of the road leading to

DeVoe Lodge. Dan and Scott were waiting for them. "Seth, come on up to the house with Scott."

Martin thanked him, but declined, saying he just wanted to be alone for a while *and my leg is killing me.* With reiterated condolences to Linda and promises to keep in touch with Scott, they all shook hands, and Martin turned up the road to the lodge.

* * *

He found Bill sweeping the front porch.

"Aha. There you are. Boy, the years have certainly changed you, Seth, or Martin, or whatever you're calling yourself now! Come on in for a cup of coffee."

"Bill, it's good to see you. The place is certainly looking great!"

"Yes, there's been a lot more changes round here since you left. But look at you! All clean-shaven with short hair. Had me fooled for a while, but I thought I recognized you yesterday. I saw you from the kitchen when you checked in. I'd sure like to hear what the Martin Steele thing's all about!"

Bill's comment led to a mutual sharing of stories. Martin giving the briefest outline of events since he had left the island, and Bill boasting unashamedly about the fame and fortune that followed Scott and Jennifer's articles.

Once the coffee had been consumed, Bill changed the offer to whiskey, and in no time, the two were seated in basket chairs on the front porch. Warmed by the late afternoon sunshine and fine malt, they continued to reminisce.

"This has been really enjoyable, Seth. But the place is full tonight, and I have to get dinner started."

They shook hands and Bill left. Martin could hear him talking to someone in the hallway.

"Take the young guy on the porch another scotch—neat. Put it on Room Three's tab."

The whiskey duly arrived, delivered, to his great surprise, by Emma Harris. He struggled to his feet.

"Emma! What are *you* doing here?" Instinctively he looked at Emma's left-hand ring finger. *I wonder if she's remarried Bill.* "How are you? How've you been? Didn't see you at the funeral. Are you still running the café?" She put the drink tray down hastily and stepped back to study their new guest. He extended his hand, and she shook it in a cool but cordial greeting.

"Well, well, if it isn't Seth Martin."

"Can you sit for a minute, Emma?"

"Sorry, we've got a full house tonight, so no, not just now. But hey, in answer to your questions, I'm doing okay, still running the café. I thought I saw you in the church, but I wasn't one hundred percent sure."

"I felt I had to come back for the funeral. What a blow for everyone."

"Yes. A huge shock. We still can't believe he's gone. Kenny's taken it real bad."

"I can imagine. Look, can we talk when you get off?"

"Oh, I don't know. Have we anything to say to each other?"

"I'd like to explain what happened. Why I left so suddenly. Will you grant me an audience?"

"Maybe. You really pissed me off, you know, when you upped and left without so much as a by-your-leave."

"Yes, I can imagine, and I'm pretty ashamed of leaving without saying goodbye.

"Well, I suppose I could meet you, but it'll be after ten."

"Okay. I'm in Room Three. I'll wait there after dinner."

"No, not in your room. It's hardly appropriate."

301

"How about out on the front porch?"

"Mmm…all right. I'll go there when I'm finished."

* * *

After she had served Martin his supper, she dropped a small, folded piece of paper on the table in front of him. It read simply: *Best guess is an hour before I can get away.*

* * *

The almost full moon hung low in the western sky, painting a streak on the unusually calm sea. Martin turned at the sound of footsteps as Emma emerged onto the porch. She paused, drinking in the stillness and beauty of the scene. He wondered if she would turn back.

"Emma, you made it. Beautiful evening, isn't it?"

"It is. Though I have to say, I almost didn't come. I'm really surprised to see you, Seth, after all this time."

He gently guided her over to a chair with his free arm. But now that they were together, he had no idea how to proceed. He paused. *Just get on with it. You certainly can't make the situation any worse.*

"Emma, I'm so sorry I left so suddenly. I came back when I heard JB had passed, but now I'm glad we have a little time. I owe you a huge apology and an explanation."

"You certainly do," she replied frostily.

"It's difficult—" he began, but Emma cut him off.

"Look, I know you were battling demons…stuff from your past. Is that why you left? Something about the bad guy Linda and Dan had to warn Sir Reg about?"

"Yes, in part…"

She waited.

Eventually, the story of his turbulent life from March 2011 to the present, came tumbling out.

When he stopped, Emma seized the moment. "But you've omitted the part about why you left so suddenly, without telling anyone. Without telling me!"

Moving a little away from her, he switched his gaze back out to sea and added very quietly, "I got involved with someone... here. Linda Wilson. JB caught us together. I only had two choices: leave before sundown and never return, or leave in the morning in a box. I know if JB had been armed, I'd have had no options, nor would I be here today. So I left before sundown."

"Wow! What can I say? I'm stunned. I had no idea. But it does explain a few things. And no one knew except JB?"

"No one, as far as I know. I'm ashamed of the whole thing. But I really thought if I got in touch with anyone or ever dared to show my face here again, JB would do as he promised, and I'd be a dead man."

She nodded. "Knowing JB, you're probably right."

They both considered the magnitude of his revelations.

After a long silence, Emma spoke. "There were a lot of rumors about what had happened to you, Seth—or Martin. Funny, I remember asking you once if Seth was your real name. You answered, 'No. not exactly,' but you never went further. Now it all makes sense. Look, Seth, I'm bushed and need to get to bed. How long are you here for?"

"I could only get three days off to come up for the funeral. I'm booked on the nine o'clock flight in the morning and have to be back at work the next day."

Martin realized all this must have come as a very big shock to Emma, and she would need time to digest, and maybe even try to understand, everything he had told her. He also knew she would be exhausted from a long day's work. He had no right to expect anything from her. But at least his conscience had been cleared—a bit.

As she started to cross the lawn to her truck, Martin called after her, "Emma...may I phone you?"

"2176."

Emma disappeared around the side of the building.

* * *

As Martin sat in Bill's noisy truck en route to the airport— *surely he could afford something a bit more upmarket now?*— his thoughts turned back to Emma and the previous evening's conversation. He wondered if her working at the lodge meant a reconciliation with Bill might be in the works. When Bill shut off the engine making conversation possible again, Martin took the bull by the horns. "Bill, I spoke with Emma last evening and I'm curious to know if her working at the lodge means you two are getting back together?"

"Ha-ha, you gotta be joking! Too much has been said and done for that to ever happen. She's a top-notch worker with a full-time job of her own but, God bless her, she's been giving me two nights a week for the last month or so, until I can find another part-timer to help. It's been working fine, but in truth, I think any more time together would really strain our 'strictly professional' relationship!"

Martin felt pleasantly surprised, even strangely relieved.

Bill pulled up alongside the landing strip and, within minutes, the plane landed, taxied in and parked nearby. Martin thanked him for the ride, grabbed his bag, and headed across the gravel.

He turned back and shook his head as Bill fired up the truck. Just as he reached the plane, Alex, the pilot, rushed past him and headed over toward Bill. The truck noise stopped and the two men talked briefly. Martin wondered what the emergency was but used the time to take a last look around. No sign of any latecomers. In fact, no sign of anyone at all.

He loaded his bag into the aircraft. He had no right to expect Emma to turn up, but he wished she would have come, even just to wave him off. He waited beside the passenger door, still silently hoping.

Soon, much to his disappointment, the roar of Bill's truck signaled his departure, and Alex came back toward the plane. "Take the co-pilot's seat, Seth," he said as he made a last-minute check of the hatches.

They were airborne in seconds.

As they banked to the left, Martin stared out of the pilot's side window, marveling at the beauty of this extraordinary island, for one last time. Through clouded eyes, he watched as the view of familiar landmarks began to shrink. Life on the ground continued, seemingly unaffected by, and unaware of, his departure. He thought he saw a vehicle of some sort come to a dusty halt near the air strip. Maybe someone had missed the plane after all.

As they climbed, he looked back for as long as he could. Then, as they skipped around the puffy white clouds, he closed his eyes. A terrible sadness triggered a crushing pressure in his throat and chest. *I don't want to leave.*

A jolt of turbulence interrupted his thoughts.

Above the scattered clouds Alex leveled the aircraft for the next 12 minutes of the 20-minute flight.

With watery eyes, Martin turned toward his side window. He had only himself to blame for the bad decisions that had brought him to this point but he consoled himself that at least now there were no more lies. He had cleared the air with Linda and hopefully made his peace with Emma. It was time for him to get his life properly back on track.

Small glimpses of the earth below started to appear and gradually his spirits began to lift. He looked over at Alex.

"Hey Alex, what are the chances of you just turning this thing around?"

Epilogue

Through the use of surveillance and cell phone video images, along with a high-tech, long, and very thorough investigation, Scotland Yard proved a Czech citizen, Mareka Krizek, was the person who murdered Edwin Henderson. Krizek had also been convicted of two other assassinations—a high-level Foreign Office official and a known organized crime leader. All three murders had been carefully planned and followed a similar pattern. Eventually conviction of all three murders landed Krizek three life sentences.

Even after the conviction of Krizek, the US interest in the murder of Henderson did not fade. The agency, along with the FBI, reopened their investigations after the trial proved Krizek to be no more than a hired assassin. In a news conference centered on another subject, DCI Mitchell responded to a question about Henderson's murder. "Mr. Henderson paid the full price for his crime, but we are not sure jealousy alone motivated him. We, together with the FBI, will continue until we are absolutely certain why Henderson did what he did."

* * *

Martin Steele's life settled into a regular routine. He still worked too much but had started cycling and enjoyed spending time with Cheryl, John, and his godson, Seth Murphy. Soon Cheryl convinced him to go out to dinner with a friend of hers, but nothing romantic developed. In fact, and to his surprise, Martin had spent much of the date thinking about Emma Harris. Driven by this, he phoned Emma several days later and planned a trip north for a week on Sandaray.

Acknowledgments

This book only took seven years to write! Juggling day jobs and a 3,000-mile separation certainly brought one or two challenges, but we got there in the end. It has been a wonderful experience, and we hope you enjoyed reading the story as much as we enjoyed writing it.

We would like to acknowledge the following for their invaluable input and support:

Malcolm "Cubby" MacKinnon, for his immense nautical expertise, endless patience, and understanding; Gwen Wilson, our first reader and number one fan, who reminded us at every turn what makes a good story; Eric Wentz, whose observations about our early efforts gave us the incentive to continue; and Captain Joe Bray, who gave us remarkable insight into life on a small island and lobstering off the coast of Maine.

We gratefully acknowledge the comments and suggestions made by Kristina Antolin-Davies and Diana Bray and, for their valuable technical and mechanical expertise, Gary Bredthauer (CIA), Thomas Gantert (journalist), Special Agent Jeffrey Heinze (FBI), Alex Kevorchian (computer guru), and Petty Officer Nate Littlejohn (USCG).

For sharing their life experiences and professional knowledge, we extend grateful thanks to Andrea Barna (BSN, RN) and Irene Walsh (RN), whose medical knowledge saved some embarrassing errors. For advice and encouragement, we thank our long-suffering friends Janet Dix and Glynis Morton. And for the image of his rugged, handsome self, we thank our cover model, Matthew Topsfield.

We are immensely thankful to our primary editor, Jean Young, whose careful work taught us how to tighten up and polish our writing, and to the team at Scribendi Inc. for teaching us the meaning of POV. Now, as we make our way through the complex and intricate world of publishing, we are greatly indebted to Dan, Michelle, Nikki, Molly, and Laura from Maine Authors Publishing, whose untiring work finally brought our book to you, the reader.

We would also like to acknowledge the following young people for their valuable contributions: Ronan MacPhee, whose knowledge of twenty-first-century computer games is second to none, and high school pupils from Sgoil Lionacleit, Benbecula (Scotland), who gave us critical feedback on the opening paragraph of *Reason to Leave*.

Finally, we acknowledge and whole-heartedly thank the great British writer Alexander McCall Smith, whose casual remark during a 2015 lecture inspired us to take up the challenge of writing a novel.

About the Authors

 After completing a degree in fine arts, Peter A. Wentz was commissioned into and worked as both staff officer and pilot in the U.S. Air Force. Later he headed the analysis department of the Burney Company, an equity management firm in Virginia. For many years he had a home on Matinicus Isle, Maine.

 Anne Wilson has worked and published as a professional archaeologist and been a museum educator, school principal, and classroom teacher. Born in the North East of England, she now lives in Scotland's Outer Hebrides, where she works as community engagement officer at the Grimsay Boat Haven and heritage center.

For more information email:
transatlanticwriters22@gmail.com